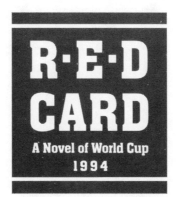

R·E·D CARD

A Novel of World Cup
1994

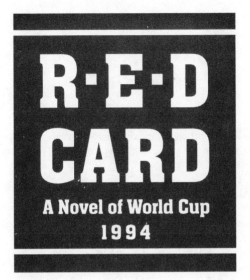

R·E·D
CARD

A Novel of World Cup
1994

RICHARD HOYT

A Tom Doherty Associates Book ■ New York

RED CARD: A NOVEL OF WORLD CUP 1994

Copyright © 1994 by Richard Hoyt

A Forge Book
Published by Tom Doherty Associates, Inc.
175 Fifth Avenue
New York, N.Y. 10010

Library of Congress Cataloging-in-Publication Data

Hoyt, Richard.
    Red card / Richard Hoyt.
        p.   cm.
    ISBN 0-312-85554-0
    1. Soccer—Tournaments—Fiction.   I. Title.
PS3558.0975R4   1994
813'.54—dc20   94-2344
                                                               CIP

First edition: June 1994

Printed in the United States of America

0 9 8 7 6 5 4 3 2 1

—for my *barkada* at the *ventanilla:*
Alburo; Canizares; Cunningham;
Monzon; Olofson; Shive; Valenzona.
So much San Miguel.
So much nonsense. Oy!

Kicks must be aimed only at the ball.
—J. R. Thring, *The Simplest Game,* 1862

AUTHOR'S NOTE

In plotting this story, I have tried to pay special attention to the four countries that have historically dominated the World Cup: Germany, Italy, Argentina, and Brazil. To do justice to Brazil's stylish, entertaining play, I have taken the liberty of putting them in the same group as the United States for the opening round robin. Also, Germany, in Group C, would not ordinarily play on the West Coast; they do so here because, being an Oregonian, I wanted to give my European, South American, and Asian readers some action on the West Coast, in addition to Chicago, Dallas, and New York. This is a genuine world tournament, and all of America is host for the finals.

Richard Hoyt
Cebu City,
Philippines,
December 1993

I

EDSON

More than 150 million athletes are registered with Fédération Internationale de Football Association (in English, the International Federation of Football Associations), headquartered in Zurich, Switzerland. This organization is ordinarily referred to by its initials, FIFA, pronounced *fee-fa*. FIFA athletes play 20 million sanctioned football matches each year.

FIFA contains representatives of national football associations in 179 countries; in the United Kingdom, England, Wales, Scotland, and Northern Ireland each have their own FA. FIFA delegates meet in a different city every other year with each FA having one vote. FIFA's Executive Committee presides over 10 standing committees, including one that organizes the quadrennial World Cup tournament.

1

The manager of the German national side was shown the yellow card shortly after he and his coaches and trainers completed a quick patrol for local street food and returned to their suite of rooms at the Jim Bowie Hotel.

When they got back, Jens Steiner and his goalkeepers and fullbacks planned to watch a tape of the Belgium–Netherlands match played two days earlier in RFK Stadium in Washington, D.C., and they wanted to have fun while they watched.

They trooped through the hotel lobby, laughing, with cardboard cartons of fajitas, tacos, and burritos. In Chicago, where they had opened the World Cup finals, they had returned with gyros drooling with sour cream; assorted subs with onions and slices of tomato poking out; hot dogs loaded with mustard and chopped onions. Now, they were in Tex-Mex country.

Although the Germans had a match remaining in their group, against the South Koreans in the Cotton Bowl, their appearance in the knockout round of sixteen was guaranteed, and the coaches and trainers were in a buoyant mood.

Steiner, a onetime striker for Leipzig and prominent defector from the former German Democratic Republic, had ordered up some more cases of beer. If there was anything the Germans felt they were unarguably good at—besides playing football, and baking bread, and making sausage—it was brewing and drinking beer.

The Germans could have bought all manner of locally and regionally made designer ales and pilsners, but they wanted to try mass-marketed American lager, which was the standard joke among European travelers returning from the United States.

They had been told that prohibition had put immigrant German brewers out of business in the 1920s. One Chicago bartender had told them the misguided Volstead Act was the result of American women getting the vote. After the unworkable nonsense was repealed, beer à la Prohibition—long on water and short on everything else—was all anybody got. The bartender, rolling his eyes, had shaken his head sadly: Thanks, girls.

In Chicago, the Germans had gone for Budweiser, Miller, Rolling Rock, Stroh's, and Michelob. They thought it was fun drinking American beer with German-sounding brand names. They had found Blatz, and Schlitz, and Meisterbrau.

Another Chicago bartender had tried to tell them there was a Griesedik beer sold in Missourah. Was Griesedik German? he asked grinning.

The Germans looked puzzled.

The bartender, laughing, gave them a round on the house, something he wouldn't have done for his American customers.

Here, in Dallas, they had the inevitable Budweiser and Miller, plus Lone Star, Carta Blanca, Dos Equis, and Corona.

They settled in front of their tube for the Belgium versus Netherlands draw. The young man who had taped the match had included the pregame show of the Camaroon versus Sweden match in the Silverdome, and they found themselves being told that this was the first time in World Cup history games had been played indoors. The Americans had gone to considerable expense and effort to keep grass alive for a month under a fiberglass dome that admitted only ten percent of natural light.

They were told that a mixture of eighty-five percent Kentucky bluegrass and fifteen percent rye was planted in two thousand hexagonal metal flats on a turf farm in Ventura, California, and that, when it was ready, the demented Americans had flown the hexagons to Detroit and fit them together in the Silverdome. They had kept the grass alive by placing banks of thousand-watt halogen lights—standard equipment for indoor marijuana growers—six to eight feet above the turf.

Jens Steiner and his coaches, laughing, decided this endeavor must be evidence of the famous American "can do" spirit, or something, that sometimes took curious forms. They suspected ordinary greed must fit in there somewhere, but it was difficult to ascertain where.

The foolishness with the grass completed, the watching German fullbacks and goalkeepers and their coaches started getting serious; it was time to study the Belgian striker Nicholas de Spoelberch working on the Dutch defenders. De Spoelberch, the RSC Anderlecht superstar, had scored three-fourths of the Belgian goals in their first round win over Saudi Arabia and tie with Holland; one of his scoring shots, a spectacular no-look backheel, had had the German defenders groaning as they watched the video replay on television. If the elusive de Spoelberch was going to pull stunts like that, there was no question they'd have to be alert if they met Belgium.

Down the hall, the German striker, Peter Tarchalski, and the other forwards and their coaches were getting ready to take notes on the match about to begin in Boston's Foxboro Stadium between Italy and Norway.

Ten minutes into Belgium–Netherlands, Elizabeth Gunderson, the comely, German-speaking FIFA security chief, called to say she was coming up with a special delivery envelope that had arrived for Herr Steiner.

1:30 P.M.

Edson. The blond man decided he would call himself Edson. Americans knew nothing about proper football players. No one would know. Mueller would get it, of course, and think it amusing. He'd call himself Edson.

Edson wore penny loafers polished to an anal-compulsive sheen. The creases of his charcoal slacks were sharp as razors, and there was not a speck of lint on his navy blue blazer. He wore a white shirt with a tie of muted green and gray diagonal stripes.

He was, for all the world, a professional gentleman of Dallas, a hustler of real estate or oil leases, possibly, or a young preacher.

"I would like to go to Delaney's Sports Bar," he told the cab driver. Above Edson's forceful cheekbones and below his formidable brow, his restless loner's eyes—a pale, bottomless blue—were as warm as Mr. Ripper's on a listless summer night.

"Eh?"

"*Donde está* Delaney's Sports Bar?"

The driver, looking back over the seat, blinked. "Say again."

"I said, 'Delaney's Sports Bar.' Do you know where that is?"

"Delaney's. Oh, sure. Over on Buckner Boulevard. Cost you about fifteen, give or take a buck."

"Take me there, please."

Edson opened the door and slipped onto the back seat. He was six feet four inches tall and so took up most of the backseat with a sprawl of his knees.

The driver tapped the button of his meter; digital numbers began counting Edson's tab. "You here for the World Cup?"

"I beg your pardon?"

"I said, 'You here for the World Cup?'"

"*Sí.* I am."

"And you're from what country?"

"Argentina."

"I was wondering. We got foreigners all over town what with the soccer and all. Everybody wants to see the Germans tomorrow. I been watchin' on TV. I don't know if you know it or not, but the Rangers are playing the A's tonight in Oakland. It might be worth watching. You look like you might be German."

As he rode, Edson remembered that when Mueller had first given him the job, he had said sport was popular for a reason. If Edson was imaginative and thought about it, he would understand that this was an unusual opportunity for someone with an inquiring mind. Mueller said sports were a substitute for combat, a form of play for human predators. What better way to understand one's adversary than to learn about his sport?

Over the years, Edson had learned that whatever else was happening in the United States in the summertime, baseball, an odd and eccentric game, continued as though nothing had happened. The World Cup was in town, and while the Americans were learning about corner kicks and throw-ins, they also remained glued to the unfolding pennant races.

"Fuckin' Rangers," the driver said. "They're loaded with sluggers, but their pitchers think they're playin' Tee Ball with five year olds. Couple a guys did this fancy computer study, turned out that pitching is forty-five percent of a club's success, and hitting's about forty percent." He shook his head in disgust. "They couldn't expect Nolan Ryan to last fuckin' forever. Noodle arms. But what you want're sluggers, not pansy-ass contact hitters. They got that right. The fuck good's a single gonna do you?"

Edson couldn't figure it. Americans complained about low scoring in football, yet loved a game in which the players spent most of their time standing around; he reasoned that the baseball players burned more calories remaining upright than in any other activity. The catcher, an anomaly, squatted. Sometimes a player fiddled with the bill of his cap, or pulled at his nose or crotch, or spat, or swung a bat, or ran a short sprint, or threw the ball, or argued, but that was about it.

After seven rounds of play, the long-suffering spectators—blood settling in their swollen feet and facing two more innings before fighting the traffic home—stood together and cheerfully shuffled their legs and waggled their arms. This "seventh-inning stretch" was, in Edson's opinion, one of the strangest rituals in all sports.

Mueller had once called the seventh-inning stretch a cheerful, even prideful acknowledgment of fan devotion to a stupefyingly boring contest; it said something about the American character, but Mueller wasn't sure what.

Edson said, "Has anybody over here ever proposed a system of divisions like the Europeans have in soccer, as you call it? The top two or three sides of one division trade places with the two or three sides that finished last in the division ranked above it. You could do it with just one side if you wanted. That way, if Yuma, Arizona, is able to win a class A baseball title, then double A and triple A, it would replace the cellar-dweller in the National League West, say the Dodgers."

The cab driver burst out laughing. "You mean if the New York Yankees finished last in the American League East, they'd have to spend a year playing in jerkwater places like Tidewater or Columbus?"

"That's right. And Tidewater or Columbus would take the Yankees' place in the American League East. You get drama at the top of the chart; who's going to be champion? And you get it at the bottom; who's going to be demoted? The Walla Walla Onions could conceivably make it to the World Series. Why, I'd have thought that would be the democratic ideal in the United States! Egalitarian and all that. A meritocracy."

The driver, Edson in his rearview mirror, laughed even louder. "Say, you Argies're real jokers, ain't you? Do you know who's in charge of the World Cup host committee for Dallas? Lamar Hunt, the founder of the Kansas City Chiefs, and he's got a big piece of the Chicago Bulls. This is J. R. Ewing country. People like the Hunts and the Murchisons do not buy sports franchises only to have them play in Amarillo or Cut and Shoot."

"I suppose not," Edson said.

"The Hunt boys tried to corner the silver market about twenty years back. Old Lamar Hunt ain't so decrepit he's forgotten how the Dallas Tornado was one of the biggies in the North American Soccer League, and people still support the Sidekicks. If this soccer tournament gets people really pumped, guess who's likely going to own the profitable new Dallas franchise?"

Edson grinned. "The Hunt brothers."

"That's Texas," the driver said.

The previous night, Edson had watched a Chicago Cubs game on television; during the seventh-inning break from the tedium, a famous elderly sportscaster led the enthusiastic fans in ritual song. Edson remembered parts of the lyrics.

Take me out to the ball game.
Take me out to the crowd.
Peanuts and popcorn and crackerjacks,
I don't care if I ever go back.

2:00 P.M.

As all professional soccer players know from the time they are school-boys, FIFA's great power stems from its ability to insist on transfer fees to control the movement of players. What was once called the reserve clause in American sports is called vincolo a vita *in Italy,* bond for life, *and the* Abfindung *in Germany. In England, where it still obtains despite being ruled illegal in 1963, it is called retain-and-transfer.*

A soccer player, once owned by a team, is its property for life, to keep, sell, or trade as it sees fit. A player can't shop for the best deal or the best place to play. He is forever stuck.

The doorbell rang, and Jens Steiner opened the door to greet the FIFA security chief, with whom the coaches and players entertained fantasies of a private showing of genuine German bratwurst. The dossier FIFA had forwarded to the Germans for their information said the German-speaking Elizabeth Gunderson was a jujitsu expert. The Germans, knowing this, had fun speculating on her other possible talents.

Unfortunately Ms. Gunderson was all business, as she had made clear from the moment she was introduced to the side she was assigned to protect. Gunderson, in her mid-thirties, was a long-legged, athletic woman with green eyes. She wore her brunette hair short, but not so short, in the opinion of the German footballers, that they wouldn't have anything to hold onto.

With her was a plump young woman from United Parcel Service with a large red and white express envelope tucked under her arm.

Gunderson said, "She says she has to get a receipt from you personally. Can't take my word for it. Our machine downstairs says the package is okay. No metal or no-no stuff."

"Of course. Same in Germany. Always rules. Regulations."

The young woman handed Steiner the envelope and a receipt. "Are you really the coach of the German World Cup team? If you could sign here, please."

Steiner signed the receipt. "Yes, I'm the manager. We're watching a tape of the Belgium–Netherlands match."

Gunderson said, "Doing a little scouting, eh?"

"If we face him, I can tell you Nicholas de Spoelberch won't be easy to mark."

The UPS woman said, "You guys look really good. I saw you on television when you beat Bolivia. I hope you win." She hesitated. "Well, maybe second place. But we all know the U.S. will win the Cup, don't we? We've still got a shot if we can tie Brazil or score three goals."

U.S. tie Brazil? Score three goals? Steiner laughed at that improbability. The Americans, bent on not embarrassing themselves as hosts, had worked extremely hard to improve their side, but still . . .

Gunderson grinned. "The game ain't over till it's over. Isn't that what Yogi Berra said?"

"Exactly right," said the UPS girl. "Reputation, smeputation, Brazil will be a piece of cake. After tomorrow, you guys will be taking notes on us Americans, you wait. Your fullbacks will be watching Luis Garcia. Peter Tarchalski will want to know more about Jerry Gotti." She set off down the hall with her FBI agent escort.

Steiner allowed himself a moment's admiration of Ms. Gunderson's rump, then retreated through the door with the envelope.

He grabbed himself another beer. Although the American public didn't know anything about football, once people realized the emotion it attracted in the rest of the world, they'd locked onto the tournament in a big way.

He supposed the spectacle was what excited the larger public. Isolated in North America, the Americans had missed out on the World Cup drama for years, and now, here they were, part of the action almost in spite of themselves and wanting more.

Steiner felt if the United States ever got its black kids booting footballs in the back alleys of their ghettos, it would become a world power. The prospect of an athlete like Michael Jordan playing soccer was scary. Europeans had better hope that after the excitement of the World Cup, America's kids stayed with the holy trinity of grid football, basketball, baseball.

2:15 P.M.

I don't care if I ever go back!

Edson couldn't remember the rest of the lyrics. He said, "I'm trying to remember a baseball song I heard on television last night. What comes after, 'Root, root, root for the home team'?"

" 'Root, root, root for the side.' " The driver thought for a moment. "I think. I'm not sure."

"That must be it. Thank you." Edson wondered what the Australians must think of that song; down under, "to root," in the vernacular, meant to fuck.

One, two, three strikes you're out,
That's the whole ball game.

Three strikes and you're out. That was the source of the attraction, he was sure. Had to be. Baseball, like life, was a game of subtraction. It was an existential drama. Which team could do the most with its allocated 27 outs?

He felt most Europeans wrongly charged American and Canadian grid football with being boring because they didn't understand it was a game of territory. Yards gained. Yards lost. The rewards of a well-executed game plan. The cost of screwing up—turnovers, in the lingo. The tension was the greatest and the action most dramatic near the goal lines. The time to go for beer was when the ball was in the middle of the field.

Edson was amused by the American practice of having ritual virgins leap up and down on behalf of their outsized, armored champions. At least cheerleaders did not get their hearts cut out as an offering to the gods of victory, as had happened to Aztec virgins.

Once, when Edson had visited a friend who worked in the Argentine embassy in Washington, he had gone to a high-school grid football game in Virginia. He remembered the ritual virgins in their little outfits leaping up and down leading the call of:

Pork chops, pork chops
Greasy, greasy,
We're gonna beat Fairfax
Easy, easy.

In proper football, the ball was almost constantly in front of somebody's goal, and the action was nonstop, fluid, and at moments downright beautiful. But, Edson had to admit, it was difficult to put the ball in the net. In World Cup play it had become nearly impossible. Perhaps, in the difficulty of scoring goals, and the necessity to remain eternally vigilant on defense, football also mimicked life.

"We're here. Delaney's Sports Bar. Fifteen it is."

Edson, eyeing the digital meter, gave him a twenty, signaling with his hand that he didn't want change.

"Thank you."

"De nada."

"They say the ribs are real good here. Plenty of meat on them, and there's a little nip to the sauce. A little ginger there, and maybe some cayenne. I hate it when they smear ketchup on a bone and call it barbecue. Also, they cook it over mesquite. Face it: if you ain't got mesquite, you ain't got Tex-Mex."

As the cab sped away, Edson stepped through a solid oak door into a hallway that functioned as a foyer of sorts. The walls were mounted, floor to ceiling with eight-by-ten photographs of sports greats. He glanced over the pictures: Jesse Owens; Rod Laver; Jean-Claude Killy.

An alcove on one side of the hall of honor contained a Dallas Cowboys section, with quarterbacks from Eddie LeBaron and Don Meredith to Roger Staubach and Troy Aiken. The larger room led into a thicket of rooms for spectators, players, eaters, and drinkers. There were rooms for eating and viewing sports on large screens, as well as rooms for dart throwers, pool players, foosballers, and videogame addicts; if one wanted to check out a chess set or a backgammon board, Delaney's had those too.

Young women possessed of remarkable boobs and butts, and wearing high heels, net stockings, garter belts, and nearly translucent black body tubes, worked their way through the tables bearing platters of beer and food: sweating bottles of Budweiser, Carta Blanca, and Heineken; plates of the Tex-Mex barbecued ribs that the cab driver had recommended; bowls of chili heaped high with chopped onions; cheeseburgers accompanied by huge, salty chunks of French fried potatoes with the skins left on.

Edson counted eight big-screen television monitors. Two featured the Italy versus Norway match in Foxboro Stadium; six were featuring a sports talk show that served as a preliminary to the baseball game in Oakland Coliseum between the Rangers and the Athletics—evidence, he supposed, of interest in the World Cup in Dallas.

He spent a few minutes in a roomful of young men watching the preliminary to the baseball game. They were talking about split-fingered fastballs, a favorite of A's pitchers. Baseball was an ideal beer drinker's game, Edson supposed. Whether at the stadium or in a bar, one could take the time to relieve oneself properly without fear of missing anything of consequence.

Finally, wondering what Mueller would conclude from a place like Delaney's, Edson settled at an empty booth in time to watch an Italian wheel and fire a shot in the middle of the crowd of defenders before the Norwegian goal. If only Mueller was there. What a good time they would have had.

2:32 P.M.

FIFA requires all professional soccer players to register with their league and with their football association. All transfers are noted by FIFA. A player suspended or disciplined in one country is likewise suspended or disciplined in all countries, as in FIFA's one-year suspension of Argentine superstar Diego Maradona for using cocaine.

This global discipline results in ever-increasing "transfer" fees paid by one club to another for the right to contract a player's services. It was FIFA's player's status committee that decreed FC Sevilla should pay Maradona's Italian club a $10 million transfer fee for Maradona's services after his suspension was lifted.

"Goalllllll!" the sportscaster shouted above the din of applause that erupted from RFK Stadium.

In his hotel room, Jens Steiner looked up at the Belgian goal scorer, a young man with long brown hair, running across the pitch, knees pumping high and arms outstretched, a look of pure joy on his face.

Qui! Qui! Qui! Nicholas de Spoelberch was mobbed by his Belgian teammates.

Steiner yelled, *"Auch du Scheisse!"*

He finished opening the envelope.

Steiner had been given a palm-sized portable telephone that he carried with him in a leather pocket on his hip. If he punched 13, a Special Weapons Anti-Terrorist squad would be dispatched immediately. But this wasn't a Code 13, if it was anything. Instead, Steiner called Elizabeth Gunderson.

Steiner asked Gunderson to come up, and she arrived a few minutes later. He handed her a yellow card, slightly larger than a playing card.

Gunderson held it by the edges. She furrowed her brows.

Steiner said, "Given by a football referee as a caution for dangerous play. A second yellow means ejection from the match. This is
what was in the envelope. What do you think, Ms. Gunderson?"

"I have no idea. But we all know the drill." Holding the card by
the edges, she slipped it back into the envelope. "A person never
knows."

Steiner said, "A warning. I don't like it. München. Remember
München. But then, you were probably a little girl then."

"I know about München," Gunderson said.

Elizabeth Gunderson called Andres Lopez of the 1994 World
Cup Organizing Committee, and Sir Roger Dusenberry, chairman
of the Emergency Committee. Gunderson's security force was paid
by the Organizing Committee, but emergencies went directly to
the Emergency Committee.

2:40 P.M.

Edson caught the attention of a waitress. He gestured toward one
of the corner monitors. "What are those television sets for, could
you tell me?"

The graphics on the silent monitors said ten minutes remained
until the eleventh day of questions on international athletic competition.

The waitress glanced at the monitor. "That's NTN, the inter-
active entertainment network. They've got more than six hundred
bars hooked up by satellite in the U.S. and Canada. Every afternoon before the World Cup game, they have a trivia contest on
international sports."

"I see. They mentioned this in the bar at my hotel. I wanted to
see for myself."

"Each week, the top twenty North American scorers get a
T-shirt. Whoever has the best single score during the tournament,
plus whoever has the best total of three scores, gets a trip for two
to the NFL Pro Bowl in Honolulu. Hotel. A helicopter trip over a
volcano. The works."

"Hawaii! Well!" Mueller would be rubbing his hands with glee.

"But you have to remember, you're looking at twelve to fifteen
thousand hotshots with remotes in their hands. The World Cup's
got everybody worked up."

"And may anyone play?"

"Of course. No charge. I can get you a remote, if you want."

"I think I'll join in, sure. Could you bring me a Beck's, please, and a remote. I'll eat after the contest. Maybe some of your ribs."

"We've got some real good ribs here."

While he waited for his beer and the remote, Edson watched the new messages being screened on the NTN monitor. Owing to the coming Fourth of July, NTN's regular afternoon trivia contest would feature questions on American history.

In a few minutes, the waitress was back with his Beck's and a remote. "All you do is log in an identification of six letters or less and wait for the first question. You're given a choice of six possible answers. The quicker you answer, the more points you score— beginning with one thousand points for answers under one second."

"I see."

"They'll give you two negative clues, then one which may be negative or positive. But if you don't know the answer by the third clue, you'll hardly score any points. If your answer is wrong, you're penalized two hundred fifty points. Right now you have to beat Easy Money."

"Easy Money?"

"A Canadian."

"How can that be? I thought players are limited to six letters?"

"E-S-Y-M-Y is how he logs in. His real name is Eugene something. They play the game in three parts with breaks so you can go to the john or order another beer."

Edson, watching the legs of the retreating waitress, turned on the remote. He tapped the ENTER button, thought for a moment, then logged in, using five of his allowed six spaces:

EDSON

The monitors said two minutes remained until the questions on international competition.

On the big screen, Norway was trying desperately to pull even with Italy, but the Italians, their fullbacks playing tenacious defense, refused to yield.

A list of Delaney's players who were logged-in and ready to play—including EDSON—scrolled past the monitors.

HERE WE GO, said the monitor.

Then, the first question.

TAMARA PRESS PARTICIPATED IN WHAT FORM OF ATHLETIC COMPETITION?

SWIMMING

BICYCLING

BIATHLON

SHOT PUTTING

EQUESTRIAN

Edson's finger was as quick as an adder's tongue.

After one second, the one thousand score on the monitor began rolling toward zero. The monitors said, NO HORSING AROUND. The first negative clue.

Another second. CAN'T SHOOT STRAIGHT. The second negative clue.

The third clue would be either negative or positive. TAKES A HEFTY MAID. Positive. Shot putting was the answer.

The game was over.

After a pause for Delaney's house computer to digest the data, the monitors all said, FAST HANDS, EDSON. Although several players had scored one thousand points by responding within a second, the blond man had been the first player in Delaney's to answer the question.

The monitors scrolled the idents and scores. Although EDSON had answered first, eight other players had scored a perfect thousand as well.

Edson looked mildly disgusted. Everybody knew about Irina and Tamara Press, for God's sake. They had pussies and male chromosomes, a formidable combination in the bad old days, and on top of that the Soviets pumped them to the eyeballs with steroids. No damn wonder they set women's shot put and discus records for years.

Edson remembered that Mueller had for years scoured the countryside looking for little girls to match them, but it was impossible; the Press sisters belonged in a carnival, not a track meet. It was said they had clits the size of a midget's dick.

Then the next question:

WHO WAS THE 'RABBIT,' OR PACER, FOR ROGER BANNISTER WHEN HE
RAN THE WORLD'S FIRST SUB-FOUR-MINUTE MILE, 3:59.4, IN OXFORD,
ENGLAND, ON MAY 6, 1954?

CHRIS BRASHER

KIP KEINO

JOSEPH CHESIRE

CHRIS CHATAWAY

BRASHER AND CHATAWAY.

Edson tapped quickly. Another giveaway thousand points.

The monitor said, NO AFRICAN.

Then, KANSAS TOO YOUNG.

Finally, RHYMES WITH THAT AWAY.

The monitor, digesting the results, said, FAST HANDS AGAIN,
EDSON.

Big deal. Edson signaled to the waitress for another Beck's.
Mueller would be the one. Nobody could beat Mueller at this
game.

The monitor said, CHRIS BRASHER DID THE FIRST QUARTER, THEN
CHRIS CHATAWAY TOOK OVER UNTIL THE FINAL 300 YARDS, WHEN ROGER
BANNISTER, A SLENDER MEDICAL STUDENT, MADE HIS RUN FOR HISTORY.

Then, WHICH OF THE FOLLOWING RACE CAR DRIVERS IS OR WAS FROM
ARGENTINA?

ARTURO NUVOLARI

PEDRO RODRIGUEZ

ARYTON SENNA

JUAN MANUEL FANGIO

RICARDO PETRESE

A fast tap.

NO ART INVOLVED.

PETERS AT EASE.

DICKS AT REST.

The monitor paused, then said, JUAN MANUEL FANGIO IS THE
STORIED ARGENTINE DRIVER, WINNER OF 24 GRAND PRIX CHAMPIONSHIP
RACES BETWEEN 1950 AND 1957. HE RETIRED IN 1958 WITH FIVE WORLD
GRAND PRIX TITLES. THE STORIED ARTURO NUVOLARI WAS AN ITALIAN,
AS IS PETRESE; PEDRO RODRIGUEZ WAS MEXICAN, AND ARYNTON SENNA,
BRAZILIAN.

Edson wasn't as strong on motor sports, but who didn't know about Fangio?

Fifty-five minutes later, when the game was finished—after three rounds of play and two five-minute pee breaks—the monitors scrolled the list of Delaney's players and their scores. At the top, with 28,600 points out of a possible 30,000, was EDSON.

Then the wrap-up from NTN central in California: CONGRATULATIONS, EDSON, OF DELANEY'S SPORTS PUB IN DALLAS. YOUR SCORE OF 28,600 IS NOW THE TOP SINGLE SCORE, PASSING THE 27,900 BY ESYMY OF THE AUSTIN HOTEL, VANCOUVER, B.C. REMEMBER PLAYERS, YOU'VE GOT PLENTY OF CHANCES LEFT TO BEAT EDSON OR ACCUMULATE THE TOP THREE SCORES. SEE YOU AGAIN TOMORROW.

Edson erased EDSON from his remote and turned his attention to the match between Greece and Colombia.

When the waitress arrived with another Beck's, she said, "By the way, you're not EDSON are you?"

Edson laughed. "You mean the one who won the game? No, I'm afraid it's not me. How many people would know who set the pace for Roger Bannister?"

"He's good. Did you see that score?"

"I certainly did."

She said, "He knew that someone named Helmut Rechnagel of East Germany won the seventy-meter ski-jump championship in 1960."

"*Helmoot* Rachnagel. Helmets are what firefighters wear."

"*Helmoot,* right. How did he know something like that do you suppose? EDSON has to be in here somewhere. The guys in the next room don't believe it. They say it's a setup."

"A setup? I don't understand."

"They're saying the guy knew the answers in advance, had to."

Edson shrugged his shoulders. He'd have to drop a note to Mueller; Mueller would be amused. He said, "I believe I'll have another Beck's and an order of your Tex-Mex barbecued ribs, please."

On the big screen, the jubilant Italian striker headed in his second goal of the day, putting Italy up two–zip over Norway.

9:00 P.M.

Edson cruised in his Saturn. Given his choice among Hertz, Avis, and a long line of other car rental companies, he had chosen Alamo, this being Texas. The Saturn was a good enough car, although he was annoyed by General Motor's bragging that it was the single largest-selling model in the world.

It probably was, yes, but everybody knew the numbers were gained by cut-rate fleet sales to car rental companies and businesses, not single buyers, which was where the money was. Not that the Japanese were any better. The entrepreneurial carbuncles from Nippon blew off profit so they could brag about how many cars they sold in other people's domestic markets. No wonder the ECC had circled its economic wagons against the pernicious little fuckers.

For the fun of it, Edson decided to take a drive and have a late supper before he went to bed. In his hotel room, he studied the map. The Cotton Bowl. Texas Stadium. Southern Methodist University. Dallas Baptist University. Christ For The Nations. Christ For The Nations? Edson furrowed his brow.

Just east of city center lay the Cotton Bowl; just west lay Texas Stadium, where the Dallas Cowboys played grid football.

Texas, second to Alaska in size among American states, was 850 miles from its northwestern to southeastern tip, that is, the distance from Copenhagen to Florence; it was 750 miles from east to west—say, from Budapest to Paris. Dallas, a prairie city famous for its fundamentalist Protestants and grid football fans, once promoted its grid football Cowboys as "America's team." Edson remembered the Cowboys' famous sideline troups of leggy dancers.

Just 75 miles south of Dallas, a spit and a holler by Texas standards—Amsterdam to Antwerp—lived the residents of Waco, Dallas's embarrassing cousins. It was in Waco that eightscore of David Koresh's determined believers had flamed their way to Armageddon. Edson wondered: Had Koresh watched the Cowboys on the tube Sunday afternoons, praying to Jesus that Troy Aikman would not be intercepted?

In the end, Edson decided to drive west on Highway 30 so he could tell Mueller that, believe it or not, he had driven past the Palace of War & Ripley's Believe It Or Not in Grand Prairie, Texas.

He drove while listening to a bluesy sax on an FM station. There were times he thought Europeans appreciated jazz more than the Americans did, the Germans and the French especially. Mueller once said that only two art forms had originated in America: jazz and private detective novels. Americans could claim one sport, basketball. And they had one original political idea— the wary citizenry's permanent division of the public trough by the separation of the judicial, executive, and legislative branches of government.

The saxophone had caused a jazz comeback, thanks, Edson supposed, to President Bill Clinton's honking and squawking. But this revival wasn't such a bad thing. This player had lips of midnight. Music for J.R.'s restless wife? Blues for a material girl?

3

LAKE WALLOWA, OREGON, 11:40 A.M., TUESDAY, JUNE 28

The earliest soccer tactic required a player to dribble toward the goal until an opponent took the ball from him. Then the opponent dribbled. A player "backed up" his dribbling mate so that, should the ball become lost, it could be quickly retrieved.

Back and forth the players went, dribbling. Nobody thought to pass the ball.

The Scots introduced the sensational new tactic, passing, in an 1872 international with England in Glasgow. Thus soccer forever changed from an individual game, based on dribbling skills, to a team game, based on passing skills.

The pinecone on the mountain in front of James Burlane, seed of the sugar pine, almost begged to be kicked by the next passer-by: *Go ahead, give me a thump, knock a few seeds out of me, and I'll start another tree.*

Burlane gave the pinecone a nudge with the instep of his foot.

Listening to the U.S. versus Brazil on his Sony Walkman, he dribbled lazily up the trail, concentrating on the action in the Silverdome in Pontiac, Michigan.

". . . The Brazilians, in their green and yellow strip, are bringing it across midfield; the Americans, after a few precious, largely wasted seconds in Brazilian territory, are dropping back once more.

"The Americans, underdogs in this tournament, have the opportunity to advance to the knockout Round of 16 if they beat or tie Brazil, which is guaranteed advancement as top seed by virtue of its wins against Russia and Sweden. Owing to the ties that have dogged Group F, the United States, Russia and Sweden are all tied at two points each. If the United States loses, it must score at least three goals, a difficult assignment against the experienced Brazilians. Anything less and Sweden advances.

"The ball goes to the front of the box, a dangerous place that has the American supporters holding their collective breath.

"The Brazilians will advance as a favored seed no matter what the outcome, but they bear proudly their reputation as exciting, skilled football players. They don't want to go into the Round of 16 bearing the ignominy of a tie or loss against the United States.

"The explosive Antonio has the ball, with the determined American defender Pat Duffy right on him. Feet wide, on the balls of his feet, hands spread for balance, Duffy is total concentration, ignoring Antonio's twisting and turning. Once again the American supporters are holding their breath."

DALLAS, 1:45 P.M.

The credit, or blame, for the dominance of defense in international competition is ordinarily attributed to the Italians, although the first modern defense dates to the 1930s and Switzerland, where Karl Rappan, an Austrian international, coached clubs in Geneva and Zurich.

In Rappan's scheme—the verrou, or "Swiss bolt," system—all players pushed forward on attack, and fell back together on defense. The forward players, retreating only to midfield, harassed the attackers as they withdrew.

The "bolt" was a defensive player—called a centerback—who slid from side to side between the goal and the line of fullback defenders. Rappan used three fullbacks in the original verrou, *with two more defenders between and immediately in front of them. The centerback "bolt" was ordinarily a large, quick, and aggressive defender.*

The importance of a judicious assigning of top seeds in the six round-robin groups for preliminary play was not to be underestimated. FIFA had naturally wanted to deliver on its announced goal of selling all of the 3.6 million seats for the fifty-two-match tournament. Previous World Cups had spectators that were either pro–South America or pro–Europe; in the United States, the traditional powers were all given home turf in the opening round.

Argentina got Group A, with two of its three round-robin games in the 102,000 seat Rose Bowl in Pasadena, with the huge population of Hispanics in the San Diego–Los Angeles urban sprawl.

Brazil lucked out with Group B, and two games in Stanford Stadium in Palo Alto, California. Stanford Stadium's field was 118 yards wide, by far the broadest in the tournament. A wide field enabled the attacking side to spread the defense; where there was space, one could actually play soccer. Better both for players and spectators.

Defending champion Germany was assigned Group C, with two games in Soldier Field in Chicago, in the heart of the German-friendly American Midwest. There were communities of Americans of German ancestry scattered from St. Louis to Milwaukee and beyond.

Argentina got Group D and two games in Boston's Foxboro Stadium.

Italy got Group E and two games in Giants Stadium, the better for Italian-American New Yorkers and Sicilian mobsters to watch the action.

Belgium got Group F and two matches in Orlando.

Now, in the Cotton Bowl, the freckle-faced striker Peter Tarchalski and the teammates who would most often be with him in the thick of the German attack—Willi Gochnauer, of FC Stuttgart; Gerd Schmidt, of Borussia Mönchengladbach; Dieter Bauer, of Borussia Dortmund; and Georg Diehl of Bayern Munich—formed a semicircle around their goalkeeper Hans Spek, of SV Werder

Bremen, who crouched in front of the net, waiting for their shots.

Tarchalski and his scoring mates wore the German national strip of white shirts, black shorts, and black socks. Spek, the goalkeeper, was dressed in a splendid, all-scarlet strip. The goalkeeper, the only player allowed to use his hands, wore off-color strip to set him apart in the heat of action.

At the other end of the pitch, the South Koreans warmed up for the match.

As Tarchalski waited for a football to be rolled back to him by Spek or a ball boy, he jogged in place, looking up at the crowd in Soldier Field. This was the World Cup, and the spectators had gathered early, wanting to enjoy the whole show, which began with the warm-ups by the German and South Korean stars. It was tournament play, yes, but it was also spectacle.

Part of the fun was comparing the players pictured in the World Cup guide with the legends and newcomers on the field. In the World Cup all players took the pitch for their native country no matter where they usually played. Most of the Germans played in the Bundesliga—their country's first division—but several, including Tarchalski, were internationals. The German midfielder Fritz Brandt played for Spain's Real Madrid, and the German sweeper Heiner Hesse played for the French club Saint-Étienne. Tarchalski played for Arsenal in the English First Division.

Somewhere up there, Tarchalski knew, someone would be studying his photograph and description in the guidebook: "Peter 'Der Wildebeest' Tarchalski, 23, striker, Arsenal, English Premiere League scoring champion, 1992 and 1993." Then they'd search him out on the field and watch him as he limbered up. When they saw him, he knew they'd smile and say, *Yes, that one's The Wildebeest, has to be. Look at those legs. And that neck of his!*

At six feet four inches, Tarchalski indeed had long legs. His long neck made his torso look short. He did not run so much as glide, and when he glided, Tarchalski's lank blond hair flopped lightly on his forehead. When he was in full-cruise stride, which was deceptively fast, he was something to behold. A writer for the *Daily Telegraph* once claimed Tarchalski looked more like a detached scholar than a passionately competitive athlete; what on earth had made this German think he could play football?

When one of his teammates looped a high pass into the box, and Tarchalski powered himself above the confusion of fullbacks, hair mid-flop, to accept the ball, he showed why he was the best striker in the English First Division. He did not just deflect the pass toward the goal. The Wildebeest, whipping his lank blond hair, boomed the ball past the goalkeeper with a powerful thrust of his amazing neck.

Herr Steiner had gathered the side together before the match and told them about the yellow card. He said nobody had any idea what the caution meant, if anything. The U.S. Federal Bureau of Investigation was looking into it.

LAKE WALLOWA, 11:15 A.M.

The World Cup was, in fact, global, not a North American competition like the American World Series. In 1992, Icelanders entered the opening rounds of the World Cup tournament with hopes as high and dreams of glory as grand as those of players from Oman, Sri Lanka, Antigua, the Faroe Islands, and the African country Burkina Faso.

Every World Cup seemed to have a surprise side of one kind or another. In 1930, a time when soccer leagues were thriving in the Northeast, the United States advanced to the semifinal round of the first World Cup tournament, held in Uruguay. The South Koreans made it to the quarterfinal round of 1966, and were up 3–0 against Portugal when they forgot to play defense and lost 5–3. In 1990, the Camerooni- ans showed the biggies how to play soccer, making it to the quarterfinal round.

If there had been two schoolboys on James Burlane's trail, or an old boy and a schoolboy—or even two old boys pretending to be schoolboys—the test would have been equally elementary and double the fun. Could a second player, without using his hands, prevent the kicker from striking the agreed-upon target?

And, just as challenging: could the defender, using only his feet, steal the pinecone ball, forcing his opponent to defend a goal?

An inflated camel's bladder on a patch of Egyptian sand or a proper soccer ball in a Liverpool schoolyard, what was the differ- ence? In the playful realm of Little Kid, all players are Pelés, and all the balls are beautiful.

Little kids of all manner of races and cultures on every continent dreamed a wonderful dream . . .

To play in the World Cup.

. . . they dreamed this dream in streets, vacant lots, pastures, and on fields of all manner of description—on grass, gravel, and sand. For soccer was a democratic sport. Africans. Asians. Size wasn't critical. Pelé at five nine was universally recognized as the best player in the history of the sport.

No, not just to play in the World Cup, to be in the final and to win it.

To play for one's country was the extraordinary kick. The juice. In the end, the Cup settled the issue of what country played the best soccer in the world. The opinions of computers, bookies, or the boys in the pub meant nothing; whoever won the World Cup got to brag.

James Burlane came upon another pinecone.

Ten yards in back of the pinecone, where the trail circled through a thicket of sugar pine, grew a ponderosa pine about six inches in diameter, with a large knot, or burl, about shoulder high.

Burlane studied the pinecone, then the burl, clearly the goal-mouth. The challenge put to the eternal schoolboy within Burlane: Could he strike the pinecone cleanly and hit the burl?

He fancied himself a striker on the American side. The ball—fortune's pinecone—was laid before him, a pass delicately served.

DALLAS, 1:55 P.M.

In 1947, an Italian named Nereo Rocco took the first step toward making defense the ne plus ultra *of soccer tactics. Rocco, named manager of Triestina, which had barely escaped relegation to the second division the previous year, went to the* verrou *for inspiration. He reasoned that if he couldn't spend as much money as the rich clubs for attacking players from South America, then he should concentrate on defense, which he could afford.*

In Rocco's insidious formation, the centerback did not move forward with the attack. He stayed put, behind three fullbacks who had three midfielders in front of them. Rocco called him the libero, or "free man"—being free to back up whichever fullback needed help. Rocco called this the catenaccio—*the great chain—of defenders.*

There had been stories in the *Chicago Tribune* and the *Chicago Sun-Times* about the World Cup excitement in German-American communities in Wisconsin, Michigan, and Illinois, and about the car caravans organized to travel to Chicago for Germany's opening two first round matches.

Characteristically, American sports stadia were huge monoliths ordinarily rising out a vast expanse of suburban parking lot. One of the big stories on Chicago television had to do with the planned tailgate parties before Germany's opening match: German-Americans from Iowa through Illinois, Minnesota, Wisconsin, and Michigan, swelled with ethnic pride, were eager to display their virtuosity with German food out of the backs of their vehicles in the parking lot.

The German players were told that the tailgate party was an American tradition in which grid football fans in their station wagons gathered in the parking lots surrounding a stadium to prepare for the game by drinking beer and eating picnic food. In time, tailgate parties had become competitive. If a family of Nebraska Cornhusker fans barbecued chicken over alder-wood charcoal before the game with the Cowboys from Oklahoma State, their neighbors responded with Rock Cornish hens over cherry-wood when the Cornhuskers faced the Colorado Buffalo. There were parking lots in American grid-football stadia where fans bought their spaces the day before and spent the night in RVs. Fans of the Arkansas Razorbacks had parking-lot hog-calling contests. In different parts of the country fans warmed up for the big game by baying like wolves, buzzing like bees, quacking like ducks, or screaming like eagles, depending on the animal name of their padded heroes.

Owing to its near-downtown location on the shores of Lake Michigan, Soldier Field did not have the usual vast parking lots to accommodate a tailgate spectacular. Still, FIFA's organizing committee, responding to complaints by the German Americans, saw to it that such space as was available, plus the parking lots at the nearby Field Museum of Natural History, were reserved for tailgaters.

Before the opening match, Peter Tarchalski and some of his teammates had taken a stroll among the assembled campers, vans, and pickup trucks, and the tailgaters were delighted to show off their sausages, venison sauerbraten, German bread, and crocks of sauerkraut and dill pickles. *Ja! Ja! Ja!*

In Peter Tarchalski's opinion, their food was every bit as good as that back home. By back home, Tarchalski meant Germany, not England, where in addition to suffering the awful English food, he was required to bang bodies with odious English fullbacks. The English, short on both skill and brains, in Tarchalski's opinion, were notorious bangers. Tarchalski's long legs were inviting targets to fullbacks who wanted him to remember them and avoid their territory next time up the pitch.

Tarchalski had Benny Burbick to feed him the ball at Arsenal; now Willi Gochnauer of FC Stuttgart would most likely deliver. Gochnauer led the Bundesliga in assists.

Tarchalski had led the English Premiere League not the Bundesliga, in scoring. In Germany, that made a difference. They played slop in England; all Germans knew that. The Germans were the ones who won World Cups, not the English.

Yes, England beat Germany 4–2 for the championship in 1966, but they were helped by a nongoal goal awarded by *das arschloch* Russian linesman.

Peter Tarchalski wanted nothing more to do with England. It wasn't that he disliked the English, especially. They were good enough people. He just wanted to be back in Germany. He missed the beer, the language, and the food.

DALLAS, 2:00 P.M.

Edson could have chosen one of Germany's first two opening-round matches in Chicago, but Soldier Field was flanked by Lake Michigan on the north, Burnham Park Harbor on the east, and an open area around the Field Museum of Natural History to the west.

The Cotton Bowl on the other hand, was located in a park east of downtown Dallas and below the principal east–west entrance to the city, Interstate 80. There was no water here to cut down on potential firing lanes. And there were avenues and boulevards running in all directions.

So here, nearly in the shadow of the Texas Schoolbook Depository, Edson would strike.

For many Americans, Edson knew, the Texas Schoolbook Depository triggered passionate arguments about the famous film Abraham Zapruder took of the assassination of John F. Kennedy. How many shots were actually fired and from where? Were there mysterious figures on the grassy knoll? Was Lee Harvey Oswald alone, shooting from the sixth floor of the brick building? Or were there others?

The Warren Commission concluded that Oswald alone killed Kennedy, firing an Italian-made, 1938 G.S. Mannlicher-Carcano carbine with iron sights, a bolt-action weapon with a minimum fire-and-reload time of 2.3 seconds. President Kennedy and Texas Governor John Connally were in an open-topped limousine 68 yards away, moving at 11.2 miles per hour when the first shot hit home.

This was where a confusion over Oswald's shooting skills began, spurring questions that remained unanswered. Witnesses said they heard three shots. The FBI said Oswald fired three shots. The Warren Commission said Oswald had scored two hits and one missed shot; one slug, it was asserted, passed through Kennedy before striking Texas Governor Connally.

Could Oswald do that with a weapon that Benito Mussolini himself would no doubt have scorned?

Encouraged by Mueller, who said fire-and-reload times varied with the skills of the marksman, Edson took a turn at duplicating Oswald's feat. He laid three hits on a moving Kennedy-dummy target in 4.6 seconds. But four of Edson's colleagues had failed, and they were all skilled, experienced marksmen with far better credentials that Oswald. Mueller didn't think Oswald had killed Kennedy alone. He argued that Edson had the advantage of years of systematic, disciplined practice with bolt-action rifles, which were standard in international match competition, and the time required to lock and load a new round decreased significantly with practice.

Mueller said that interests in sports and weapons were masculine, complementary, and natural to the human male. Sport was ritual combat. Humankind, the slowest and weakest of predators, owed its triumphant survival to intelligence; man was the most advanced user of tools in the animal kingdom, and firearms, death tools, extended his ability to draw blood, which was what being a predator was all about. Skill in killing with a high-powered rifle, the ultimate masculine art, was obtained by sheer, bonehead, stubborn practice; by constant drill one imprinted the requirements for success in one's brain.

Mueller said it was equal folly to compete with second-rate equipment. Since one always had access to the best—at least Mueller did—then get the best. Mueller's people had the best of whatever they required—shoes, skates, poles, pistols, name it.

Unfortunately, intelligence and nerve couldn't be bought, Mueller said. Some had it; some didn't. Intelligence. Nerve. Concentration. The will to persist. That was the test of competition in all its many forms, ritual and otherwise. It was nature's way of separating winners from losers.

Mueller said democratic politics reflected the collective will of losers, while progress demanded that winners be allowed to win. Mueller said FIFA was a perfect example of this phenomenon, the results of which were unsurprising. With every football association having one vote, the object of FIFA's grave deliberations and complicated politics was to regulate football in such a way as to prevent domination by a few clubs or countries. The refusal to adjust the rules to encourage offense was the result.

Did countries with limited pools of talent want liberal substitution rules? No, they did not.

The disinclination to add another official was another result. As things stood, only the referee could call penalties and fouls. It wasn't so much that the football associations were too cheap to hire more officials or couldn't train them properly, but that one referee, having just one pair of eyes and modest peripheral vision, could not control the hacking and shinning on defense.

Penalty minutes, as in hockey, would have the same effect: to reward expensive offense at the expense of cheap defense.

And did countries without television want to interrupt a game for commercials?

And the result of FIFA's conservatism?

One of four countries—Argentina, Brazil, Germany, and Italy— had been in the championship match since the first tournament in

1930. Uruguay and Argentina had won it twice; Brazil, Germany, and Italy had each won it three times. And a handful of clubs, recognizable to most football fans, had dominated play within countries: Saint-Étienne in France; RSC Anderlecht in Belgium; Borussia Mönchengladbach and Bayern Munich in Germany; Ajax and Feyenoord in the Netherlands; Juventus and AC Milan in Italy; Real Madrid and Barcelona in Spain; Liverpool and Manchester United in England; the Celtics and the Glasgow Rangers in Scotland; Independiente and Boca Juniors in Argentina; Fluminense, Flamingo, and Botafogo in Brazil; Penarol and Nacional in Uruguay.

Clearly, those clubs with the most resources inevitably found a way to win. Mueller couldn't understand why, if the little guys were going to be losers, they chose to lose while playing boring defense. Why not lose in an entertaining way? The way football was now played, no wonder fans in the profitable American market had balked.

Mueller came to the conclusion, in one of his and Edson's last sessions of talk, that a failure of this sort was what ultimately brought down the Soviet empire; there had been no television when FIFA was conceived in 1904, just as there were no computers or television when the Bolsheviks launched their experiment in 1918.

Now, eyeing the Cotton Bowl in the city where John Kennedy had fallen thirty-one years earlier, Edson worked the ultra-smooth bolt of his Steyr-Mannlicher match rifle. The Austrian-made rifle fired .308 Winchester rounds, the same as 7.62 mm NATO rounds; it weighed nearly 12 pounds with the silencer attached to its 25.6-inch barrel.

Edson had mounted an American-made Leupold telescopic on the Steyr-Mannlicher. The Leupold gave him a field of vision from 5.7 feet wide to 14.8 feet wide at 100 yards. The scope was a big one, 14.2 inches long and a full American pound, but it was extraordinarily clear and accurate.

The amused Mueller had once told Edson that when the American gunsmith Samuel Colt went to the U.S. Army with his curious invention, a pistol with a revolving cylinder, he was mocked as a crackpot. The Texas Rangers didn't laugh; when they learned how to knock redskins off their horses at close range, they worked their thumbs raw cocking their single-action revolvers. Judging from the number and variety of weapons David Koresh and his Christian soldiers had amassed in Waco, Edson assumed that most Texans remained tolerant, if not outright fond, of shooting irons.

Edson felt he understood Americans who did not want to cede one inch of their right to own guns. They didn't want to own guns because they wanted to kill people, but because they wanted to have them around to play with and show their friends. They liked to feel them. To hold a pistol in one's hand was to hold instant death. A pistol felt cool. It had heft. It was precision killing.

Mueller said most males with the standard dose of hormones got a physical rush out of holding a high-powered rifle; it didn't make any difference if they were college professors, cops, or kids on the street. A pimpled adolescent with a firearm in his hand was suffused with power, bearing lightning as surely as Zeus. Thus even Lee Harvey Oswald, creep, was able to qualify as a footnote to history.

In South America and Asia, Edson had seen young men staring in open-mouthed rapture at posters of guns photographed lying on purple or red velvet; as though they were naked women in a magazine: a Kalashnikov AK-47 leaning against a flowered wall in an angle of lethal repose; a Colt Python revolver, .357 magnum with an eight-inch barrel, on a pink pillow, cocked.

In examining the gun posters, Edson was convinced that the photographers routinely airbrushed the barrels to spiff up the wicked shaft of reflected light. Pretty pussies and beautiful pistols. Edson almost laughed out loud at the suggestion that the many wars and armed disputes that raged around the planet had anything to do with injustice.

Mueller said the drama of life lay in the cycle of creation and death; those who denied the obvious, ordinarily the losers of the world, simply refused to let truth stand in the way of their righteous ideals.

Of course, few Texans or anybody else would publicly admit that their affection for killing metal had anything to do with

Mueller's forthright, if unnerving views. Edson was amused at the thought of showing the folks in Dallas what real shooting was all about.

DALLAS, 2:10 P.M.

A tie on the road had long been considered the equal of a win at home, and so the catenaccio *was first used at away matches. Then clubs began using it at home, going so far as to add a fourth fullback in front of the* libero, *leaving only two offensive players forward—a striker and perhaps a winger.*

Then the big clubs started using the catenaccio, *and since they had more money to spend, they did it even better. Inter Milan won the European Cup twice using the* catenaccio, *and defensive play became the mark of Italian soccer.*

Slowly, this defensive play spread to the rest of the soccer-playing world. The English called the libero *the "sweeper." In addition to a fourth fullback, some clubs put yet another defender in front of all these, the "screen," who moved from side to side facing the point of attack.*

Players scored 140 goals in the 1954 World Cup, an average of 5.3 each game. They scored 89 goals in the 1962 tournament, an average of 2.7 goals a game, and the play remained defensive from then on.

Peter Tarchalski knew the American fans in the Cotton Bowl were also listening via radio to the end of the match in Detroit, where the overachieving Americans were holding Brazil to a nil–nil tie. Detroit and Dallas were in the same time zone, but the U.S. versus Brazil match started an hour and a half earlier.

Tarchalski and his teammates had watched the match on television in the locker room until it was time to take the pitch and warm up. After a while, the bad luck of the Brazilians had become nearly comic.

The German players all agreed they would prefer to have the luck-out United States advance to the knockout Round of 16 than someone who could be dangerous later on. The question was, how on earth did the Yanks propose to score? The Americans were earnest and hardworking, yes. And they had proven they could defend. But they had to score goals in order to advance.

It felt good to be playing with Germans again. Tarchalski's English mates were both friendly and fun, and he spoke good English, but still, it wasn't the same. German was his language. He'd always be more comfortable speaking German.

Tarchalski braked a shot with his left foot and looped an easy ball over Hans Spek to make him stretch. The score in Texas was obviously still nothing to nothing; there had been no communal groan in the RFK Stadium to signal a Brazilian goal.

In Europe, they whistled their jeers. In the United States, they booed, individually and in raucous chorus. In East Asia, he supposed, soccer fans would most likely ape the Americans they watched on television. The idea of sport, that is, organized, playful contests, as opposed to outright, barbarous bloodletting, was European in origin, spread to Asia by displaced Europeans living in North America.

LAKE WALLOWA, 12:12 P.M.

On June 29, 1950, the wire services reported, to the disbelief of the planet, that the United States had defeated England 1–0 at Belo Horizonte. Journalists from the U.K. who watched this game voted it England's best match of the year, except that the Englishmen forgot to score any goals.

The American goal was scored when Walter Bahr, later the soccer coach at Penn State University, took a twenty-five-yard shot at the far post; the free-spirited, acrobatic American center forward, Joe Gaetjens, misdirected the shot with his head, putting it past the diving English goalkeeper, Bert Williams, who was following Bahr's shot.

Later, it turned out that Gaetjens was traveling on a Haitian passport, never mind that World Cup rules required him to be an American citizen.

James Burlane, in the Zone of Little Kid, told himself that if he kicked the pinecone and hit the burl on the tree, it would be a good omen, and the Americans would upset the Brazilians—past winners of three World Cups. Unknown to the entire world, he, James Burlane, would have scored the winning goal in the Wallowa Mountains of eastern Oregon. All he had to do was hit the burl with the pinecone.

Under Burlane's rules, a pinecone soccerball that missed the goal became an ordinary pinecone before it hit the ground—a Cinderella pinecone. But the next pinecone was another matter. The next pinecone would be the magic one, a wonderful pass perfectly delivered, and he'd find another target for a goal.

And if he hit that target, well . . .

He closed his eyes and entered the zone of imagination.

Ah the dream . . . The glory . . . A goal in World Cup competition.

He saw it all, and it was so grand . . .

Jimmy Burlane in the World Cup against the proud, eccentric Brazilians, they of the stylish, soft feet. Their skill with the ball was legendary; they used their chests and feet to catch the ball rather than simply control it. It was said Brazilians played soccer with the same panache as they danced the samba and the mamba. They nearly embraced and caressed the ball with their bodies and feet. The drama was the thing.

In the opinion of Brazilians, the Western Europeans had bodies that were posts, but the Eastern Europeans, vulgar bangers, were even worse. And the Americans? It was to laugh. The Americans, having hired the best coaches in the world to teach them how to play, were yet unable to excel; their well-known deficiencies—feet of stone and lack of style—were borderline genetic in origin, right up there with the Brits ability to throw Japanese darts and the ability to understand Zen.

DALLAS, 2:28 P.M.

The modern concept of soccer, total soccer, was pioneered by the Dutch in the early 1970s when Feyenoord of Rotterdam won the European Cup in 1970, followed by Ajax of Amsterdam from 1971 through 1973.

In this blending of offensive and defensive skills, the formations shifted, with players pushing forward and dropping back according to the situation and the combinations of their individual skills. A good player had to be fit, have good ball skills, and be smart.

The German side Bayern Munich won the European Cup from 1974 through 1976, as the Germans, known for their fitness, discipline, and uncomplicated tactics, emerged as a perennial power in international competition.

There were not a few suggestions that Hamburg's Dieter Bauer ought to be Germany's main man, not Tarchalski. Tarchalski was sensitive to suggestions, made both in the U.K. and Germany, that he was an overachiever with an indifference to the pain of getting kicked in the legs.

He put up with getting kicked all the time. The secret of his success! Not that Tarchalski couldn't head the ball in, or couldn't shoot with either foot, or wasn't good at passing in traffic. No, no. He was good because he could take the hammering in front of the goal mouth.

Also, there was that business of his going to England.

Signing a contract with Arsenal had been the biggest mistake of Tarchalski's life. When Arsenal's owner, media mogul Harry Beauchamp, had secretly and generously charmed him, in violation of FIFA's rules, Tarchalski should have been careful.

Only later, too late, locked into a FIFA-enforced contract, did he learn that no amount of British pounds could compensate for having his club's owner publicly mock him for failing to score a goal in a critical match.

Tarchalski had done everything he could to bail out of Arsenal and return to Germany to shut the doubters' mouths, but it was impossible.

Screw FIFA.

But now, after all the lawyers and arguing and bitterness, Peter Tarchalski was out of there, out of the horror of playing for Harry Beauchamp, out of London and on his way back to Germany as the striker for FC Cologne. The transfer fee had been paid. It was a done deal except that Harry Beauchamp's newspapers loved to gloat that Arsenal's striker was the chief German goal scorer, never mind that he'd be gone come next season.

So, the deal was not technically complete until after the World Cup.

Then, release. Freedom.

5

As the host country, the United States got an automatic slot in 1994, but the Americans earned their way to the World Cup in Italy in 1990. They gave the host Italians a 1–0 scare that had soccer fans from the Alps to Sicily twisting their prayer beads in anxiety.

The earphone of James Burlane's Sonny Walkman exploded with the action from The Silverdome. "Yes," he shouted to the Wallowa Mountains, "Yes, yes, yes!"

On the Walkman, Halloran:

". . . and once again the Brazilians were thwarted by the brilliant goalkeeping of Jerry Gotti, as the goalkeeper for the Blackburn Rovers made another acrobatic stop in the confusion in the box. The Brazilian striker, Antonio, shook his head in dismay as somehow, incredibly, Gotti twisted and managed to deflect the point-blank shot over the bar.

"Gotti is in the center of the box now, shouting defensive instructions to his teammates as Rubio, the star of Italy's powerful FC Inter Milan, gets ready for the corner kick. Gotti is in command here. His mates will do as they're told. Pointing with his hand, shouting instructions, he tells them where he wants them. The rangy Antonio, frustrated, takes the far outside corner of the box, he'll come forward with Rubio's kick . . .

"A hard, tight curve—out and in toward the box. Beautiful! Ohhhhh, Antonio got his head solidly on the ball, when out of nowhere, a leaping Pat Duffy returned the favor with his own noggin, redirecting the ball over the top of the bar."

"That's not robbery, Don Halloran, that's statutory rape. Jerry Gotti and Pat Duffy have these amazed and delighted fans on their feet in appreciation of their inspired performances. We're nearly eighty minutes into the goalless game, and the Brazilians must be wondering what it takes to get a ball past the demonic Gotti, who continues to defend the goal with a passion, and Pat Duffy is driving the Brazilian superstar Antonio up the wall. Bonkers. Bananas. Unhinged."

"Name the cliché."

"There you've got it, Don. Around the bend. Off his nut. Loonie-woonie. If the Brazilians don't watch out, the Americans will figure out a way to repeat their amazing upset of England in 1950. On that day too, the luck was with the Yanks. England played extraordinary soccer, but couldn't find the net."

"Antonio dribbling again. Duffy is on him like a terrier after the mailman. Oh, and Duffy tackles the ball out of bounds, and the Brazilians will have to throw it in. Did you see the look Antonio gave the American?"

Burlane concentrated on the burl.

He studied the pinecone ball.

He took a practice swing with his foot. He'd strike the cone with his instep. He told himself: *Concentrate on the goal and strike it solidly.*

With Halloran describing yet another Brazilian theft at midfield, Burlane swung at the pinecone . . .

. . . and watched it sail wide by at least a yard.

He'd let the side down. Idiot! Laughing at himself, he ran up the trail in a panic. There was still time. It was still possible. He could do it. Never quit. Never.

Detroit, 2:50 P.M.

Luis Garcia fogged out. There was no other accounting for it.

One moment, the all-American forward from the University of Washington had the ball.

The next, it was in the possession of Rubio, who, unmarked, dribbled straight at Jerry Gotti.

Luis Garcia's blood sugared.

As Gotti came out to meet Rubio.

Rubio chipped the ball neatly over Gotti's head . . . but the ball took an unaccountable twist to the left and hit the goalpost.

Garcia leapt in jubilation. Deliverance. Reprieve.

Dallas, 3:10 P.M.

Argentina defensed its way to the 1990 final in Rome; except for such breakaway opportunities as presented themselves, its players nearly refused to leave their end of the field. The Argentinians committed 152 fouls in getting to the final game against West Germany: one offense for every three minutes and fifty-seven seconds of playing time.

Argentina's fabled star Diego Maradona got just one goal in the entire 1990 tournament, a penalty shot that beat the Italians 1—0 in one semifinal. A penalty shot put West Germany past England in the other semifinal game of this most defensive of all World Cup tournaments.

Going into the final, Argentina was missing four starters who had been banished for receiving yellow cards in previous games.

It was shaping up as an entertaining match to watch; the fit Germans, with their discipline and lovely one-touch passing, always moving, probed the South Korean defense every way possible.

For their part, the South Koreans, understanding their limitations, had apparently trained using videotapes of the Italians. While they had mastered the art of tenacious defense, they lacked the complementary skill for which the Italians were also famous: the ability to successfully counterattack in swift, mercurial strikes. The misanthropic Italians, spirited kickers of shins, invited their adversaries to come at them. Then, just when their opponents thought all the Italians could do was defend, they were leaping and dancing for joy at having scored a surprise goal.

On one attack, the Germans mixed it up in front of the South Korean goal; the next time up the pitch, Willie Gochnauer or Dieter Bauer looped a pass in to The Wildebeest, hoping for a header.

In their first attempts to cross midfield, the Koreans were repelled by the German fullbacks and retreating halfbacks. But the danger remained that a screwup could lead to a Korean goal; if that happened, Korea would almost certainly follow the Italian formula and establish a *catenaccio* in front of their goal.

The Germans felt that if they persevered and concentrated, the Korean defenders would inevitably succumb to the pressure and let a hint of daylight through, along with a goal.

Tarchalski regarded the Koreans as barking dogs. Let them kick him and slam into him and grab him and do whatever they could get away with. He was bigger than they were and tougher and more determined. If Tarchalski could handle odious English fullbacks week in and week out, month after month, he could take anything the Koreans threw at him. If he had to, he would show them what a pissed-off kraut was capable of doing with his elbows.

Let there be no doubting his determination: in the end, the Germans would teach the Koreans how to play *futuboru*.

DETROIT, 3:14 P.M.

Luis Garcia was conceived in Chihuahua, Mexico, but born in San Angelo, Texas. His mother was five months pregnant with Luis the night in the summer of 1969 that she and her husband and their five children waded across the Rio Grande. As a kid, Luis picked cherries and apples and worked in asparagus and watermelon fields in Washington State's Yakima valley.

Now, the American national side counted on Luis Garcia for goals. He didn't want people laughing at the stupid wetback who choked in the clutch. He was the pride of every Mexican-American household, and he was determined not to let them down.

Garcia glanced toward Coach Bora Milutinovic. He had missed Coach's initial reaction, but he knew Milutinovic's mouth must have turned dry. But the Yugoslav-born Milutinovic—who'd guided Mexico to a sixth-place finish in 1986, and Costa Rica to the second round in 1990—was cool. Or as cool as he could be under the circumstances.

Milutinovic turned his palms down and waved his hands slowly back and forth, the gesture, combined with the expression on his face, saying: *It's okay, Luis. It's over. No harm done. Now concentrate.*

Then Milutinovic, compressing his lips, doubled his right hand into a fist and rammed it skyward. This time his body language said: *Now put it to the bastards, son. Do it.*

DALLAS, 3:20 P.M.

In the sixty-fifth minute of the Rome final in 1990, Pedro Monzon of Argentina was shown the red card for viciously chopping down German striker Jurgen Klinsman. In the eighty-fourth minute, Roberto Sinsini brought down Rudi Voller in the box, enabling Voller to score the game's only goal on a penalty kick.

Three minutes before the end of the game, the desperate Argentine striker Gustavo Dezotti got a second yellow for half choking the German

*defender, Jurgen Kohler. A second yellow yields the same result as a red:
Dezotti got the hook.*

The German opportunity came without warning or buildup, as
is often the case in football.

Dieter Bauer, with the ball on the right wing, maneuvered
enough room to whip a quick pass in to Tarchalski, who went for
it, along with the *libero* who was marking him and the other South
Korean fullbacks. The ball popped out of the crowd and landed at
the feet of Willi Gochnauer, standing just midfield of the action.

Gochnauer, facing a confusion of bodies, one-touched the ball
back to Tarchalski and moved quickly to his left, hoping for space
and an angle.

Tarchalski could have turned and shot—the *libero* had been
knocked off his feet—but he didn't because there were other
defenders behind him . . .

. . . and because he saw Willi Gochnauer, unmarked.

He tapped it back to Gochnauer.

Who fired . . .

. . . high and toward Bauer's wing, against the flow of action.

Peter Tarchalski was every bit as joyous as Willi Gochnauer
when the ball sailed past the outstretched hand of the South
Korean goalkeeper and hit the back of the net.

Ja! Ja! Ja!

The Koreans liked to play defense. Now it was Germany's turn.
The Germans had the luxury, if they felt like it, to pile on defense
like sauerkraut over bratwurst. The Koreans had a taste for defense;
let them have a helping.

Perhaps the Koreans could abandon their Italian models and try
imitating the goal-scoring Brazilians. Shake a leg. Dangle a hip.
Dribble through a crowd. See how that worked.

Ja! Ja! Ja!

6

The luck-out of Rubio's miss gave the already fit Garcia a sudden burst of energy and confidence. The score was still nil–nil. Shots on goal didn't count. Goals did. This late in the game, one goal would do it.

Beside him, Rubio was disbelieving.

João Blanco, the Brazilian midfielder, looped a soft, exquisitely timed pass over the heads of the American defenders to Rubio. It was a sweet pass, but it took a sour bounce off Rubio's chest.

Rubio, jarred back into the game, recovered the ball quickly, and seemed alert, dancing confidently on the balls of his feet.

But Rubio was perhaps casual about Luis Garcia, as though Garcia didn't count.

Or Rubio flat didn't see him.

Luis Garcia dropped to the ground and tackled the ball . . .

. . . and scrambled to his feet in a continuing motion.

And there, squirted well out in front of him, was the ball.

And behind the ball, grass.

Nothing but grass. And the Brazilian goal.

It was as though, pursued by Rubio, he ran in a glorious dream.

In a handful of life's ticking seconds—the memory of which Garcia would later replay countless times in his mind's eye, more than a few times bringing tears—the 56,500 people mashed into RFK Stadium, the collective ghost of Bobby Kennedy, rose as one.

He was aware of this as he ran.

Aware that he, Luis Garcia, American, Chihuahua-born, was the bearer of big dreams of his countrymen.

A vortex of noise, a din, a roar, rising . . .

In front of him, the ball . . .

. . . and in a heartbeat: the Brazilian goalkeeper Rodolpho Teixiera, *El Gato*—"The Cat." With nearly all the action taking place at the American end of the field, the cat had been a sleeping pussy.

Not time for yawning now. Teixiera, hands stretched above his head, raced toward Garcia.

Should Garcia attempt to lift a shot over El Gato's head now, as Rubio had done with Gotti?

Too late.

He caught Teixiera's eyes.

He glanced right. Playground move.

El Gato hesitated.

As Luis Garcia tapped left. Eyes on the goal, he hooked the ball with the side of his foot . . .

. . . as Rubio, running full tilt, flattened him from behind.

DALLAS, 5:20 P.M.

More than once, Fredrich Mueller had told Edson that the key to a successful offense in team sports was the ability to anticipate the adversary's defense. Mueller said all great coaches had a knack for it, whether Vince Lombardi in grid football, John Wooden in basketball, or Martin Bukovi's "Flying W" offense of the famed Budapest football club Voros Laboga in the early 1950s.

Edson, drinking a cold bottle of Budweiser Dry and eating Chee-tos that turned his fingers a salty orangish yellow, opened the window and laid the barrel of his Beeman/Feinwerkbau on the sill. He adjusted the Leupold to give him a 10-foot-wide stage at 200 yards, and swept the territory several times.

In the parking lot, two buses waited.

The German players, laughing, feeling good after their victory, began strolling across the parking lot toward the buses.

Edson calmly surveyed the players from rear to front, until he found Peter Tarchalski. He isolated the left side of Tarchalski's head, cross hairs on his ear.

Edson released a round.

Then he found Willi Gochnauer.

7

LAKE WALLOWA, 9:00 P.M.

James Burlane turned off his radio after the 2–0 German victory over the South Koreans. Now, the sun was low on the horizon as

Burlane paddled a canoe over lovely Lake Wallowa, which reflected silver with the setting sun. In the Wallowas in late June, it didn't get dark until nearly nine-thirty.

With alplike, jagged mountains looming above the south shore, he beached his canoe, removed his fishing gear and two large rainbow trout, and walked up a path to a neat cabin nestled among evergreens.

He went inside. By the time he laid the trout in the sink and got out his salt and pepper, flour, and corn oil, it was 10:00 P.M., Pacific time—1:00 A.M. Eastern. The phone rang.

The man on the phone had a southern English accent—public school and likely finished off at Oxford or Cambridge. "Major Khartoum, my name is Roger Dusenberry. I'm an official of the International Federation of Football Associations. Have you been following the World Cup action?"

"That would be FIFA. Yes, I have. I listened to the U.S. play Brazil on my Walkman this afternoon. Wasn't that something? Our Frito bandito put it right square in the net a megasecond before Rubio ran over him. Gave me goosebumps. All right Luis Garcia! Right up there with Joe Gaetjens's header, Terry Bradshaw's Hail Mary to Franco Harris, and Bobby Thomson's home run in the Polo Grounds. In your face, Brazil!"

"But you didn't listen to the Germany–South Korea match in Dallas, I take it."

"Oh, sure, but I turned my radio off after it was over and went back to my peace and quiet. A scrimmage for the Germans. Arsenal's striker and Willi Gochnauer are quite a pair, aren't they?"

"Mmmmmmm. Yes . . ."

"The Korean fullbacks mob the big kid, and he coolly lays it back to his partner to put it in the net. German discipline for you. My partner Ara Schott will be knocking back the celebratory schnapps."

Dusenberry sighed. "Major Khartoum, Peter Tarchalski and Willi Gochnauer were both murdered after the match."

Burlane was stunned. "What?"

Dusenberry's voice was grave. "By a sniper. In the parking lot outside of the Cotton Bowl. They were on their way to the team bus. Major Khartoum, it's on behalf of FIFA that I'm calling you tonight."

"Oh?"

"We wish to hire an investigator for our security force, and you've been recommended. We would like to talk to you in New York in the morning, if that's possible. The committee will take care of your expenses, including the rental of a private plane to get you to Portland or Seattle for a connecting flight east. Whatever it takes."

"It'll probably be an all-night project getting there, but I'll do my best."

"Thank you, Major Khartoum." Dusenberry sounded relieved.

"Did you talk to Ara by any chance?" Schott, Burlane's bookish and reclusive partner in Mixed Enterprises, a man of Germanic calm, was a former director of counterintelligence at the CIA.

"Yes, we did. Mr. Schott says he'll keep in touch with us at this end. He wants you to call him at your earliest convenience."

"I was about to ask you for a seat for Ara at our breakfast."

"Taken care of."

"Dallas!"

"I know. I know. It had to be Dallas. We'll be having breakfast in Harry Beauchamp's hotel." Dusenberry pronounced this *Beechum*; Beauchamp publicly corrected people who called him *Boochamp* or *Bow-champ*.

"Mr. Media Baron himself?"

"Mr. Beauchamp, who is the owner of Arsenal, Peter Tarchalski's English club. He is concerned about justice for his murdered player."

"Justice? Well, aren't we all?"

"That's at the Norman Hotel on Park Avenue. In the morning, then, Major Khartoum. Perhaps the two of us could have a cup of coffee before joining the others. Eight-thirty, say, or as soon as you can make it."

II

PLAY OF THE GAME

Teams from 141 countries entered the World Cup qualifying draw in New York on December 8, 1991. When round-robin qualifying rounds in six international zones ended in November 1993, 22 winning sides qualified for the 1994 final, joining the automatic entries, defending champion Germany and host United States.

Twenty-three national sides from North and Central America and the Caribbean qualified two teams for the finals, including host United States. Asia's 29 entries qualified two. South America's nine sides qualified four. Africa's 37 nations qualified three. Thirteen of Europe's 36 sides qualified for the finals, including defending champion Germany.

1

They made their rendezvous in the Norman Hotel on Park Avenue in midtown Manhattan, which had been in place and buzzing with talk of power and money since well before Lincoln took the bullet. This was Harry Beauchamp's temporary digs, which James Burlane found somehow appropriate given Beauchamp's storied avarice—the Norman was where Boss Tweed, Emperor of Tammany, was said to breakfast with the colonels of corruption in the late 19th century.

The Democrats were no longer as obvious as the soldiers of Tammany. Now, they ruled by a bureaucratic device known as a filing form, which, coming as it did with attached rules that challenged the federal tax code in complication, enabled the ruling Democratic party to disqualify unblessed candidates for using the wrong color of ink, or touching a line in a box, misspelling a word, failing to dot an *i* or cross a *t*, or any number of Extremely Important Rules. Since nobody could negotiate these bureaucratic hoops, even after weeks or months of concentrated study, nobody could challenge the authority of the party favorites, that is, the Entrenched Shits who suckled the city's treasury.

The Norman was a citadel against the insistent blacks and ethnics and recent immigrants who daily leaked onto Manhattan from Brooklyn and Queens and down from Harlem and the Bronx, muddying the sidewalks with the smell of garlic and their brown eyes, brown skins, and curly if not kinky hair. New York was no longer an island city of Irish and Italian Catholics and Greeks and Jews, dominated by blue-eyed WASP males; it had become a Fourth World country, flooded with Puerto Ricans, Haitians, Koreans, Filipinos, and Africans, Arabs, and South Americans of uncertain origin.

But the Norman was not part of that yucky mess. Here, there were proper linen tablecloths. Here, far from the bump and bustle of the streets and the rattle and bang of subway trains and the howling urban roar, Sir Roger Dusenberry and James Burlane could have a leisurely cup of coffee and a get-acquainted chat before they met with Harry Beauchamp, FIFA's security chief, Elizabeth Gunderson, and Burlane's partner in Mixed Enterprises, Ara Schott.

Although his hair was silver, Sir Roger Dusenberry had jet-black eyebrows over his outsized, hawklike nose. His face was long and bony. His complexion was ruddy and windblown, with prominent squint marks at the edges of his blue eyes. He had an almost–Kirk Douglas cleft on his chin. It was easy for Burlane to picture Dusenberry on the golf course with a fellow royal, his thinning brown hair whipping in the wind, perhaps sharing an Irish ethnic joke.

James Burlane himself wore jeans that were well broken in, but without patches, a short-sleeved cotton shirt with snaps, not buttons, and a multi-pocketed cotton photographer's vest, good for dispersing valuables. The pockets had nylon zippers, a prophylactic against the curiosity of thieves. Burlane regarded this vest as mandatory apparel in the Third World and New York.

He wore burgundy-colored Saucony running shoes—chosen because he had found them on sale, and because he had never heard of the brand name. Also, he could slop chianti on them, and nobody would know the difference. In deference to the presence of British royalty, he had tied a red bandana around his neck. A neckerchief could be used to mop sweat, clear one's sinuses, or fashion a tourniquet; a proper necktie was only good for the latter or hanging oneself in a Turkish prison.

Burlane said, "I grew up on a farm, you know. An American peasant. When I sit down to have a simple cup of coffee with an English peer, I feel like the Slav in *From Russia with Love* who tried to pass himself off as a proper Englishman. They were on a diner on the Orient Express, remember, and he ordered red wine with fish. James Bond knew immediately he was bogus; an Englishman and a gentleman would know one drinks white wine with fish."

Dusenberry said, "Sean Connery gave him such a withering look in the movie. Wasn't that wonderful?"

"The Russian felt like a pile of excrement. Our own Alexander Hamilton wanted inherited titles, I suppose you know that. He wanted dukes, earls, the works. Can you imagine what the results would have been? Viscount Nixon. King Jimmy. Baron Reagan."

"Hamilton himself was illegitimate, I'm told."

"Yes, a bastard born in the West Indies. But a smart and well-intentioned bastard for all his faults. He thought the future lay in making widgets; Jefferson believed it was in growing turnips. Turned out they were both right, although we had to suffer a civil war to find that out."

They paused while the waiter brought them their coffee. Burlane said, "My partner Ara Schott says he reads that you fish and play golf with Prince Charles. Is that true?"

"Somebody has to fish and play golf with Charles, I suspect. He's really not as stern a figure as he's made out to be. Are his critics all happily married forever after, do you suppose?"

Burlane grinned. "The world would be truly boring if they were."

"He's a companionable chap, really, quite clever, and he has a wonderful wit. And to be cuckolded by such a . . ." Dusenberry closed his mouth, his lips white with fury. "He never has any privacy. He's borne the burden quite well, to my way of thinking."

"So how is it that you were put in charge of FIFA's Emergency Committee, Sir Roger?"

"Charles had a lot to do with it, I suppose, at least in the beginning. Football arouses terrible passions, Major Khartoum. In 1969, the rancor between El Salvador and Honduras was so great following a 0–0 tie that it spilled into the streets following the match." Dusenberry grimaced. "Two thousand people were killed in the war that ensued. Yes, literally! War! Charles and I were trout-fishing when that awful business happened in Brussels in 1985."

"Oh?"

"Liverpool was playing Juventus of Rome for the European Cup when rioting English drunks managed to kill thirty-nine people.

Someone was needed to seriously study and confront the problem because English sides were in danger of being forever banned from play on the continent, which Charles felt would be both tragic and embarrassing. English sides *were* banned for a while, as you probably know. He said if I was willing to devote all my time to the subject, he'd see to it that the English Football Association gave me some kind of title. They named me the FA's director of security—as though crowd control had anything to do with the problem."

"Which was?"

"A form of tribal custom evolved among bloody drunken sods with nothing better to do than make fools of themselves. They're bored. What they need is something to do. Work. A sense of responsibility. A believable future, not rhetoric, which is all the government can give them, I'm afraid. Short of an economic miracle there's nothing we can do except make the fun not worth the risks."

"Clap them in jail."

Dusenberry sighed. "Unfortunately, spending a night in jail is a badge of honor to them; it seems a large part of the sport is being carried off in a police van with one's sodden mates. A form of initiation. The anthropologists have the best explanations, in my opinion. Banning them from the matches hurts them the most, but it's hard to enforce."

"We've got problems of our own, if you've seen the Bronx."

"Have I seen the Bronx? Through the window of a train on my way to Connecticut. But I'd never get off there, I assure you. Heavens!"

Burlane laughed. "You don't look like you suffer from a death wish."

Dusenberry said, "Should you decide to take the job, we propose to make you a special assistant to Elizabeth Gunderson, who is in charge of the security for the tournament. The FBI have assigned a small army to the case, but both the Executive and Organizing committees feel FIFA should, as a matter of form, be active as well. The Emergency Committee concurs. Ms. Gunderson was a longtime assistant to the FBI's principal big-event security expert, Ladd McAllen. She was deputy chief of security for the 1984 Olympic games in Los Angeles, and was a stadium security consultant until FIFA hired her. She speaks fluent German, which is why she is following the defending champions."

"Mixed Enterprises would work for Ms. Gunderson, then?"

Dusenberry glanced at his watch. "For the security force, under the Organizing Committee. Correct. But when something goes wrong, Ms. Gunderson reports to me. As chairman of the Emergency Committee, I'm responsible to the Executive Committee.

"You know, Major Khartoum, it strikes me that you Americans may be innocent of the passions aroused by international competition of this sort. You cheer your American athletes on in the Olympic games, yes. But, believe me, that is a far, far different matter than city against city, country against country, or continent against continent in organized team sport."

"Is it possible that we've avoided it, saying soccer isn't our game? We are only interested in something if we're the best. Otherwise it's for garlic eaters and Englishmen."

Sir Roger raised an eyebrow. "Yes, well. Shall we go up? I'm sure everybody has arrived by now. Our host will be most anxious."

9:10 A.M.

Burlane and Dusenberry took their seats on elegant chairs and waited for ear-ringed Puerto Ricans in tuxedos and polished shoes to put the finishing touches on a glass table with a silver coffee urn in the center.

The waiters surrounded the urn with platters and bowls of croissants, German bread, Dutch rolls, butter, marmalades and jams, cheeses, pâtés, caviar, sausages, rashers of crisply fried bacon, slices of ham, and a duke's mixture of mustards, both foreign and domestic. This was Harry Beauchamp's idea of a modest continental breakfast they could enjoy while he coarsely used a dead soccer player to push his weight around.

Burlane was exhausted and hungry after a long night of traveling. When the gong sounded, he was prepared to go for the grub with gusto.

Behind the polished cherrywood table, lace curtains were pulled on the windows overlooking Park Avenue, eight stories below them.

The balding Harry Beauchamp took a seat at the end of the table facing the curtains. Beauchamp had a plump face with neat bags under slightly lidded blue eyes, and a network of tiny red veins on his cheeks like secondary highways on a *Reader's Digest* road map. Burlane assumed this manly rouge was the result of an affection for the bottle, but it could have been Beauchamp's genetic inheritance, high blood pressure, or even windburn. But judging from his round body, he didn't spend a lot of time in the gym.

FIFA's security chief, Elizabeth Gunderson, sat to Beauchamp's left. Ms. Gunderson was a good-looking woman in her mid-thirties, with a rangy figure and full lips. She wore a suit that was an imitation of the standard male issue, except that it had a skirt rather than trousers, a white blouse instead of a shirt, and a red necktie wider than the noose preferred by males. As she poured her coffee she eyed Burlane, across the table.

Dusenberry sat at the end of the table opposite Beauchamp.

Ara Schott was seated between Sir Roger and Burlane. Schott was a reclusive bachelor possessed of a scholar's detachment and an intelligence officer's paranoia. His sister, declaring that she was tired of his looking like a computer nerd or shoe salesman, had recently commandeered the buying of his clothes. She sewed codes on the insides of the jackets and trousers so that he now wore combinations that sort of matched. On this occasion, he had unaccountably gone preppy, choosing penny loafers, charcoal slacks, and a tweedy-looking jacket.

When the waiters were finished with their chores, Beauchamp began helping himself, followed quickly by his guests. The spread was far better than a truck-stop fat fry, and Burlane wasn't so foolish as to pick delicately at it rather than appear boorish. His mother had always said she appreciated a good eater.

Gunderson, pouring herself another cup of coffee, said, "My people say they've heard all manner of stories about you over the years, Major Khartoun."

Burlane nodded. Gunderson had all the outward appearance of

the prototypical career woman that feminists were urging their fellow women to admire. Burlane didn't mind career women. Good for them. But he found it difficult to believe they were capable of emotionally neutering themselves. Were they capable of short-circuiting their hormones through ideology, he wondered? He suspected they weren't, but he would never argue the point with them. Gunderson certainly looked beddable enough.

Gunderson said, "Ten years ago, you allegedly died of dysentery in Mozambique. But it was a trick, they said."

"Oh?" Burlane went for a slice of ham. The best tactic with someone like Gunderson, he suspected, was to play the game by her rules. He would be professional all the way. All business. She would have no way of knowing he admired the line of her thigh and ass, coarse male that he was.

"Specifically, your invention. A form of editorial comment." She made a whistling sound.

Mmmmmmmmm. Burlane made a sandwich of some cheese and a Dutch roll. No suggestive comments. No hanky-panky. Eyes off her chest. Show her he could do it. Then, just then, maybe . . .

Dusenberry raised an eyebrow. "Dysentery in Mozambique?"

Gunderson said, "You should hear some of the stories."

Dusenberry smiled. "I've heard several."

Burlane considered a plate of sausage. For now he'd have to limit his sensual pleasures to food. "Oh? And who were these informants of yours, Sir Roger?"

"The MI6 chaps who recommended you to FIFA, which was corroborated by Ms. Gunderson's former associates at the FBI."

"I see," Burlane said. Out of deference to his MI6 admirers, he speared a British banger; on his deft retrieve of the sausage, he casually snagged some bacon and reeled it in as well. This was streaky bacon, English style, a different taste than pork fat treated with savory chemicals, which was the allegedly carcinogenic American preference, but still good.

Beauchamp said, "Tell us, Major Khartoum, how is it that you decided to, what do I say, go private?"

"I was sacked years ago, actually, and didn't feel like settling in as a guard at Kmart. My business associate and I stay busy. We get a job here. A job there. The action's international these days, as you well know." Burlane reached for some more English cheddar. "Boy, this is some spread."

Gunderson said, "From all the many stories, I would have imagined you to be a little longer in the tooth, Major Khartoum."

Burlane bit into his sandwich with appreciation. His jaws grinding, he said, "Why thank you, Ms. Gunderson. I'm still ambulatory, but to tell you the truth, sometimes I feel like I can hardly get out of bed in the morning. I do my best, though. I know how to get vegetables in and out of a wok before they're destroyed. I eat lots of garlic for spiritual and aesthetic reasons. I take vitamin E in quantity and vitamin C. That's not to mention all the spinach." He took another bite from his sandwich, then added, "I, uh, drink ginseng tea. They say it has remarkable properties."

Gunderson said, "So I've heard."

"I buy the ginseng by the kilo. Keep it in the freezer. It's a tuber, you know, looks something like gingerroot."

Gunderson glanced briefly at the ceiling, as though appealing to the gods.

Beauchamp said, "No matter what you have read in the papers, Major Khartoum, I want you know that Peter Tarchalski and I liked and respected one another."

Dusenberry looked down the table. "Is everybody ready? If there are no objections, I think we should proceed as we eat. Under the circumstances, this is no time to dally."

9:30 A.M.

Sir Roger Dusenberry said, "We all know what happened to Peter Tarchalski and Willi Gochnauer after the match in Dallas yesterday. What we haven't made public yet is that Jens Steiner received a yellow card by express delivery on Saturday afternoon while the side was watching a tape of Belgium playing Norway.

"Then, when Steiner finally returned to his room last night, it was to find another envelope waiting. This one had one red card and two yellow cards in it. The red had Tarchalski's jersey number written on it, and the two yellows had Gochnauer's number. As followers of international football may know, one of the Argentine players ejected from the 1990 final match in Rome was given a red; the other received two yellows."

Beauchamp said, "He was my player. Mine. Part of the Arsenal family, and I had to hear about it on the telly. Bloody FIFA sods. And they swan around pretending to be such fancy gentlemen. Sportsmen!"

Burlane said, "Where were they hit exactly? Can you tell me that, Sir Roger?"

"Ms. Gunderson. I believe you know more about the details than me."

Gunderson said, "Gochnauer was hit in the ear. Tarchalski in the neck just below the ear."

"By what?"

"The police say a .308 Winchester, same as a 7.62-mm NATO round."

"In what order were they hit?"

"Tarchalski first, then Gochnauer."

"No shots were heard, I take it."

"None. They were apparently fired at some distance, and he no doubt used a silencer."

"Elapsed time?"

"About two-point-five seconds. Two rounds. Two dead-on hits. From a distance. He is very, very good. Better than Lee Harvey Oswald."

Dusenberry said, "The Germans are scheduled to play in the Round of 16 in six days. Knockout play." He removed his glasses and massaged his eyes.

Burlane said to Gunderson, "I take it the Dallas police department and the FBI are doing their thing."

"They're doing everything they can. But they don't have a lot to go on. One yellow card. Two shots fired. Two hits. Then a red and two yellows. They're searching the area to find where the shots were fired from in hopes of gleaning some evidence there."

"And, of course, they're reviewing their list of known fruitcakes on the loose." Burlane took a sip of coffee.

Gunderson said, "Oh, sure. The players at the Cotton Bowl yesterday were protected the old-fashioned way, same as John Kennedy was in a moving automobile in 1963. Perimeters."

"Perimeters at Troy. Perimeters at Leningrad. Perimeters at Dienbienphu."

"Our perimeters started at the edge of the field in the Cotton Bowl. We thought we were safe. We had them out of there."

Dusenberry grimaced. "Ms. Gunderson and the security people are not to blame for what happened; everybody understands that. The FBI and the police agencies involved have all given their assurances that they will put every resource and effort into this, and they've acted quite quickly. But we all know there'll be a chorus of demands that somebody has to be held responsible. There will come a day when fingers will be pointed at us. Am I not right, Mr. Beauchamp?"

"You're damned right you are." Beauchamp narrowed his eyes.

Dusenberry said, "People will expect us to have done something positive, to have taken action immediately. 'Young men's lives were at stake. What did you do?' they'll ask. 'Sit there like ninnies?' We trust that all the law enforcement agencies involved will prove capable of protecting the German players if they are still in danger. But FIFA have to protect themselves." From Beauchamp's mouth, he might have added, something, but he didn't speak. "That's why we called you and Mr. Schott."

Burlane glanced at Schott. "I see."

"Ms. Gunderson has the responsibility of liaising with the FBI and overseeing a security force under siege. She speaks fluent German. It makes sense that she remain with the German side for the time being. She agrees that we need someone who can roam, if necessary, to ask questions."

Beauchamp said, "I take it that as owner of Peter Tarchalski's football club, I would be privy to the progress of Major Khartoum's investigation? I didn't fly all the way from London to stand around while my player's murderer goes free."

Dusenberry seemed unsurprised. "Oh, yes, of course. Certainly. That goes without saying. But first, we have to determine if Major Khartoum and Mr. Schott are interested in our proposal?"

Burlane checked with his partner.

Schott nodded his head yes.

Dusenberry said, "We'll see to it that you receive your usual fee."

Beauchamp added quickly, "If necessary, I'll pay for your services out of my own pocket, Major. It's perhaps not as deep as people think, but it's deep enough for this."

Dusenberry said, "It strikes me that the business of one red and two yellows given the dead players is too much of a coincidence for us to ignore the possibility of Argentinian revenge. As it happens, I have an acquaintance there, Detective Inspector Hector Villanueva, who is an expert in stadium security. He's a former captain of the Buenos Aires police department side. If I give him a call, I know he'll be more than happy to cooperate with a FIFA investigator."

Beauchamp ripped off a hunk of French bread. "You're thinking the Argies are still sore over the ejections in 1990? All they can do is trip people and kick them in the legs when the referee's back is turned. They're vile, filthy-mouthed complainers, and they got what they deserved in Rome."

Dusenberry looked mildly at Beauchamp. Then, to Burlane, he said, "Do you suppose you could schedule a flight to Argentina as your initial assignment, Major Khartoum? The FBI will no doubt send someone to Argentina themselves, but Inspector Villanueva is a special friend of FIFA's—part of the family, so to speak—and I think he might respond better to someone from FIFA."

Burlane said, "I can do that. No problem."

Gunderson grinned. "A regular cowboy."

Schott said, "Thinks he's the Lone Ranger, I agree, Ms. Gunderson. Give him a little mask, and he'd be happy."

Beauchamp said, "Peter Tarchalski was like a son to me. You ask anyone. Like a son."

3

Santa Barbara, California, 2:00 p.m.

Edson, chewing on a hamburger, retrieved some limp french fries from the passenger's seat of his rented Chevrolet and chewed thoughtfully while he appreciated the expansive La Casa Blanca. He took another bite of hamburger, then a sip of Coke from the red paper cup.

He checked his watch. He still had plenty of time to catch a flight to San Francisco and get a good night's sleep.

When he first saw it, Edson thought that the estate, which was surrounded by fortresslike walls, looked like the Alamo. Well, no, it didn't either. The Alamo, if the American John Wayne movie he had seen was in any way authentic, was a regular fort with a proper gate that opened to let the last doomed Texans inside.

The estate's original owner, he had learned, was Bert Hammond, a vaudevillian song-and-dance man turned silent-movie actor. Hammond built the house in 1922, calling it La Casa Blanca and putting the name in three-feet-high carved oak letters in an arch at the beginning of the curved driveway.

In the 1920s, La Casa Blanca became famous for its lavish parties, where prohibition gin flowed freely and aspiring, therefore compliant, actresses abounded. Fatty Arbuckle and Clara Bow partied there. Stan Laurel and Oliver Hardy amused the guests on several occasions.

Shortly before his death from cancer in 1931, Hammond sold the estate to a Los Angeles businessman. It was put back in show business hands in 1987, when it was bought by the Argentine pop singer Tony Artes, a Julio Iglesias wannabe. Edson failed to understand the public's enthusiasm for either singer, although what he knew about music didn't make spit.

Inside the battlements, La Casa Blanca was a sprawling, split-level Spanish- or Mexican-style house with white walls and red-tiled roof.

Through the staves of the black wrought-iron gate, Edson could see a putting green rolling to the left of the house. There was a tennis court on the right. Although he couldn't see it, Edson knew there was a swimming pool below the court, on the seaward side.

The complex dominated a bluff that overlooked a rocky beach. There was a trail down to the beach where, Edson had been told, one could get to within fifteen or twenty yards of the seals that sunned themselves there. When not sunning themselves, they cavorted in the surf. Edson decided that seals were something not to be missed. When he finished his business, he would hike down to the beach.

4

Sir Roger Dusenberry was lodged in the Plaza hotel on the southern end of Central Park, which Elizabeth Gunderson thought was a classier choice than the Norman, where Harry Beauchamp was billeted.

They met for a quiet drink in the Plaza Lounge so that Gunderson, and Dusenberry could review the day's events and consider the challenge before them. The Plaza Lounge, was imitation Polynesia, minus the heat and bugs and lethargic boredom of those faraway, thus presumably happy islands. Gunderson was an unashamed fancier of drinks made of rum and fruit juice, a specialty of the Lounge, and so ordered a Maui Wowie, while Dusenberry, out of class consciousness, taste, or loyalty to the UK, ordered a Scotch, neat.

"So what do you think, Sir Roger?" Gunderson said. She took a sip of her drink, wondering if the management of Plaza Lounge was aware that Maui Wowie was a term used for marijuana grown on that island. This Maui Wowie boasted four kinds of rum, layered according to color, and was served with a sprig of fresh mint in addition to a maraschino cherry stuck on the lip of the glass. Gunderson could have passed on the syrupy cherry. Yuch! "Well, Sir Roger, will FIFA play or not?"

Sir Roger Dusenberry bunched his lips, considering his answer, then said, "Controversy is the currency of democracy, Ms. Gunderson. Where it is not minted according to plan, it is counterfeited to prevent boredom. If the law required that public officials be sent packing after their third unfulfilled dire prediction, we would all be better off. In the present circumstance, I am rather like your Attorney General Janet Reno in that terrible cult burning in Waco, Texas. Everybody can later lie about what they would or wouldn't have done except for Ms. Reno, and in this case, me. Only I am held responsible. I am damned if I do and damned if I don't."

Gunderson said, "If the FBI lucks out." She sighed. "You never know. Remember the Arab who demanded the deposit back on a rental van that'd been used to bomb the World Trade Center?

That's world-class dumb. If the FBI investigators don't luck out, which is more likely the case, and it takes weeks or months to come up with the stingiest of clues or no clues at all, then they're incompetent morons as the media always suspected."

"I don't have to tell you that I can use whatever information you get as soon as you can get it. Dr. Coelho and the Executive Committee wish to be informed immediately of any major breaks."

"Ladd McAllen and the FBI are doing their best, I assure you. They've lifted fingerprints from the penalty cards. They're checking on referees who have served military duty or had other reasons to have their fingerprints taken. That will take a couple of days, I'm told. They're backsighting the murder site to see if they can locate where the marksman was hiding. Maybe he left some physical evidence behind. The German police agencies are combing their lists of known screwballs. While I ask questions, Major Khartoum is on his way to Buenos Aires."

"Have you had a chance to have a chat with Harry Beauchamp yet?"

"I have an appointment to talk to Mr. Beauchamp tomorrow afternoon. I talked to the team last night, and I've been on the phone all morning talking to friends and teammates of Gochnauer and Tarchalski in Germany. Gochnauer was married, and left two small daughters. He and his wife owned a greenhouse and four flower shops in Frankfurt. There doesn't seem much that he's done to offend anybody unless it's score goals. Owing to the large transfer fee F.C. Cologne paid for him, Peter Tarchalski is another matter."

Gunderson checked to make sure her tape recorder was working properly. "Sir Roger, at breakfast this morning, Mr. Beauchamp said he and Peter Tarchalski had a father-son relationship. Do you believe that?"

Sir Roger Dusenberry smiled. "Are there hippos that sing, do you suppose? Elephants that fly?"

"It was such a palpably untrue and stupid thing to say. I was curious."

"It's Harry's sense of drama, Ms. Gunderson."

"How long have you known him?"

Dusenberry raised an eyebrow. "How long? It's been three years now, I suppose. Since he bought Arsenal. Why do you ask?"

"Are you at all surprised that he showed up?"

"I would have been surprised if he hadn't. He never misses an opportunity."

"An opportunity? For what?"

Dusenberry hesitated. "To, uh, express himself, I guess is one way of putting it. Most owners with players in the tournament are probably here. They've got the money, and having a player on a national side makes them an insider. Gives them a little extra pride. No harm in that."

"Harry Beauchamp didn't come here until Tarchalski had been murdered."

"You have to remember, Ms. Gunderson, Peter Tarchalski was a German international, not an Englishman. Harry showed up because under the circumstances we couldn't keep him away. You're not thinking he had anything to do with the murders are you? Harry Beauchamp?" Dusenberry, suppressing his amusement, shook his head. "That'd be rich."

"Can you tell me about him, please, so I can at least pretend I'm earning my oats?"

"Are you serious?"

"Certainly I'm serious," Gunderson said. "Two athletes are dead, ambushed in the deepest woods of human passion. There are footprints everywhere. It won't do to decide in advance which prints belong to the innocent and which to the guilty. Who knows where a single set of prints will lead? Do you see my problem?"

"Yes, I do. But I'll have to deal with Harry when this is all over. You understand that."

"What you say goes no further."

Dusenberry looked uncertain.

"I really do need a full context," Gunderson said. "You need to think about this. Ladd McAllen and his people will be asking you the same questions."

Dusenberry sighed. "If the legend building is to be believed, Harry began as a copy boy for the *Times of London*. He says he quit because they wouldn't give him a shot at being an apprentice reporter, but nobody at the *Times* can place his face. He turned out to have a knack for buying and selling things. First it was commodities, then oil options, then media property. He piled deal upon deal, and before anybody understood what was happening, he'd bought half of Fleet Street. He bought everything he could lay his hands on: radio and television stations; magazines of every description; publishing houses; newspapers, including the *Times of London* and *The News of the World*."

"Ambitious!"

"Yes. Then, when the government began to get concerned, he cheerfully stopped. It was fairly obvious a backlash was developing after the unfortunate crash of Robert Maxwell's empire. Anyway, Harry said that for the moment he had what he wanted."

Gunderson said, "Leaving open the possibility that he'd start buying again once he consolidated what he already had."

"There you have it. There's little doubt that he'd overextended himself. But Harry thinks ahead, you have to give him that. When he had been buying property, he was nowhere to be seen. There was nothing to dislike about him; he was the mysterious Harry Beauchamp. After his moratorium on acquisitions, when the word was that he was skirting bankruptcy, he, uh, introduced himself, in a manner of speaking."

"Introduced himself?"

"He said any fool could make money off commodities and securities. The editors of the *Times* had once scorned him. Now, he was going to show people he knew how newspapers were run."

"I see. And did he?"

"That's open to conjecture. I'm not one of his accountants, so I don't know. His editors know which side of their bread is buttered. I'm probably not the only citizen of the U.K. who has grown weary of Harry's, uh, views."

"His opinions?" Gunderson ventured.

Dusenberry smiled. "The bill for his lawyers must be extraordinary. When he limited his attentions to Fleet Street, I was able to ignore him and mostly did. All I had to do was turn the page or flip the channel. I'll never forget the day I sat down to my morning toast and coffee and discovered that he was the new owner of Arsenal. It was a Monday morning, I remember. My wife brought me my orange marmalade and my *Daily Telegraph,* and said, 'Dear, you had better brace yourself.' " Dusenberry closed his eyes. "He announced that he had been a midfielder as a schoolboy at Rugby, the public school he allegedly attended. He was going to take Arsenal all the way to Wembley."

"Allegedly?"

"The headmaster at Rugby says that's news there."

"Did he take Arsenal to Wembley?"

Dusenberry said, "He came within a couple of points on the table last season—with the help of Peter Tarchalski and others. But, he did come close, that's true. Shut our mouths, I suppose."

"I see."

"Then he said he was going to bring the Football Association into the twentieth century. His first objective was achievable. The second perhaps rather less so, things being what they are."

"Had he been a midfielder as a schoolboy?"

"There's apparently no record of it at Rugby."

"Perhaps he means matches held in local pastures."

"That seems to be the case."

"He's an Aarry, not a Harry?" Gunderson smiled.

"I believe that would cover it."

She raised an eyebrow. "And the truth of his relationship with Tarchalski?"

"If Peter'd been better than Pelé, Eusebio, Franz Beckenbauer, and Johan Cruyff combined, Harry wouldn't have been satisfied. For the money he was paying him, Harry expected a goal every trip up the pitch."

"I see," Gunderson said. "So what does Harry do with himself now that he's made all that money and achieved all that power?"

"He spends most of his time on yachts. He's had a series of girlfriends, but he never married. His former lovers hint of a dark, vindictive temper, but the evidence is anecdotal. Once in a while he pops off abroad to check on his foreign properties. But surely you don't suspect Harry Beauchamp of being any sort of villain here. He may have his eccentricities, but he's no murderer."

"A talented goal scorer is an expensive piece of property, Sir Roger. It strikes me that any sensible owner would try to be aware of anything that threatens to reduce the value of his investment, which is what a player is. The use of drugs, say. Hanging out with gamblers. A fatal woman. Whatever. A careless player can cost his owner a lot of money. Am I right?" Gunderson cocked her head.

"He can indeed."

"Have you heard any untoward rumors about Tarchalski? He doesn't have a secret trick knee or anything?"

"I don't think Harry sold Cologne damaged goods, if that's what you're thinking."

Gunderson said, "If the killer's not a total nut case or hired by Arabs, he may have been after Tarchalski or Gochnauer, and it makes a difference which. Other than working together to score goals against the Koreans, a motive for killing both is hard to figure."

"I see what you mean."

"What about Beauchamp's renewed vow to take Arsenal to Wembley? What will happen to that now that Tarchalski is gone?"

"Arsenal's a solid side. If Harry can work a deal with his Costa Rican phenom, and he's as good as Harry's sportswriters claim, they'll remain strong next season. The Costa Rican is supposed to know only a few words of English. If he's smart, he'll learn only enough to order food and communicate with his mates on the pitch."

"The Costa Rican perhaps being less expensive than Peter Tarchalski."

"I would say considerably cheaper, yes. Harry knows how to spot a deal, there's no denying him that."

Gunderson said, "Before we wind it up here, Sir Roger, you might be able to help me with something that's been puzzling me. We call the game 'soccer' here in the United States, while you people in the U.K. usually call it 'football.' But the term 'soccer' is British in origin, as I understand it."

"The term comes from a nineteenth-century split over how football should be played. There was a faction from Mr. Beauchamp's much-fancied Rugby, a public school near Coventry in the Midlands, in favor of using the hands and kicking the legs of one's opponents, a practice called 'shinning' or 'hacking.' "

" 'Public school' meaning 'private school' in British-ese."

"In English, yes." He smiled. "Correct. The proponents of the finesse game—no hands or hacking—were centered at Cambridge University in southern England. In 1863, proponents of the Cambridge game formed the Football Association in London. Students were then in the habit of adding 'er' or 'ers' to a word, often dropping the last syllable. 'I'll have baker and egger for breker and chicker for luncher.' Add 'er' to the last three letters of the abbreviation Football Assoc.—soc-er—and there you have it: soccer. Rugby football was called 'rugger.' "

Gunderson laughed. "Well, you've got that one down, Sir Roger."

Dusenberry smiled. "You're not the first American to ask the question, Ms. Gunderson."

"No shining and hacking in the gentleman's game."

"We do our best to keep it clean," Dusenberry said.

SAN FRANCISCO, 10:00 A.M., THURSDAY, JUNE 30

It was a lot of expense and effort for one or two practice sessions, but Edson knew it was smart to follow the advice of Mueller, who had told him it was foolish to play a match without a warm-up.

Edson could have rented a two-thirds replica of a romantic-looking Spad or Fokker, but he resisted the temptation. He had flown the Fokker replica, and it was fun, but not the best for what he had in mind. Biplanes had a good lift from having two wings, so they had a low stall speed; they were also good for certain kinds of aerobatics: it was possible to snap roll a biplane so fast a spectator could hardly see it.

Unfortunately, the extra drag from two wings made biplanes slow on the climb. Never be ruled by sentiment, Mueller had said, and he was right. Get the best equipment for the job, then practice. Even if he could only get a couple of days in, practice was practice. Great athletes practiced.

To be legal in the U.S., an ultralight couldn't weigh more than 254 pounds, carry more than 5 gallons of gas, fly faster than 55 miles an hour, or stall at anything over 27 miles an hour. There were low-wing, aerobatic ultralights that looked like sleek World War II fighter planes, but Edson didn't want the wing underneath him. He wanted to see the ground. The high-winged craft looked dopey, but when you were flying at low speeds and low altitude you wanted to be able to see the ground, not the clouds.

What Edson wanted, and got, was a Kolb Starfire, an odd-looking but aerobatic ultralight. The wing was neither above nor below the pilot; it was above and behind him. Also, there was no propeller in front of the pilot. The Rotax engine was mounted at the rear of the wing. There was nothing about the Kolb that could properly be called a fuselage; it had, rather, a slender, braced staff that supported the tail.

The result was an ultralight that looked like a large flying insect, a bee or a dragonfly. The pilot, protected by a curving Plexiglas windscreen, sat in the insect's bulbous chest.

If he removed the windscreen, a pilot in the open cockpit could aim a pistol above, below, or directly in front of him. Thus, as with a bee, the Kolb's stinger was in front of and below the furious buzzing. The Kolb Firestar traveled at a leisurely firefly speed, but like an insect, it had a low stall speed.

Edson chose his practice site because of geography and weather. And, ultimately, because of Mueller. Mueller scoffed at the notion that politics, that is, human will, could somehow displace or compensate for the pernicious inequities of weather, calling it one of the dumber popular conceits. All one had to do was look at a map and see that all of the economically productive areas of the world, whether in Eurasia, North America, or Australia, had temperate or subtropical climates. The tropics were universally screwed.

And so, Edson, curious, had started paying attention to ocean currents and prevailing winds.

He was amazed by the similarities of geography in disparate parts of the world. He agreed with Mueller that to be well traveled, one should have experienced the major climates of the world as charted by meteorologists, in addition to the major cultural and religious zones.

The north–south running Sierra Madres formed a long spine that ran down the eastern border of California. The Mediterranean climate west of this slender ridge of mountains, with its pre-automobile sun—once a hallmark of southern California—was a major reason early moviemakers settled in Hollywood.

At San Francisco, the weather yielded to dominant, moist marine winds coming off the Pacific onto northern California, western Oregon and Washington, and British Columbia. While Los Angeles was famous for its movies, and presumably moviegoers, Portland and Seattle, Edson knew, were among the leading American cities in the consumption of books.

The moisture from the prevailing easterlies coming off the Pacific was scraped off by a narrow coastal range and the taller Sierras, at whose summit the landscape shifted abruptly from conifers to desert scrub and mesquite. This desert climate of cold, dry winters was shared by eastern Oregon; the republic of Kazakhstan, northwest of the Caspian Sea; and the Argentine pampas.

If Edson's Bartholomew was to be believed, the Sierra Madres from Lake Tahoe north to the Oregon border didn't have much in the way of human activity. There would be a few log trucks maybe, and a scattering of cattle on government range land.

This was where Edson would go.

He checked out of his hotel near the San Francisco International Airport at 8:00 A.M. He had catnapped on his late-night flight from Chicago, and so he was reasonably rested. He drove his Mitsubishi minivan north and crossed over the San Francisco–Oakland Bay Bridge and then north, passing Berkeley. Ninety minutes later, he was on Interstate 5 heading north toward Oregon.

He turned east at Red Bluff, taking California Highway 299 to Susanville and beyond. He was soon in the foothills of the Sierras.

As the sun set behind his back, Edson pulled off at a highway rest stop. The piney air was crisp and good. He decided the quality of the air was what was missing from the John Ford westerns he had seen.

6

Elizabeth Gunderson took another sip of her martini on the rocks. She and Harry Beauchamp were in the Reading Room Bar of the Norman Hotel, which contained a handsome stone fireplace and was lined with shelves of musty-looking books whose titles were, tantalizingly, too far away for her to see very well.

She did spot a handsome edition of Mark Twain's *Huckleberry Finn*, of which she approved. Was it a first edition? she wondered. Probably not, or somebody would have lifted it by now, even in the Norman; not all thieves in Manhattan roamed the streets.

Gunderson spotted Thorstein Veblen's *The Theory of the Leisure Class*. It was Veblen who had coined the phrases "captain of industry" and "conspicuous consumption." Did the Reading Room Bar also have Charles Beard's *An Economic Interpretation of the Constitution*, in which Beard investigated the men who wrote the Constitution and found that with few exceptions, they were extraordinarily wealthy by the standards of their time?

She said, "I do hope you don't mind my little recorder, Mr. Beauchamp. It helps me remember exactly what I asked, not almost."

Harry Beauchamp laughed. "No problem. I suppose you program all this into computers."

"I'm pooling my information with the FBI. Their computers process the data. Our problem is time. We have just three more days before Germany plays Poland on the West Coast. When I finish here, I'm on my way to San Francisco."

"Ask what you want. I want this bleeding sod caught as much as you."

Gunderson smiled. "Well, thank you, Mr. Beauchamp. I had a talk with Sir Roger last night. I'll talk to everybody involved before I'm finished."

"The earnest Sir Roger."

"I read that he had a large hand in getting the Continentals to accept English sides back on their soil."

"Sir Roger did do that, I admit, and for that he is to be commended."

Gunderson said, "Tell me, Mr. Beauchamp, how was it that you managed to take Arsenal from the bottom of the table and in three years move it to within two points of Wembley? That's what you did, isn't it?"

Beauchamp's drink was finished. He saw that Gunderson's was, too, and signaled for another round of drinks.

Gunderson said, "Really, how did you do it? Was it just money? Or luck? Or did you have some kind of plan? How? There are some American sports franchises, like the Tampa Bay Buccaneers, that never go anywhere. Others, like the Los Angeles Dodgers, may be down one year, but the other clubs have to keep an eye on them next season. Everybody knows they'll be back; the question is when."

"I owe it all to FIFA and the gentlemen of the English Football Association."

"How is that?" Gunderson asked.

"By being their wonderful selves, they gave me the opportunity, that is, the money, to buy the players I needed, including Peter Tarchalski. You see, in order to maintain the lofty ideals of gentlemen and sportsmen—and to keep hustlers and high rollers out of football, that's people like me—FIFA early on declared that 'football shall not be used as a source of profit to its directors or shareholders.' Isn't that grand? 'Shall not be used a source of profit.' All you have to do is substitute 'football' for 'capital,' and you understand how generations of bureaucrats remain ensconced at FIFA as the Stalinists once did at the Kremlin, calling the shots over their empire and planning for the parties at their meeting every other year. There are whores to be lined up. Food and booze to be ordered. These bureaucrats are the dictatorship of the sports proletariat. Wherever football is played, from Mozambique to Peru, it is in such a manner as pleases FIFA."

"It's all about power."

"Never trust high-minded rhetoric, Ms. Gunderson. Never. In keeping with the spirit of FIFA, the English FA put a seven-and-a-half percent limit to the profits earned by any shareholder, and decreed that a club's director was to work for free. Good enough reason for unemployed royals to run a working man's game."

"People like Sir Roger," she said.

"He's what you call the genteel rich. He was given this job so he could keep the electricity hooked up; everybody knows that. As I understand it, he and his wife have turned their estate into a fancy restaurant while they live in the servants' quarters in a stand of trees out back. People admire the Dusenberry family pewter while they're eating their soup." Beauchamp looked disgusted.

"In the matter of Arsenal's success."

"We came close to winning the FA Cup, but won the money-making contest hands down, and that's what really matters in the end, isn't it?" Beauchamp looked pleased. "The Spanish side Real Madrid showed the world how to get around FIFA almost twenty years ago. FIFA might control the *pesetas* Real Madrid made off admission tickets, but not what they earned from the activities of a private club. Right?"

"I guess," Gunderson said. "Clever Spaniards!"

"They charged their members an annual fee and monthly dues and gave them magazines with articles about their heroes, and schedules of upcoming events. For members willing to buy bonds to help pay for them, they built and maintained tennis courts, gymnasiums, swimming pools, and playing fields. They established a professional basketball team and built an arena for it to play in, plus they built a skating rink, a restaurant, and a track-and-field stadium. That is, Ms. Gunderson, they turned their fans from spectators into participants. They quickly grew to sixty thousand strong, with an impossible queue for new members. Football clubs in São Paulo and Rio de Janeiro did all that plus added theaters, nightclubs, and resort hotels."

"I take it, in England things remained rather more staid and manageable, if less profitable."

Beauchamp held up his hands in mock despair. "It wasn't that there was anything illegal about the Real Madrid model, it was just that kind of promotion wasn't done in England with such, uh . . ."

"Zeal?" Gunderson grinned.

"It was said to be cheap and coarse, uncivilized, and so on. Legality has little to do with it. For example, the English courts ruled the retain-and-transfer illegal, but FA still enforces it. I built things for Arsenal that the fans really wanted. Some pubs with first-rate snooker tables and dart boards. A resort hotel at Black-burn. We've got fan tours of Portugal. It's cheap there, and they like Brits and our money.

"I peddle an Arsenal just about whatever you want to name. Arsenal ale mugs. Arsenal shirts. Arsenal hats. Arsenal exercise togs. Arsenal wool blankets. I even sell an Arsenal ale for them to pour in their special Arsenal ale mugs. They have a longing to belong to something that means something. Politics, the rest of it, has become so much warm poop. Arsenal is the People's Army, don't you see? They're eager soldiers."

"Cross your palms with silver!"

"You take the profit you make from your private club to buy strikers like Peter Tarchalski and fullbacks who can whack shins without being found out. How did I do it? There's your answer."

"And the objections of the FA?" she asked.

"I believe there are two major ones. First, I did it and they didn't. I take that back, there are three objections. Two, I didn't ask their permission. Three, it takes too much sweat and imagination. They just want to go watch the chaps knock a ball about once a week, then go to the party after the match. If they prefer to sit back telling themselves how civilized they are, let them. Once I get to the top of the table, I'll be generating enough income to buy the players necessary to stay there, and they know it."

"How about the fourth objection?"

"The fourth?"

Gunderson said, "I bet they don't like it that you use your newspapers and radio stations to tout Arsenal, do they?"

"Oh, that. Well, yes, they don't like that either. The owners cry foul. Let them buy their own papers. Nobody's stopping them." Beauchamp looked amused. "Say, Ms. Gunderson, I find this place insufferably pretentious. We both know the philistines in here are only after money, they don't read books. Have you heard of Cucumber's, by any chance?"

Gunderson laughed. "I sure have."

"Have you ever been there?"

"Well, no I haven't, as a matter of fact."

"How would you like to finish this chat in Cucumber's? We're big boys and girls."

"I don't see any reason why not."

"More in line with real people, I think. It's just a few blocks from here, isn't it? I've been reading about it so much, I want to see for myself. I'll have them fetch us a car and a driver. No reason to have our talk in such boring surroundings. Won't solve the case any sooner." Harry Beauchamp summoned a waiter with his hand.

2:15 P.M.

Cucumber's was decorated with photorealistic plastic replicas of fruits and vegetables that looked like human genitals, buttocks, and breasts: cucumbers, gourds, and zucchinis served as penises, and plums, apricots, and persimmons as testicles; canteloupe, watermelon, and pumpkin buns were in abundance, and there were admirable breasts of squash, pear, and papaya sporting cherry, raspberry, and radish nipples. And much more.

Elizabeth Gunderson and Harry Beauchamp were squired to a table underneath massive papaya thighs spread out from a deformed eggplant that was remarkable in its resemblance to a pussy.

Beauchamp, having ordered drinks, said, "This is more like it. Everybody knows what makes the world work, and it's definitely not those fusty books in the Reading Room Bar. A purple pussy and yellow thighs. Complementary colors. My word!" Beauchamp laughed. "Would you look at that magnificent gourd across the way?" He was referring to a speckled yellow gourd that was an enormous dong, correctly shaped. The gourd penis had red apple testicles.

"Quite a specimen, I agree." Gunderson turned on her recorder.

Beauchamp said, "The people who own this bar know how to make money. In six months, they'll have bars like this all over Europe, mark my word. You Americans can be a creative bunch on occasion, I'll grant you that, Ms. Gunderson. Look there: a potato dick!" Beauchamp was amused.

"To pick up where we left off at the Norman, Mr. Beauchamp, can you tell me what happens to the transfer fee?"

"Transfer fee?"

Gunderson said, "For Peter Tarchalski's move to FC Cologne. FC Cologne had to pay you a transfer fee, didn't it?"

"You foolish woman, Ms. Gunderson. Of course they did. Indeed! Peter was the top goal scorer in the English Premiere League. Or are they calling it the Premier Division these days? The most valuable player. They paid nine million of your U.S. dollars, as you know from the papers."

Gunderson looked surprised. "You're telling me, this murder cost FC Cologne nine million dollars?"

Beauchamp grinned, shook his head. "No, no. Heavens! Lloyd's of London gets nicked for nine million buckaroonies. I understand that FC Cologne judiciously bought an insurance policy to cover that period between the payment of the transfer fee and when they got their player. Standard practice, but whether they did or didn't, it's no skin off my nose."

"You have to give it back?"

Beauchamp laughed. "Give it back? What sodding for? Why, I used it as a down payment for a newspaper in Michigan."

"I don't get it," she said. "I thought you're worth hundreds of millions or whatever."

"Well, in December I had, what is the moronic phrase, a 'cash flow' problem."

"You were close to broke."

"No, no, I was doing quite well financially, thank you. I just needed fast cash to legally steal a newspaper. It was cheap, but going, going . . . You won't get anywhere if you leave nine million dollars in a savings account. My heavens, Ms. Gunderson!"

"I guess not."

"There was no problem moving Peter. Any number of clubs wanted him. Defenders are like human donkeys, you know, but goal scorers come at a premium. I rather fancied having my striker carry the German side in the World Cup, so I compromised: if Cologne paid me in December, so I could buy the Michigan newspaper, Tarchalski could join them on the pitch in August. If he topped the scoring charts another year, I could get Maradona money for him, and they knew it."

"It was either your way, or 'sorry.' "

"When you're talking about a footballer as good as Peter Tarchalski, that's it," Beauchamp said.

"What did Lloyd's have to say about all this?" she asked.

"What can they say? They took FC Cologne's money, didn't they? They'll try to weasel out. I've never yet seen an insurer that liked to part with money. They're keen on collecting it, but they don't fancy paying it, do they?"

"His health was okay. He wasn't damaged goods or anything?"

"Damaged goods? What are you saying? He was the most valuable player in the Premiere League. Peter was a hard worker. He was quite fit."

Gunderson said, "So what happens to Arsenal with him gone?"

"Now, I bring on Ricardo Montana."

"The Costa Rican phenom."

"A brilliant young lad who learned his ball skills on the beach. On the beach, yes! But oh, you should see him move when he's got a proper pitch under his feet. He's quicksilver. Those Latins are easy enough to handle. I'll feed him all the beans and rice he can handle, and if he needs spiritual help, I'll ring the Pope, no problem. Fiber and faith and a fuck now and then, no offense; that's all it takes. Do you really suppose I'd have sold Peter unless I had somebody to replace him?"

"An article in *Newsweek* said you once publicly accused Tarchalski of walking around in wet shoes because he couldn't hit the loo."

Beauchamp laughed. "*Newsweek* guy standing there, and I didn't know it. Squish. Squish. Squish. Peter deserved it, dumb kraut. He missed a goal an old lady could have scored. What's the matter with a little truth now and then? Just because he was good doesn't mean he never dropped a turd in the pudding. Now that's he's dead, they're saying he was one of the greatest goal scorers in the history of the game. Twaddle. Ms. Gunderson, do you suspect me of having Peter Tarchalski murdered?"

Gunderson said, "I wouldn't be a very good investigator if I let a nine-million-dollar question go unanswered, would I?"

"Why on earth would I want to kill Peter Tarchalski? I bought him cheap and after I found a replacement, I sold him dear. My risk, my profit." Beauchamp waggled his hand for another round of drinks. "One more round," he said.

Gunderson considered that. "Mmmmmmm. I see by the national dailies in the U.K. that they haven't yet found the cause of the fire last week. What's the name of your company again?"

"Nottingham Ltd." Beauchamp looked sore. "It was deliberately set, had to be. Bloody sods. The fire gutted the production lab. Three of my computer artists asphyxiated." He looked chagrined. "So now I have all manner of people lining up to file suit against me. Some of their relatives, it seems. Several friends. And as far as we can determine, even one total stranger, an obvious queer."

"To file suit? What for?"

"The police say the technicians choked because of uncollected refuse piled in front of the escape route. I'd been stupid enough to hire a company of sodding Paks to maintain the building. Be generous, they said. It doesn't make any difference if they're bloody bomb-toting Micks, or Paks, or sticky-fingered Boogie Woogs. They're all citizens of the U.K. If we don't keep them off the dole, they'll get restless. Hire them. So what if they relieve themselves in the elevators? Let them pile their prayer rugs and comic books and chips bags in front of the fire doors. Idiots!" Beauchamp looked sour.

Gunderson said, "The story I read said they'd just finished a 'visually enhanced' version of *Alice in Wonderland*, although I'm not sure I understood what that means."

"It's the next generation of technology beyond *Terminator II*. It means we were able to cast a photo-perfect Marilyn Monroe as Alice, and comrade Lenin straight out of old photos as the Mad Hatter, and Saddam Hussein as Humpty Dumpty, among the many characters. Easy enough to plump him up for the part. More fun than the stupid lizards in *Jurassic Park*, the way I see it. It's a thoroughly modern *Wonderland*, Ms. Gunderson, as though at Sarajevo we had collectively tumbled through a hole into the twentieth century. At the other end, Sarajevo again. Now this. Just look at the progress we've made."

7

BUENOS AIRES, 8:00 P.M.

It was winter in Buenos Aires, but it didn't feel that way as a balmy wind scurried down the boulevard. James Burlane loved a city with real, honest-to-God boulevards, and Buenos Aires, which had a European look about it, had them in abundance.

There were admirable cities farther north, in the tropics, but they were condemned by the dreadful, pervasive heat and humidity. In Buenos Aires, the eviscerating equatorial swelter was mercifully lacking. Vigor replaced torpor. Here, the men walked with a spring in their step—minus the tropics, pervasive, goatlike stench of sweat that was, by necessity, communally ignored. It was possible for young Argentinian women to look stylish and fresh rather than wet and wilted and to smell of soap instead of body alcohol.

A civilized bottle of wine replaced all the weak beer one knocked back in the tropics to fight dehydration. And the idea of beans and rice, culinary staples of the banana republics, was enough to make an Argentinian shudder. Argentinians, who had the vast pampas to produce proper beef and grain, liked their steaks and vegetables and properly baked European bread.

Burlane thought surely the man was right who said Argentinians were Hispanicized Italians and Germans who thought they were Europeans. They had been through some hard times, but still, the residents of Buenos Aires—*porteños*, they called themselves—had a stylish, cosmopolitan, if slightly standoffish, way about them that said: This is not another banana republic, Señor Norteamericano. This is Argentina!

Burlane wondered if Buenos Aires might not be like Paris, yielding great pleasure to a traveler with patience and forbearance. Language was ordinarily the key to the fortress of pride, and sure enough, Inspector Hector Villanueva let down the drawbridge when he discovered that Burlane spoke a little Spanish.

And so now, Burlane and Villanueva waited in a *casa de carne* on the corner of Las Pampas and Bolívar. They had a seat looking out onto Bolívar, where stylish Argentinians escorted elegant women in tight-fitting dresses and high heels in and out of taxis. In the rear of the restaurant, chefs wearing huge, puffy white hats presided over smoking banks of grills where they cooked beef loins, ribs, tongues, you name it, *amigo*. The chefs were part of the entertainment and so cooked with style and panache, slinging a T-bone here, a tongue there, whop, plop, in just the right place. As Burlane watched, one ho-hum flipped a huge rib-eye behind his back while he checked the time on a languid wrist.

Slender waiters dressed in black trousers, white shirts, and red bow ties presided over the confusion of tables. It was a terrific place. The wine was good. Burlane could hardly wait for the meat to begin arriving at their table.

Inspector Hector Villanueva, a large, bearish man with curly black hair and a five-o'clock shadow over pale skin, poured another glass of Argentinian Pinot noir. He glanced up with deep blue eyes. "Surely, it should not be difficult to imagine our fury, Major Khartoum. They ejected two of our players in Rome. Not one, but two!"

"Dos. Ay!" Burlane shook his head in sympathy.

"Caramba! It was an outrage! They yanked four of our best players for yellows before the final even began. What chance did we have after that? They gave the match to the Germans."

Burlane grimaced.

"The business of throwing a player out of a game is too much."

Burlane said, "They might try handing out penalty minutes like they do in hockey or lacrosse. A team might have to play short for five or ten minutes, but not forfeit a player for the rest of the game."

Villanueva smiled. "Try something different? Actually change the game? Do something sensible? Why you must be loco, Major Khartoum. Such a joker. Surely you are aware of the reputation of FIFA. FIFA will never change anything. To them, fútbol is immutable. They will play now and in the future the exact same way as they played in the past. The mere suggestion of change is controversial. They feel they are custodians of a heritage. Dios mio!

"Enough of an outrage to move an enraged Argentinian to murder, do you think?"

"Señor!"

Burlane sucked air between his teeth and used a toothpick to pry something loose from his lower jaw. "It would take an extraordinary motive to murder two football players. Or a madman with motives impossible to imagine, I suppose. We can't afford to overlook possibilities out of diplomacy."

"Well, I don't know. There's Juan Carlos Rodriguez, but surely that's all talk."

Burlane refilled his wine glass. He cleared his throat. "Could you tell me about that talk, please? If it goes nowhere, it goes nowhere, at least I can say I checked it out."

"Juan Carlos Rodriguez owns the *fútbol* club Independiente and felt passionately about the ejections in Rome. After Argentina lost the championship match to Germany, Rodriguez vowed he would have his revenge for the ejections that had stained the reputation of Argentine football, but I'm sure that would have to be written off as so much *macho* hot air."

"A proud man, I take it."

"A proud man, and he's had plenty of time to calm down. It's been four years." Villanueva grinned. "Of course, with Anna Maria Varga involved, calming down might be difficult."

"Anna Maria Varga?"

"If we are to believe the stories, Rodriguez's passion for revenge was cubed when he met a television actress named Anna Maria."

"I see. Do you want to tell me about that? On the off-chance."

Villanueva leaned back in his seat. "There's nothing to it, I'm sure. Rodriguez, who is thirty years Anna Maria's senior, was smitten by her at a party given for the returning Argentine side in 1990. This wasn't the first rich and powerful man who had fallen for Anna Maria. In fact, at the time she was officially, uh, what would be the English word, 'taken'?"

"I bet that would cover it."

"Out of sight, out of mind. She collected rich men. She'd charm one and videotape him and spend his money until she got bored with him. Then it was onto someone more famous or with a fatter wallet."

"Videotape him?"

"She keeps a sort of diary with a videocamera. When she goes to a fancy party, the sweet and beautiful Anna Maria carries a videocamera in her handbag so she can share the moment with her adoring fans on television talk shows. This is what it's like to be a famous actress being squired about the jet set on the arm of a rich and powerful man. They read about the parties in fan magazines, then she gives them a little glimpse of the fun on television."

"I see."

"Anna Maria was enraged by the red card travesty in Rome. Where were Argentinians with hair on their chests? Witnesses claim that when Rodriguez was introduced to Anna Maria, she repeated her disappointment. Rodriguez liked what he saw and, in a gesture of chivalry, vowed that he would see to it that the red cards were avenged. "The gentle lady asks for justice. I, the mighty Juan Carlos Rodriguez, will give it to her." Villanueva grabbed his crotch. "It is a vow from *los cojónes*, Major Khartoum. *Los cojónes* make men behave like fools. They say things they don't really mean."

"Poor Rodriguez. So much in love!"

SUSANVILLE, CALIFORNIA, 5:00 P.M.

Exhausted and dehydrated from a long day of driving—and yearning for a hot shower—Edson pulled into the parking lot of Chihuahua Charlie's Mexican restaurant in Susanville, where he had *chiles rellenos* and refried beans, which he had come to like, and a leisurely three sweaty bottles of cold Dos Equis.

He started to cruise motel row, but thought the hell with it; he was too tired to worry about the best deal. He settled quickly on Big Will's Wild West Motel, just an Arby's and a Taco Time down the street from Chihuahua Charlie's. Will's, which offered color TV, cable, and X-rated movies, turned out to be run by Hindus. A certificate on the wall of the office informed patrons and passersby that Mr. Chanda Sayani, the proprietor, was a member in good standing of the Susanville Chamber of Commerce.

As Edson paid his bill, dark-skinned children with large, shy brown eyes watched him from the shadows of the motel courtyard.

The furniture in Will's room was covered with genuine imitation wood, that is, artificially grained, plastic, pretend-wood glued onto the real article. A soft drink machine just outside the door contained Coke, Squirt, Sprite, Orange Crush, and Dr Pepper as necessary to top off the gentleman's whiskey or vodka. Edson had visited America often enough to know that in rural areas one was apt to hear a farmer or cowboy order a "Seven and Seven," meaning Seagram's 7 Crown whiskey mixed with 7UP. Yuch!

The lid to the toilet was secured with a paper band by way of demonstrating to the gentleman or his lady that this was a clean, therefore civilized place to bed down for the night. Or afternoon. Or whatever. In the United States, the Chinese and Vietnamese had their restaurants; the Koreans had their corner stores; and the Hindus, for some reason, had bought old hotels and motels. Edson wondered how these particular Hindus had come to settle in Susanville, California. What did they think about the business of putting paper bands over the drinking glasses and toilet lids?

Edson tossed his valise into the rear of his Mitsubishi van. This was one week after the summer equinox, and—with American daylight saving time setting the clock ahead an hour in the summer—it would not get dark in the mountains until close to ten o'clock.

He thought of an American cowboy song, in which the lyrics were interspersed with rhythmic hand clapping:

Stars are white, big and bright
Clap, clap, clap, clap
Deep in the heart of Texas
Deep in the heart of California

No, substituting California for Texas didn't work. Too many syllables.

9

BUENOS AIRES, 9:00 P.M.
Villanueva refilled their wine glasses as a waiter arrived with their first course, arranged dramatically on a large, peasant-looking, carved wooden platter: smoked tongue and horseradish sauce; handsome T-bone steaks; slices of loin, crisply grilled and served with a mustard sauce; and a generous loaf of French bread to rip apart and smear with spiced marrow.

Burlane sampled a bite of wonderful tongue. "And, you say, Rodriguez is in the United States now?"

"To watch the World Cup matches, yes. He took Anna Maria Varga, by the way. *Que tetas!*" Villanueva's eyes lit up, and he cupped his hands, weighing imaginary breasts.

Burlane grinned. "A television actress, you say? What kind of television actress?"

"She's a soap opera star. You'll find her on the covers of Spanish-language women's magazines from here to Mexico. To the United States, in fact. Her soap opera is a standard cable offering in American cities with large numbers of Spanish-speaking people."

"Los Angeles, Miami, and New York, I suppose."

"Yes, of course. Throughout the West and Southwest."

"Heroine or villainess?"

"She has huge green eyes and hair that falls to the small of her back. She portrays Annabella, a simple, working-class girl who marries into the world of a ruthless television mogul and his glamorous, politically powerful family."

"I see. Horny too, I'll bet. Coveting their neighbor's wives. Much hiding of determined sausage. Fortunes won and lost."

Villanueva laughed. "It goes without saying. The big question in the gossip magazines is: Is the real-life Anna Maria anything like the saintly Annabella, who suffers one soap opera tragedy after another, accepting them in noble silence, crying buckets of tears? Some say she's a lovely, sweet thing cast by the producers to play herself. She always remembers her fans. Others say no, that in fact Anna Maria is *una muchacha* who knows how to get her way and gets it. *Una vagina con los dientes.*"

A vagina with teeth. Burlane grinned.

"It does seem that Anna Maria is in love with Rodriguez, or something approaching it. From all appearances, she actually likes the guy."

"Not just another rich hulk to share with her maybe fans?"

"Maybe not."

"In any event, she apparently knows how to flip Rodriguez's switch."

"*Que verdad*, Major Khartoum. In this case *es posible* it is the only button she needs to flip. Did you know what she did to the English who came down here to show *La Prensa* and TV-PORTI how to do business?" Villanueva grinned at the memory.

"No, I don't believe I do. Who was that?"

"The guy who owns Arsenal in the English First Division."

"Harry Beauchamp?"

"*Sí*, that was his name."

"Peter Tarchalski played for Arsenal. I guess you know that."

Villanueva thumped the heel of his hand against his forehead in dismay. "*Dios mio. Sí, sí*, I'd forgotten. I hadn't made the connection. Harry Beauchamp!"

9:30 P.M.

James Burlane studied his red wine. He said, "I have a friend who maintains that if you fly flour, sourdough culture, and water from San Francisco to Seattle and bake it in an identical oven, it won't taste as good. San Francisco sourdough is inimitable. Horseshit, I say. My palette was educated on mom's homemade, true, but I bet a Frenchman would have a tough time matching this wine." Then, almost as an afterthought, he said, "Do tell me about Harry Beauchamp, Inspector."

Hector Villanueva refilled Burlane's glass. "Harry Beauchamp was down here issuing edicts at the headquarters of his new properties, La Prensa and TV-PORTI, when he met and fell in love with Anna Maria Varga, who was then the ladyfriend of Juan Carlos Rodriguez. TV-PORTI produced Ms. Varga's soap opera, *La Vida.*"

"I see."

"Harry fell in love with her, and for several weeks they were seen everywhere together. Anna Maria had lost two brothers and a cousin in the Falklands war, and was supposed to be a furious hater of the Brits, and here she was screwing this arrogant British *mierda* who bought *La Prensa* and TV-PORTI. How could she do that?"

"Good question" Burlane helped himself to a crisp slice of loin. *Mm-mm.*

"Everybody thought the answer was obvious when Dusenberry's London film company showed up to film two adventure movies with her as the female lead. Harry didn't seem to mind that the first movie was awful, but a few days after the second one was in the can, he packed his bags for London. A few weeks later, he sold both *La Prensa* and TV-PORTI. Anna Maria returned to the arm of Juan Carlos Rodriguez as though nothing untoward had taken place."

"I see."

"On television talk shows, she'd tell her Argentine audience how Beauchamp loved to clown around for her while she taped him. All she had to do was bat her eyes, and he'd go goofy. Do whatever she wanted."

"Letting the viewers imagine just how goofy, I take it."

"Exactly. Then rumors and suggestions began surfacing in the gossip columns in fan magazines about embarrassing 'mystery tapes' featuring Beauchamp as the star."

"Oops!"

"Anna Maria supposedly had embarrassing videotapes of Harry Beauchamp that Juan Carlos Rodriguez liked to show at parties. A jet-set acquaintance of mine claims to have seen three: Harry masturbating as he leafs through pornographic magazines; Harry dancing and flipping his genitals about as he sings 'Blueberry Hill'; and Harry sipping a double martini while he fondles a teenage girl."

"What did Anna Maria say about these rumors?"

"She denied them indignantly, but not without a mischievous look in her eye. The consensus seems to be that Anna Maria figured out a way to drive Harry Beauchamp out of town and coolly pulled it off, complete with the leaked rumors. If he got stubborn, she'd have some more fun at his expense. The Big Man was down here having a good time showing off, then he suddenly packs his bags. What other explanation is there?"

"Anna Maria is still the star of *La Vida*, I take it."

"She sure is. And the likelihood that she figured a way to single-handedly send the hateful Brit packing has made her even more of a star. She accomplished what the Argentine army couldn't do. Major Khartoum, without Anna Maria Varga, *La Vida* would be *nada*. Anna Maria is happy. TV-PORTI and *La Prensa* are happy. Now that we have gotten rid of the generals and got our finances straightened out, the country is prospering."

10

SUSANVILLE, 8:00 A.M., FRIDAY, JULY 1

Edson parked his van at a Denny's on the outskirts of Susanville and studied the map while he had an American breakfast of bacon, eggs, and hash-browned potatoes. He decided to take a loop down onto the Nevada desert—toward Reno—to see if what he wanted was down there.

Edson liked the desert weather. Here a day had seasons. The cool mornings, carrying the promise of spring, began with the purple edge of the sun that warmed quickly to red, then yellow. By midday, the white-hot sun seared bone-dry air, thus attending to the needs of snakes, lizards, and insects, if not human beings. Edson had been told that at times, in parts of Arizona and Nevada, it got hot enough to fry eggs and bake brains.

He finished his breakfast, then drove east on a curving, two-lane blacktop that dropped off the Sierra Madres toward Winnemuca in northern Nevada. There wasn't much in the way of foothills here. The Sierra Madres rose straight out of a flat desert floor.

Twenty minutes out of Susanville, he got a good view of the highway below him, which shot straight east through the desert. He knew it was unlikely he was going to find what he wanted down there. It was too open; a vehicle would be visible for miles. Also, it was perhaps a little too barren for him to scare up any help for his practice sessions. Not much out there except for snakes and nocturnal mice.

He turned his Mitsubishi around and returned to the mountains, eventually taking the road north from Susanville to Alturas. Edson took his time exploring the isolated roads that led off the main highway, slowing to consider each prospect.

In the first hour, he turned down two spurs that promised trees and isolation and a little space. In one case, he found cattle, which suggested the presence of cowboys. The second road followed a stream, but when Edson spotted a fisherman standing in white water, he turned back to the main highway.

Finally, he found his spot, down a side road about twenty miles east of Alturas.

Edson pulled back the Mitsubishi's sunroof and stood up. Below him, barren folds of land flattened into bumpless desert. In the foothills, juniper and buckbrush were nestled into the bottoms of narrow arroyos. In there, Edson knew, there would be mule deer, sleeping it off in the heat of the day.

Farther down, where the real desert began, there would be jackrabbits and an occasional coyote. It was, in fact, similar to the spot Edson had picked out for his and Mueller's retreat, tucked up against the eastern foothills of the Andes.

The weather will be like this Mueller. There will be cool mornings. The temperature will rise quickly, but the air will be crisp and dry.

PALO ALTO, CALIFORNIA, 9:14 A.M.

Eee!-Eee!-Eee! Eee!-Eee!-Eee! Eee!-Eee!-Eee!

Elizabeth Gunderson snuffed her beeper. She dialed her number on her cellular phone and was patched through to James Burlane. He said, "You said to call immediately if I find anything worthwhile. Well, I've found a definite maybe. I'm calling from the cabin of a Boeing 747 on its way to New York. Just finished watching *Terminator II.* It's amazing what they can do with computer graphics. Photo-realistic. They're electronic Andrew Wyeths, except that their images move and attempt to scare the shit out of people instead of trying to drown them in sentiment. A form of high-tech comic book. Do you suppose we were born too soon, Ms. Gunderson?"

"What have you found?"

Burlane told her of his conversation with Hector Villanueva.

When he had finished, she said, "My God! What does that all mean, do you think? That Rodriguez had those men murdered to avenge the players ejected in Rome?"

"Beats hell out of me."

"And this business of Harry Beauchamp and Anna Maria Whatever-her-name-is."

"Anna Maria Varga."

"And Harry Beauchamp!"

"The very same."

"So what do you think we should do? Tell Ladd McAllen and hope he can score a warrant to search Rodriguez's stuff?"

"That's what I'd do."

"Then have a chat with Harry Beauchamp."

"I don't think I would if I were you."

"No?"

"Somebody's gotta talk to him, of course. I'm headed for New York; you're on the West Coast. I think you should let me do it. Then I'll fly on to San Francisco to do my thing in Palo Alto on Saturday. Wire me and listen in if you want. Also, Harry seems to see himself as a heroic individualist jousting the lethargy of the British establishment."

"And you see yourself as some kind of a soul mate."

"Not exactly that, but I think he's interesting. For all I know, he had his own player murdered, but I'd like a shot at him before he starts posturing for the media, which he'll almost certainly do once Ladd McAllen goes official on him. Put a mike on me so you can make a transcript. I won't muddy any waters."

Gunderson said, "Okay, put what you told me in a witnessed affidavit from Inspector Villanueva; and fax it to Ladd."

"What about me talking to Beauchamp?"

"By the time you land, it will be arranged. Call our number in New York, and they'll give you transcripts of my sessions with Dusenberry and Beauchamp yesterday. You might want to read those before you talk to him."

"Thank you, Ms. Gunderson. I appreciate it."

"You're welcome, Major Khartoum."

11

James Burlane assumed Willard's was an American imitation of a English gentleman's club. The walls, of a dark brown, oiled wood no doubt hard enough to be nearly bulletproof, were covered with smoky oils of manly boxers, horsemen, fishermen, billiard players, and shooters splashing waterfowl on Long Island Sound.

Their age and crusty frames suggested that some of the sporting scenes might have been rendered by known artists; the walls served the function of intimidating proletarian interlopers so boorish as to require prices on the menu or who ordered foo-foo drinks instead of honorable beer or proper Scotch.

The gentlemen of Willard's—the women customers were conspicuous by their presence and tolerated only according to the dictates of the new order—dined in an atmosphere of satisfied manly murmur punctuated by the muted clicking of glass and cutlery. Tolerance of females was one thing; acceptance was quite another. However often the pushy broads showed up, pretending to be one of the gang, some going so far as to wear pretend neckties and padded blue jackets with elegant pinstripes, they had only hair between their legs, not the requisite swinging horn.

Burlane had come from "I seen," "it don't," "lean it up agin the barn" country, and there was a time, when he was an adolescent, that such pretense would have turned his mouth dry with insecurity. Now, if his lower bowels had been in the mood, he would have squeezed out an audible fart, an editorial ripper or proletarian squealer.

Harry Beauchamp, who surely had once been concerned with such nuisances as prices, had ordered clams and chips for both of them, the equivalent of ordering a hot dog in a fancy steak house. He had ordered with assurance and without consulting anything as plebeian as a menu, and Burlane assumed that the puzzled chef—who would no doubt have done a bang-up job of steamed halibut cheeks in crabapple and tamarind sauce—had done his best to fulfill the crass order. Even without practice, Burlane thought, a professional chef should have done better. Was this an example of the much-talked-about lack of skilled labor?

Beauchamp dipped a strip of clam into a paper tub of an over-salted, whitish yellow goo spiked with minced dill pickles and vinegar.

Burlane, chewing on a clam strip, said, "That glutinous gel is what we call tartar sauce in the U.S. It's supposed to be made of mayonnaise."

"I was wondering," Beauchamp said.

"Also, the cook seems not to know that the purpose of hot oil is to seal the outside of food and lock the juices in. If he impatiently crowds the fryer with too many clams, the temperature of the oil plunges and the clams come out sodden with grease. Do it right and you hardly have any grease at all."

Beauchamp said, "Yes, it appears something wasn't done properly."

"The trick is to slowly add the pieces to be cooked a few at a time in order to maintain a high temperature. Keep that oil hot. Double, double toil and trouble. Fire burn and caldron bubble."

"The way these things taste, a person would think you had an Englishman in the kitchen, if you don't mind my saying. Perhaps a starving Catholic chap fled Northern Ireland."

"Also, these clams might well have been genetically engineered at MIT. You ever think of that? They started out with a grant from the Pentagon to perfect a new kind of rubber and wound up with chewy clams."

Beauchamp made a face. "There's a Mexican café I ordinarily fancy, but this afternoon I thought I'd try something different. Lesson learned."

James Burlane finished his Harp lager and caught the waiter's eye; he tapped his empty bottle with his finger. As he did, he snagged another strip of fried clam. He said, "Harry, Harry, Harry. We're talking two murders and the World Cup here. We have to be serious. It's okay to call you Harry, isn't it?"

"You already have."

"I want you to fess up about that business between you and Anna Maria Varga. I had to go all the way to Argentina to find out about that craziness. Shit!"

"Oh, that!" Beauchamp looked disgusted. "I suppose the Argie you talked to was aware of all the amusing details."

"He told me about scurrilous rumors that found their way into fan magazines. He knows someone who claims to have seen three videotapes with you as an unwitting star. Please be a good media baron and tell me the truth. What happened?"

Beauchamp's face tightened. "That bitch took videos of me naked, and I was dumb enough to oblige. Do it for me, *amor, por favor*. I adore men who know how to play, *amor*. Express yourself, *amor!* Be free! It was premeditated, Major Khartoum. She did it deliberately. While my attention was glued to her patriotic Argie tits, she was focusing her camera on my crotch. My God. I sold *La Prensa* and TV-PORTI to put that all behind me. In any event, it's completely irrelevant to any of this."

Burlane said, "Just because the connections don't mean anything now, doesn't mean they won't with a little effort. Did you know about Rodriguez's threat to avenge the ejections Argentina suffered in the 1990 championship game?"

Beauchamp made a farting sound with his tongue. "I pay no attention to anything that issues forth from that Argie's mouth. He's of no interest to me whatsoever."

"But you do remember Rodriguez's so-called vow to give retaliatory ejections to the Germans?"

"Now that you mention it, yes. The hairy-chested *El Señor Machismo*. He's going to do this. He's going to do that. Yawn. I assure you, the very last thing on my mind is Anna Maria Varga. She is one of those women, that when you first see her, you think you'll never forget her. Your ego swells like a balloon with Anna Maria on your arm. Then, when you really get to know the bloody bitch . . ." Gloomily, Beauchamp dipped a clam in his tartar sauce.

"Ahhh. Well . . . If I had a nickle for every woman who drove me crazy. They intuitively know where our brains are located."

"That crazed little episode cost me a whole lot more than a nickel, I can tell you."

"Speaking of nickels. There's one more thing that bothers me, Harry. I still find it hard to believe that Lloyd's of London is prepared to passively fork over nine million bucks to FC Cologne on this deal. That flies in the face of all reason. I mean, what if there was something wrong with Tarchalski? Some reason he wouldn't be able to perform?"

"I thought I went over that with Ms. Gunderson yesterday. And the people from the FBI."

"I know you did. I read a transcript of your talk with Ms. Gunderson. You answered a question with a question. You asked how could there be anything wrong with Tarchalski if he won the Premiere League scoring title?"

"Well, how could there be?"

Burlane said, "What if there was some kind of biological glitch that wouldn't hamper his performance immediately, but would in the long run. Is that impossible?"

Beauchamp laughed. "Oh, come on, now. How on earth would I know something like that? If I were a doctor, perhaps." He popped a slice of clam into his mouth.

"Nothing embarrassing that would be disasterous if someone like Anna Maria ever found out about it?"

"Not that I'm aware of," Beauchamp said. "To my knowledge, Tarchalski wasn't a closet drag queen or anything like that. I don't know what it would be."

"I know your Costa Rican is supposed to be good, but he isn't yet tested in Premiere League soccer, is he? In all honesty, I have to say that question bothers me. Soccer is a competitive business. It's natural enough to want your side to win. But we both know that being the star of the beach at Punta Arenas or at Frijoles Grande in San José doesn't mean you have the stuff to take an English side to Wembley. Let's be realistic." Burlane took a swig of Harp.

Beauchamp grinned triumphantly. "Ricardo Montana is all that he's billed, believe me, Major Khartoum. He has soft feet, and he can slam 'em. He's a stout wide-body, like Maradona. Aggressive as all get-out. Sprinkles Y chromosomes on his eggs for breakfast. And as for Peter Tarchalski, both Lloyd's and Cologne gave him a rigorous physical exam. He passed without reservations. The transfer was legally executed, and correctly registered with the FA and FIFA duly informed. As I told you, Tarchalski kept in shape. He was fit."

"If he molested little girls on the side or something equally abhorrent, I don't suppose that would show up in a physical exam, would it?"

"You're reaching, Major Khartoum. He was clean, I assure you."

"Tell me, if it could be proved that Tarchalski had been murdered for the insurance money, would Lloyd's have to pay?"

Beauchamp narrowed his eyes. "Just what are you getting at, Major Khartoum?"

"Let me put it to you this way. An ugly way to put it, I know, but I have to, it's my job."

"Put it any way that pleases you, Major Khartoum."

"What if there was something wrong with Peter Tarchalski? What if you had peddled the Germans damaged goods and nobody knew it?"

ALTURAS, 10:00 P.M.

In Alturas, Edson stayed at the High Desert Inn, a motel with cable television, an X-rated channel, paper tape over the toilet, and the soda machine outside, just like the place in Susanville.

He showered and later, enjoying a cold Budweiser and a pipeful of overpriced hashish that he had bought in San Francisco, he turned on the X-rated channel. He watched an energetic young couple for a few minutes, but he was far too tired to get excited about watching other people do it. Even the frenzied slurping of genitals looked boring.

He flipped on to a channel featuring the San Francisco Giants playing the New York Mets in Shea Stadium. The Americans and their baseball! He reloaded his pipe and took a draw. Baseball was a stupid game, but at least the Americans didn't go at one another for five days straight like the Brits and their silly cricket.

He watched the Giants and Mets with the sound turned off and fell asleep in the sixth inning.

Later, when he got up to relieve his bladder, the baseball game was over; on the screen, a long-faced man with dimpled cheeks and an enthusiastic, boyish way about him stared straight at the camera, mouth moving. His eyes, wells of a weird, possibly artificially colored green, said, or meant to say: sincere, sincere, sincere. He used a reassuring grin—showing outsized, horsey teeth—as a form of punctuation. A flash of equine chompers functioned as a comma. A down-home smile served as a dash. The full yowza, yowza, spread of outsized ivories functioned as a period, full stop.

Edson found himself starting at the man's athletic upper lip, which was almost a solo performer. Was he about to whinny or neigh? What was he after? Another helping of oats? Edson turned up the sound.

The horse-faced man, spittle flying, said he only wanted $150 for a set of six videotapes on how to be a success. He said if the viewers really wanted to succeed and weren't afraid of a little hard work, it was the deal of a lifetime. There was virtually no limit to what they could accomplish. But they had to remember, these tapes were for hard workers only. Otherwise, forget it; all bets were off.

Edson punched off the television and prepared to go back to sleep, but then something occurred to him. Americans were taught to be respectful of religion. He suspected that this was culturally enforced because churches had tax-free money to spend and politicians were always sucking up to them. Ronald Reagan had been a master at that.

Edson remembered that the guru of the Rajneesh Puram cult in Oregon had collected twenty-eight Mercedes Benzes on his tax-free collections taken from his followers, so given to obedience that they poisoned local salad bars. Christian lawyers, concerned that the profitable god business might be challenged, entered briefs on behalf of Rajneesh Puram as friends of the court. And when Christians looned out as they had at Jonestown or in Waco, Texas, they were judiciously called "sects" out of deference to Christians who did not want to be identified with madness.

If you were religious in America, you were given that extra, critical mark of respect and presumed good motive, a wonderful advantage in front of the goal mouth.

Edson wrapped a towel into a makeshift turban. It was part of a Sikh's religion to wear a turban and a metal bracelet. No problem with that. And males were required to carry a knife in their turban, a fact known by airport security people, but few others outside of India.

He put the terry cloth turban on his head and looked at himself in the mirror. The quiet and calmly efficient Sikhs, with their exotic turbans and handsome beards, commanded respect because they were tall and trim and took care of themselves. They were bank guards in Hong Kong, hired for decor as much as anything else, Edson suspected. With their reputation for scrupulous honesty and loyalty, they had traditionally guarded the prime minister of India until one of them assassinated Indira Gandhi.

Other than that oopsie to mar their dignity, one did not question an elegant Sikh. It wasn't done.

Edson had contacts with brown lenses. No problem with the beard certainly, or to darken his skin with a little makeup. Sure, he could see it. A godly Sikh.

12

ALTURAS, 8:00 A.M., SATURDAY, JULY 2

Edson ducked down and opened the locks on a box of tools. He started removing the Kolb's tail assembly from the back of his Mitsubishi van, when, seemingly inspired, he grabbed a soccer ball that rested among the parts. He hopped out of the Mitsubishi and jogged in place, bouncing the ball on the tops of his thighs.

For you, Mueller.

He kicked the ball straight up, as hard as he could. Grinning, he ran after it, trying to catch it. Then . . .

"Ay!"

. . . the sun!

Grimacing, he squinted his eyes to block out the light. He had lost the ball. He didn't know where it was coming from. At the last second he saw it and leaped up, heading it away.

In addition to the inflated soccer ball, the disassembled ultralight, and the tools necessary to put it together, Edson retrieved a cardboard box filled with twelve deflated soccer balls and two tanks, each no larger than a propane tank in the kitchen of an RV. He used a hand pump to fill the soccer balls through their rubber needle valves. Then he numbered each ball with a felt-tipped marker pen. Finally, he topped off each numbered ball with a measured squirt from the green tank and checked the final pressure with a gauge. On a pad, he recorded the number of the ball, the exact pressure, the time, and the size of the squirt from the green tank.

Then he lined the balls up in a row and returned to the business of assembling the ultralight. As he was working, he suddenly saw them, out of the corner of his eye. He froze, watching.

Two big-eared doe mule deer crossed the meadow about thirty yards in front of him. They were fine-boned and delicate. They daintily savored the odors in the air with their wet black noses. Connoisseurs of scent, they were. They hadn't smelled him because of the direction of the wind.

Then, the breeze shifted.

They stopped, noses still up.

Spooked, they scoped the smelly stranger, and, in a heartbeat, bounded off in great, graceful leaps, their tiny hooves making a rhythmic *chop! chop! chop!* on the ground.

Yes, there was action out there.

He checked the balls with his pressure gauge. Oops! Ball number 12, which had taken the heaviest dose from the green tank, was fast losing its poop. He noted the time on the pad.

Santa Barbara, 8:30 a.m.

The Federal district judge in Los Angeles was at first reluctant to issue a search warrant based on a faxed affidavit from a detective in Buenos Aires. Who knew what knives Hector Villanueva was sharpening? Villanueva was down there, and the judge was up here, in righteous *gringo* land.

Ladd McAllen's request would have been easier to grant had it had been made by an officer of the U.S. embassy acting as an official of the American courts. The fact that James Burlane was FIFA's hired hand was of negligible weight. Rodriguez vowed this; Rodriguez vowed that. Really? Villanueva offered only hearsay, which was low-octane legal fuel; Burlane's "definite maybe" would almost certainly cause pings in the overloaded engine of justice.

Also, Juan Carlos Rodriguez was a wealthy and powerful man, although not a brand-name biggie in the United States. Despite protestations to the contrary, it was far easier for a judge to issue a warrant to search a cabdriver's digs than an industrialist's domicile; lawyers for people like Rodriguez could recite civil rights precedents in their sleep.

The U.S. attorney claimed the entire World Cup was threatened; this was a search warrant, not a warrant for Rodriguez's arrest. The judge was aware of the public consequences if he said no out of noble sentiment and Rodriguez was responsible for the death of more soccer players; also, an Anglo judge in Los Angeles could ill afford to indulge in stereotypes about the excitable Latin temperament.

After demonstrating proper caution, the judge proceeded as though the evidence was overwhelming and Inspector Hector Villanueva was a model of near-Japanese calm. He approved the search warrant.

FIFA investigator James Burlane, still suffering jet lag from his night flight from New York, accompanied Elizabeth Gunderson on the thirty-minute flight from Palo Alto to Santa Barbara.

On the way Gunderson told Burlane that she had served as McAllen's apprentice for six years before she accepted the job at the Los Angeles Olympics. In the luck of the career draw, McAllen had wound up the FBI's chief specialist in stadium security. Where there were crowds and worried cops, McAllen was summoned. He had been to the last twenty Super Bowls without seeing more than a few plays in any of them.

McAllen was the one who had taught Gunderson how to work the nut lists. He taught her how to establish defensive perimeters. He taught her tactics for drunks, tactics for victory celebrations, and tactics for psychopaths.

They were met at the Santa Barbara Airport by the barrel-chested, six-foot-five-inch McAllen, almost totally bald with a Van Dyck beard and a disinclination to tie his necktie. McAllen and five special agents in government sedans drove Burlane and Gunderson south toward Los Angeles to La Casa Blanca, overlooking the Pacific. Rodriguez and his lady were staying at the estate while they watched World Cup matches in the Rose Bowl and Stanford Stadium.

Tony Artes, the owner of La Casa Blanca, was on a European singing tour. He had offered the house to Rodriguez while Rodriguez was in California to watch the matches.

McAllen said there were seals on the rocky beach that could be seen from the grounds. Fatty Arbuckle was said to have been fond of watching them from poolside, preferably when he was thoroughly pickled. McAllen said Gunderson and Burlane would have to watch carefully because the seals blended in with the rocks. They couldn't see any.

An American flag fluttered atop a flagpole in the turnaround before the main entrance of the Spanish hacienda, or whatever it was supposed to be.

Burlane and Gunderson stood to the rear of McAllen and his shotgun-toting agents as McAllen, brandishing his search warrant, banged the brass knocker and rushed past the maid who answered the door.

A man shouted in Spanish.

Then a woman.

Agent Ramon Fernandez, a broad-chested, curly-haired Hispanic American, the party's translator, shouted in Spanish.

McAllen said, "Easy, easy, Mon." "Mon" was Ramon Fernandez's nickname.

"Ay!" the woman screamed.

Burlane followed Gunderson inside to see McAllen standing face-to-face with an enraged Latin man who had a thin Cesar Romero mustache and a chest matted with curly gray hairs. He was swarthy, thickening with middle age, but solid and manly. He wore a Mickey Mouse terry cloth bathrobe, including tail, and fluffy slippers that were flop-eared Goofy with black plastic eyes. Except for his Walt Disney costume, he looked like a swashbuckler gone only slightly to seed. This, presumably, was the inestimable corned beef baron and football afficionado, Juan Carlos Rodriguez, owner of the Argentine club Independiente.

Behind him was the single most beautiful woman James Burlane had ever seen. Her face was a showstopper, part Ava Gardner, part Sophia Loren, that is, dominated by large, languid eyes, outsized, sensual lips, and breasts that belonged on a larger rib cage.

She was perhaps five-five, but her willowy figure made her look taller; it also made her breasts look larger. Burlane had once read that since the camera made people look larger, actors and actresses tended to be little people. Perfect little people. Surely, this petite siren, provocative in the extreme, was an example of this. Her black hair was wrapped in a turban of flowered towel. Her thimble-sized nipples thrust provocatively against a Los Angeles Lakers T-shirt, the bottom of which barely covered her naked butt.

This was Anna Maria Varga . . .

And Anna Maria was pissed! *Ay!*

Stomping a foot, she sailed a vase in the general direction of McAllen.

McAllen, eyes wide, ducked, saying, "Aw shit!" as the vase crashed into the wall. "You know her lingo, Mon. Talk to her."

Fernandez did his best to tell Rodriguez in Spanish what was happening.

Rodriguez, eyeing the automatic weapons, took a step back. This was serious business. He tried to hear what Fernandez had to say, but couldn't, as behind him, his lady's tirade of Spanish continued; her shrill voice, rising in intensity and pitch, spit vowels like bullets fired full automatic.

Suddenly, Rodriguez turned and bellowed: *"Valgame Dios! Calle la bóca! Pare!"*

Anna Maria began wailing, *boo hoo-hoo, boo hoo-hoo.* Tears streamed down her face. She wept. She wept. Oh, how she wept! Her little body shook pathetically. Poor little Anna Maria. *Boo hoo-hoo.*

Rodriguez, knowing he was in some kind of fix, but not knowing why, gave McAllen a What-am-I-going-to-do-with-her-now-woman? gesture with his hands. His face pleaded with the bearers of automatic weapons to be patient. Then, looking sympathetic, he attempted to comfort Anna Maria.

But Anna Maria was in no mood to be placated. She yanked back from him, blubbering, tears rolling. Her look condemned Rodriguez: He was mean. He had yelled at her. Sweet little Anna Maria. How could he? What had she done to deserve that?

Burlane wondered how on earth any human could contrive to sound so utterly wretched. Anna Maria was demonstrating Force Ten grief.

Rodriguez, grinding his jaw, coming to the end of his patience, said evenly: *"Calle la boca!"*

She wept on.

Without warning, Rodriguez popped her hard on the ass and pointed to the rear of the house, to the bedroom or wherever, shouting, *"Vaya! Mujer loca! Por Dios!"*

Anna Maria, sniffling, lower lip still bobbing up and down, did as she was told. Holding her chin high and shoulders back to maintain her pride, she strode from the room and entered a hallway. Her admirable buttocks bounced all ways at once; the rising and falling of her T-shirt flashed glimpses of those unhappy campaigners in action.

She stopped at the first door in the hall and turned, showing her profile to Rodriguez and the federal officers. She poked her rump out. The T-shirt rode up, baring her stinging rear. She rubbed it with her hand, giving Rodriguez a red-eyed, pouty look. Her feelings were hurt. Her lip quivered. She sniffled. Having thus established to the males in the room that she was fuckable in the extreme, and they could lope their goats for an eternity as far as she was concerned, she disappeared.

Rodriguez turned suddenly morose. He looked like he'd gotten caught whipping a puppy.

McAllen said, "Mon, give this man the warrant and explain what it means. Tell him his rights and why we're here. Let's get this over with!"

Fernandez did as he was told.

Rodriguez, his attention yanked from the empty hallway where Anna Maria had stood, looked astonished. *"Caramba!"* he said. He jabbered in a blue streak of Argentinian Spanish, ending with *"Hijo puta!"* His brown eyes blazed.

Fernandez said to McAllen, "He wants to know if we're crazy. Does he look like the kind of man who would run around shooting football players? He says to do what we have to do and please go. We're upsetting Señorita Varga, as we can see."

McAllen looked relieved. "Do it then," he said, and waved his people forward into the house.

Rodriguez, his face intense, said something to Fernandez. Much palaver in excited Spanish. He ended with, *Mierda! Ay!*

Rodriguez translated. "He asks what kind of lunatic country is this? A banana republic? Do we know who we're talking to? He is Juan Carlos Rodriguez. He is a millionaire in U.S. dollars. In Argentina, he is as well known as the owner of your New York Yankees in baseball. He owns Independiente. Argentina is playing in the World Cup. They are in Group A. They play two games in the Rose Bowl. He is a sportsman. This is madness." Fernandez had translated *mierda* as "madness" when everybody in the room knew it meant "shit."

McAllen sighed.

Anna Maria was suddenly back, still in the inadequate Lakers T-shirt, but with black exercise tights stretched like a second skin over her lower half. She could now scratch her neck without tormenting males. She had unwrapped her hair and given it a quick blow-dry, so that it now tumbled, jet black, glistening, nearly to the small of her back.

Smiling a grand smile, showing perfect teeth, she gave Rodriguez's arm an affectionate squeeze as though nothing out of the ordinary had happened. She molded herself against him. She held him tightly, her tiny, earnest biceps bulging with the intensity of her squeeze. She gave him a big, wet kiss on the cheek and cooed into his ear in breathy Spanish.

The squeeze and the kiss had an immediate tranquilizing effect on Rodriguez. He wilted instantly from bluster and bravado to charm and cool. One minute a killer Doberman, the next, a cocker spaniel puppy.

The suddenly congenial Rodriguez spoke earnestly to Fernandez.

Fernandez said, "The *señorita* would like to apologize for her outburst of temper. She had just gotten up when we arrived. She is a very private person and was shocked by the sudden appearance of strangers. What if we had been bandits? These things can happen in Argentina. She has invited those of us who aren't busy with the search to have a cup of coffee with her and Señor Rodriguez on the patio. She will have her maid grind coffee beans that were hand-picked in an area of Colombia that is dangerous because of cocaine smugglers."

McAllen looked relieved. "Thank her, Mon. Tell her we'd be

pleased. Tell her the Germans play Poland on Saturday, so we're under a great deal of pressure. We'll complete the search and be out of the house as quickly as possible."

Anna Maria quickly added something in Spanish.

Fernandez said, "Also, she wants to know if she can have our permission to shoot the group with her videocamera? She tapes a kind of diary. Easier and more fun than trying to write everything down, she says."

"She what?"

"She wants to be able to show her friends the American FBI agents who burst into her house in California one morning flashing a search warrant."

McAllen sighed.

Anna Maria squealed with joy and raced off to get her Minicam.

Burlane was amazed: Anna Maria had screamed, cried, pouted, seduced, apologized and charmed—all with little or no emotional transition. When she wanted Rodriguez upset, he was upset. When she wanted him calm, he was calm. She had coolly shifted Rodriguez's emotional gears as though his cock was a stick shift. If this was acting, it was an Academy Award performance, but Burlane felt what he had seen was the real deal, the genuine Anna Maria Varga in action.

Burlane, Gunderson, McAllen, and Mon Fernandez joined Anna Maria and Rodriguez for a stroll to the patio, where they took seats at a redwood table overlooking the rocky beach and the Pacific. Burlane had a terrible time keeping his eyes off Anna Maria, who was now in her Annabella mode, sweet and demure, as she moved around the table, her camera humming. He was torn between her beautiful face and her provocative nipples.

When Anna Maria was finished with her diary-taping, Fernandez translated the small talk, in which Burlane, Gunderson, and McAllen asked Rodriguez polite questions about La Casa Blanca and Argentina's chances in the World Cup. Above them, squawking terns rode the wind like airborne sailors, sliding this way and that with minute corrections of their wings. Then Burlane spotted four seals on the beach. He pointed out the seals, and in a few minutes everybody at the table was watching them.

Burlane knew that, like himself, Ladd Mcallen and Mon Fernandez were having to work at watching seals sunning themselves on the stupid beach rather than enjoying Ms. Vargas's charms. This was the unusual woman to whom Rodriguez had allegedly pledged revenge for the penalty cards given Argentina in 1990. Was she unusual enough to be a motive for murder?

During a lull in the conversation Gunderson leaned toward Burlane and said quietly, "Well, what do you think?"

"About what?" Burlane blinked.

"Now just what do you think?"

"I think Ms. Vargas *es una vagina con los dientes.* All this is found in Ulysses."

Gunderson looked puzzled.

"Anna Maria's a siren sitting atop dangerous rocks. Sailors beware."

"I see."

"I take my cue from popular fiction."

"Which is?"

"I think the thing to do is to be sensible in one's choice of pretty girls. The tactic is to ride into town on a white horse and defeat the bad guy, that, and keep drinking ginseng tea." He pretended to scope Gunderson's rump.

Gunderson said, "Oh, for Christ's sake," but Burlane thought she was secretly pleased.

Ten minutes later, one of McAllen's agents returned to report the find of a waterproof plastic container stashed in a toilet tank. The container held newspaper clippings about the murder of the German players that had been published in the Spanish-language edition of the *Miami Herald,* a brief biography of the Austrian referee Reiner Schmidt, and architects' drawings of the Rose Bowl and Joe Robbie Stadium in Miami.

ALTURAS, 1:00 P.M.

When the Kolb was ready to go, Edson cleared himself a runway and in a few minutes was aloft, with his Uzi 9 mm assault pistol in his lap and a bag of ten loaded 32-round clips. The pistol, which could be fired semi- or full-automatic, weighed a hefty 3.8 pounds and had a 4.5-inch barrel.

The air was crisp and cool. Edson, wearing goggles and feeling good in the open cockpit, cruised at about thirty-five miles an hour about 300 feet high, eyes trained on the arroyos and copses of juniper below him.

Then suddenly, action.

Five mule deer, including a nice buck, two does, and two fawns. They bounded high with that tell-tale chopping of their tiny hooves.

Edson banked his wings and dropped, as much like a falcon as the Kolb would allow, and squeezed off the buck and one doe with crisp singletons. The shot on the buck had been slightly off the mark and he thrashed and hopped in his death throes. Although the dying deer would eventually cease his struggles, Edson flew down and gave him another hit behind the ear. The Uzi was a slick little pistol, but it took some getting used to.

Edson's sentimental interruption for a *coup de grace* allowed the surviving doe to gain some distance on him.

He flew up to about 300 feet to spot her, bounding flat out through the scrub and juniper. She was making a spirited run, he had to admit. He replaced the clip, closed on the doe, and exploded her head with an entire clip at full automatic. The volley of 9 mm rounds sent her somersaulting down the side of an arroyo, tail over outsized ears, hooves flying. Her slapstick descent almost made Edson laugh out loud. What a kick!

Edson circled back to find the fawns, but could find only one of them, which he dispatched with a singleton. He would let a coyote enjoy the sport of running down the other. He had given the buzzards and maggots a free lunch. There were more fawns in the Sierras. Who was to complain?

Edson didn't see what got the greenies and environmental nuts so worked up. Life was fluid. Water into cloud. Cloud into rain. Rain into grass. Grass into deer. Deer into grass. The eater and the eaten. All bugs and beasts were conduits for fluids. Trees, bees, fleas, and peas were all temporary repositories. Mueller said that was the way the world worked, and he was right. Freed of the cholesterol of sentiment, the system functioned perfectly.

Edson returned to the Mitsubishi for more gas and a sandwich and cold beer from his Budweiser cooler, then took off again, this time down to the Nevada flats looking for jackrabbits. Jackrabbits were quicker and smaller than mule deer and so more challenging targets. Even better if he could happen onto a coyote. A coyote was fast and agile, a good test of Edson's flying and shooting skills. A jackrabbit was probably harder to hit, but there was something about a coyote, maybe because of the cartoon character Wile E. Coyote, that made it extra fun to waste.

Edson didn't believe there were roadrunners this far north. To prang a roadrunner from an ultralight would be a real challenge.

13

SANTA BARBARA, 4:00 P.M.

Outside the windows of the federal office building in Santa Barbara, the sun inched its way toward the Pacific. The search of Tony Artes's estate having come up positive in the morning, the lethargic gears of justice, goaded by the gravity of the situation, had begun to turn, however slowly.

While Ladd McAllen and Elizabeth Gunderson checked the forensics report one last time, the other four waited: James Burlane worked the crossword puzzle in that morning's edition of the *Los Angeles Times*; Mon Fernandez doodled on a yellow legal pad; Juan Carlos Rodriguez chewed on his lower lip; Rodriguez's lawyer, Armando Brilliante, studied the back of his hand. Brilliante, a Hispanic celebrity lawyer, was a Miami Cuban who had made his rep keeping drug dealers out of jail.

McAllen picked up the clear plastic envelope that contained the *Miami Herald* stories about the murders outside Soldier Field. He said, "Your fingerprints and those of Señorita Varga were found all over these clippings. How do you account for that?"

Burlane looked up from his crossword puzzle to watch Rodriguez answer the question.

Brilliante said quickly, "He is not required to answer that." He whispered into Rodriguez's ear. Rodriguez, listening, nodded yes. He understood. He replied in Spanish.

Fernandez translated: "As you know, he owns Independiente, a soccer side in Buenos Aires. In Argentina, this is like owning the New York Yankees. He came here to watch some World Cup matches. Argentina played two opening round matches in the Rose Bowl, as you must know. He flew to Orlando to see the Argentina–Greece match, but he stayed in Miami Beach. Why would he stay in Orlando? To watch Mickey Mouse? Miami is where the action is. Naturally, he was interested in the murder of the soccer players. Yes, he read the *Miami Herald's* Spanish-language edition. But he did not cut out the stories. Someone else did that."

"Who?"

Rodriguez knew what "Who?" meant, *"No se."*

"Señorita Varga?"

Rodriguez understood that too. His eyes narrowed. He fired a question at McAllen in Spanish.

Fernandez said, "He says that's preposterous. He wants to know why should she do something like that? He says he wants Señorita Varga left out of this."

Rodriguez spoke to his lawyer.

Fernandez, raising an eyebrow, said, "He's telling Mr. Brilliante that he doesn't want Señorita Varga involved. He wants to know if you're allowed to make suggestions like that."

McAllen snapped, "You tell him he can bet his sweet cheeks I am."

"You really want me to say that?" Fernandez said.

McAllen smiled. "No. Fix it for me, please, Mon. You should join the foreign service."

Brilliante spoke to Rodriguez. Then, in English, he said, "I told him it's all right, Mr. McAllen. You're just doing your job and meant no offense to Señorita Varga. He's a Latin man, you have to understand. He's worried about Señorite Varga's career."

Rodriguez, placated by Brilliante's efforts on his behalf, had something more to add.

Fernandez said, "He says when he and Señorita Varga were staying at Miami Beach, they read the same paper at breakfast every morning. She read the soccer stories just like him. He says naturally her fingerprints were on them."

McAllen said, "Ask him why he hid a biography of Reiner Schmidt in his toilet tank."

Brilliante held up his hand before Fernandez could ask the question. "It hasn't been established that Señor Rodriguez hid anything in the toilet tank. It isn't *his* toilet tank. You say you found something, fine. The question is: how did it get there? And who, by the way, is Reiner Schmidt?"

McAllen said, "Okay, Mon. Ask Señor Rodriguez if he knows an Austrian named Reiner Schmidt."

Fernandez asked the question.

"*El no sé.*"

Fernandez started to translate, but McAllen cut him off. "I got the '*no*' part. Tell him who Schmidt is."

Fernandez did.

Rodriguez shrugged. "*El no sé.*"

Brilliante said, "He doesn't know any Schmidt. I don't know how he can make it any clearer. Does Schmidt's biography have Señor Rodriguez's fingerprints on it?"

"No."

Brilliante turned his palms to the heavens. "Why then anybody could have put it there, couldn't they?"

McAllen looked pensive. "Mon, ask him why his fingerprints were found all over the architectural blueprints of the Rose Bowl and Joe Robbie Stadium tht we found in his toilet tank."

Before Fernandez could say anything, Brilliante said, "The Germans were murdered outside the Cotton Bowl in Dallas, Texas."

"Please ask the question, Mon."

Brilliante said, "They're playing World Cup matches in Orlando, not Joe Robbie."

"Joe Robbie was on the original list of proposed World Cup stadiums considered by FIFA. Mon?"

"He doesn't have to answer this one either." Again, Brilliante whispered into Rodriguez's ear.

Rodriguez, smiling, whispered back. Brilliante seemed pleased at whatever he had to say. Then, Rodriguez answered McAllen's question.

Fernandez listened, then said, "He is a member of a committee appointed by the mayor of Buenos Aires to study the possibility of building a new stadium. He said in the last ten months, they have reviewed the plans of scores of outdoor stadiums in several countries. The Rose Bowl holds more than one hundred thousand people. Joe Robbie Stadium is considered versatile, and was relatively inexpensive to build. The Miami Dolphins paid for it, not Florida taxpayers."

Brilliante said, "Were there other fingerprints on the blueprints?"

"Yes," McAllen said.

"Whose?"

"We don't know yet," McAllen said.

Brilliante struck himself in the forehead with the heel of his hand. "You don't know? Ay!"

McAllen said, "Ask him how he thinks the blueprints came to be in the toilet of Tony Artes's house where he was staying? Did the little people put them there? Fairies?"

Fernandez looked at Brilliante.

Brilliante checked with his client. After an exchange of whispers, he waved his hand disdainfully in a be-my-guest gesture.

Fernandez translated the question, omitting references to little people and fairies. He relayed Rodriguez's answer. "Señor Rodriguez says there was a break-in at the commission's office a few months ago. Nobody could figure out what the intruder had stolen, if anything. He says the stadium blueprints were kept in an unlocked metal filing cabinet. If somebody had lifted the ones for the Rose Bowl and Joe Robbie, nobody would have noticed."

"How many commissioners are there?"

Fernandez repeated the question.

"Doce," Rodriguez said.

Brilliante said, "See, a logical answer for every question. This is foolishness. Are you going to arrest him because an unknown idiot is playing fun and games with a toilet tank, is that it? Try to hold him up for impossible bail because he is a rich Argentinian? A casual jerking around, *a la gringo?*"

McAllen said, "No, we're not going to arrest him, Mr. Brilliante." To Gunderson, he said, "Do you have any questions, Elizabeth?"

"I'll probably think of a half dozen an hour from now, but none for the moment."

"Major Khartoum?"

Burlane looked up from his crossword puzzle. "I need a six-letter word for Polo's destination."

McAllen grinned.

"Cathay," Burlane said quickly. He filled in the box.

To Fernandez, McAllen said, "Mon, please thank Señor Rodriguez for his time, and tell him we appreciate his cooperation. Tell him he is free to go. We hope he and his beautiful lady enjoy the World Cup matches, but tell him we still want the United States to win the cup."

Mon Fernandez translated.

"*Los Estados Unidos? La copa del mundo?*" Rodriguez burst out laughing.

McAllen grinned. "Tell him desire and heart will do it."

Fernandez said, "And defense."

"That too," McAllen said.

Fernandez rendered the Spanish.

Juan Carlos Rodriguez, rising from his seat, extended a hand to McAllen. "*Los Estados Unidos? Ay, señor!*"

PALO ALTO, 9:00 P.M.

Elizabeth Gunderson called James Burlane at his hotel to tell him the story of the FBI's forensics score, reported to her minutes earlier. Fingerprints on the penalty cards matched those of a former German soldier, now an Austrian citizen. The Austrian was currently in the United States to help referee the World Cup tournament.

"Really?" Burlane sounded impressed.

"A German sports firm markets the cards in several Western European countries. There were clear prints on the cards. Whoever last handled the cards no doubt enjoys sausage."

"Sausage?"

"The card had a residue of pork fat, seasoned with salt, sage, summer savory, marjoram, and black pepper."

"That's it?"

"Isn't that enough?"

Burlane said, "Pizza before he refereed his last game. Has McAllen found him?"

"They've found him."

"Okay! They're going to talk to him, I take it."

"Tomorrow morning in San Francisco."

"And the referee's name?"

"Herr Reiner Schmidt."

"Reiner Schmidt's fingerprints were all over the penalty cards?"

"Clear prints and a perfect match. What do you think?"

"About Juan Carlos Rodriguez or Reiner Schmidt?"

"Either one."

"Beats hell out of me," Burlane said. "In Rodriguez's case pride is powerful firewater. Maybe McAllen will learn something good when he talks to Schmidt in the morning. Wrap up the case."

"God, I hope so."

You're going to tag along, I take it."

"Oh sure."

"They're, ah, still taking notice of the comings and goings of Señor Rodriguez and his lady, I take it. Tapping their phones. Going through their garbage. Charting the timbre of their farts. All that good stuff."

Gunderson laughed. "Ladd McAllen has his troops in their shorts, guaranteed, Major Khartoum. If he tries to make contact with the killer, Ladd will know immediately."

14

SAN FRANCISCO, 9:30 A.M., SUNDAY, JULY 3

Regardless of whether or not the FBI prevented more red card murders, two dead players were enough to later provoke a tangle of career-destroying accusations and blame laying. Whenever the bureau's institutional propellers ran into a shit storm, there was no shortage of opinions on how the turds of accusation could have been avoided.

If the transcript of Reiner Schmidt's interrogation revealed any-thing other than scrupulous adherence to every step of the proper legal drill, the media would later use it to flay the FBI in print, and Ladd McAllen knew it.

McAllen, in the neat, sterile, functional interrogation room in the FBI office of San Francisco's federal building, suppressed the urge to chew on his lip. Actually, "debriefing" was the word ordinarily used, a euphemism intended to dispel rumors of high-handed agents in a democratic state; "interrogation" smacked of the evil Gletkin in Arthur Koestler's *Darkness at Noon*. Herr Schmidt was to be debriefed rather than interrogated.

The debriefing room had a desk, three chairs, a small mirror on the wall that was obviously two-way. The wall opposite the two-way mirror was given to shelves of law books as though to reassure dry-mouthed people being questioned that everything was legal. The interior was professionally wired so that conversa-tions could be shared with one's colleagues. The room was painted institutional mauve and cream, such colors intending to soothe, McAllen supposed. He was anything but calm. He checked his notes.

"Herr Schmidt, the reason we want to talk to you today is because we found your fingerprints all over a yellow card that was sent to Jens Steiner before the game with Japan, and on a red card and two yellow cards subsequently sent to Steiner. The red card had Peter Tarchalski's name on it, and the two yellows had Willi Gouchnauer's name on them."

Schmidt blinked. "My fingerprints? You think I murdered Peter Tarchalski and Willi Gochnauer?"

McAllen said, "We are not now charging you with any crime. You are entitled to a lawyer at any time. You may answer our questions or not answer them as you see fit. Under American law, you may decline to answer any question you feel may incriminate you. If you prefer, we can postpone this until we can reach some-body at the Austrian consulate. Do you understand?"

"Yes, I do. I answer your questions of my own free will." Reiner Schmidt, lean, trim, blond, was dressed in khaki slacks and a Dallas Cowboy sweatshirt.

"You speak English very well, Herr Schmidt, but should I talk too fast or use an expression you don't understand, I want you to stop me immediately and ask for a clarification."

"I don't think I will have any problem, but if I do, I will let you know."

"I say again, I apologize for any inconvenience we are causing you. We certainly don't mean to harass visitors to the United States. Tomorrow is July Fourth, our independence day. We will celebrate the establishment of a nation of law, not of whim."

"Of course. I don't know why you want to talk to me, but if there's any way I can help you find the killer, I will do my best. My fingerprints on the penalty cards? You found my fingerprints?"

"They were also on record with the German army. Could you tell me your full name please, and your occupation, home address, and your date and place of birth."

"My name is Reiner Karl Schmidt. I was born on October seventeenth, 1951, in Munich. I live at two-twelve Muellerstrasse, Salzburg, Austria. I own a bakery. I am a football referee with the Austrian first division."

"Do you have a family?"

"I've been married fifteen years. My wife is Erika. I have an eleven-year-old son, Jurgen."

"Why are you now in the United States, Herr Schmidt?"

"FIFA selected me as one of the referees for the finals."

"Tell me, how was it you became a referee?"

Schmidt paused. "That's a long story."

"Will you tell it to me, please."

"I began as a football player, a winder for an amateur side in Rosenheim, a small town halfway between Munich and Salzburg. I was said to be quite good." This was obviously a story Schmidt didn't like telling.

"What happened, Herr Schmidt?"

"In 1972, when I was twenty-one, I was invited for a tryout by Bayern Munich. Bayern Munich is one of the most famous German sides. It would be like a tryout with your baseball Yankees when they were champions. Franz Beckenbauer played for Bayern Munich. In a practice game, I slammed into a fullback and was knocked out. I woke up in a hospital a week later. I had been in a coma." Schmidt grimaced.

"What happened then?"

"I was up and about in a few hours. After a few days I felt all right. I was young. I was fit. I felt I could play as well as before the accident. I got banged on the head, yes, but I had recovered. Unfortunately, nobody would insure me. No insurance, no Bundesliga." Schmidt closed his eyes momentarily.

"How did you feel about that?"

"Bitter. I felt bitter, at first. But that was twenty-two years ago. Time passes. Life goes on."

"What did you do then?"

"I took a job with my cousin, who owned a bakery in Salzburg. I played amateur football, and when I got older, I bought my cousin's bakery and became a referee. I've always been interested in sports, and it was fun to participate in some way. I'm pleased to say I'm quite good, which is why I was selected as a World Cup alternate. It is quite an honor."

"You're carrying an Austrian passport. You're a naturalized Austrian citizen, is that correct?"

"Yes, it is. I owned a bakery in Salzburg. I married an Austrian woman. I felt I should become an Austrian citizen."

"You were in Dallas to stand by in case the referee assigned by FIFA for the Germany–South Korea game was downed by a blocked colon or whatever. Is that correct?"

"In the event something happened to Meneer Guyen of Holland, yes. I was an alternate for that match."

"Where were you during the game?"

"I watched it from my assigned seat."

"What happened when the game was over?"

"I left."

"Immediately?"

"Yes. I joined the crowd and filed out of the stadium."

"Where did you go?"

"I prefer not to answer that question, if you don't mind."

McAllen, who did mind, blinked. "No? Why not?"

"You said I didn't have to answer a question if I didn't want to."

"Yes, I did, and I stand by that statement. Do you have witnesses to your whereabouts after the game?"

"I'm sure people saw me, but I'm not sure they would remember me."

"Do you own a gun, Herr Schmidt?"

"What?"

"I said, do you own a gun?"

Schmidt hesitated. "Well, yes."

"What kind of gun?"

"An antique German shotgun that I inherited from my father. I have it mounted on the wall of my living room. I've never fired it because I don't know if it could withstand a modern load."

"Did you learn to shoot in the army?"

"I was a company clerk, but yes, they taught us to shoot. I . . . I did quite well on the range, actually."

"If you're innocent, it is extremely important for you to tell us where you were when the German players were killed. As it stands now, it doesn't look good, does it? For all we know, what happened to you twenty years ago has been grinding at you ever since. What if your switch to Salzburg was out of bitterness and not a bakery? If so, you had both motive and opportunity. We have to be suspicious. It's our job. The Germans are our guests at an international tournament. We are responsible for their safety. We have an obligation to be thorough."

"I think I would like to talk to someone from the Austrian consulate."

"On Sunday? On the Fourth of July weekend? We'll try."

10:22 A.M.

Next door, James Burlane took a sip of coffee as Elizabeth Gunderson turned off the monitor on which she and Burlane had been watching McAllen's interrogation of Reiner Schmidt.

"What do you think?" Gunderson asked. She poured herself another cup of coffee from the stainless steel percolator in the corner, stirring in a packet of yellowish chemicals to lighten the color.

Burlane said, "It could be somebody stole his cards."

"If he's innocent, why doesn't he tell us where he went?"

Burlane shrugged.

McAllen came into the room. "We finally got the Austrians. They're sending a man over. It'll be a few minutes." He grabbed a cup and helped himself to some coffee. "What do you two think?"

"Beats me," Gunderson said.

Burlane said, "He sounds sincere enough."

"We'll see," McAllen said.

A few minutes later, a representative of the Austrian consulate arrived, a polished and personable man carrying a leather briefcase. His name was Joseph Rothman.

McAllen gave Rothman several minutes alone with Schmidt, then went back inside the room to continue his interrogation.

10:32 A.M.

McAllen said, "I take it Herr Schmidt has told you everything. We have his fingerprints on penalty cards sent to Jens Steiner. Herr Schmidt denies having anything to do with the killings. He says he left the Cotton Bowl immediately after the game, but declines to tell us where he went."

Rothman nodded. "He told me what you asked him. I guarantee, Mr. McAllen, I want to get to the bottom of this as much as you do, but I have to respect Herr Schmidt's rights as an Austrian citizen."

"Of course. As do we," McAllen said.

Rothman said, "Reiner, if you think you may be in serious trouble, you have every right to have a lawyer present. That is the law here in the United States, and it applies to foreigners as well as American citizens."

"Mr. McAllen told me that."

"I can get you a lawyer if you like," Rothman said.

"I don't need one."

"If you don't require counsel, if you're innocent, you must tell this man where you went after the match. I find it hard to believe the FBI would lie about something like your fingerprints. This is important, Reiner."

Schmidt sighed. "All right, I'll tell you where I went. But I will only do it if I'm wired to a lie detector. I don't want there to be any question as to my innocence. When I'm finished, I want to be free to walk out of here and go about my business without fuss. I'm scheduled as an alternate this weekend."

McAllen said, "Fair enough, if that's okay with you, Herr Rothman."

"Of course," Rothman said. "This is the best way, Reiner. If you're innocent, prove it, and I'll take you out to dinner."

"If he's innocent, I'll buy," McAllen said.

Schmidt sighed.

"Kansas City T-bones," McAllen said.

"See there," Rothman said. "A T-bone steak."

"Ja, ja," Schmidt said. He looked dispirited.

11:10 A.M.

The polygraph operator was the bulbous-nosed Miles Templeton, a distracted-looking man in his early sixties. Templeton appeared for the examination of Reiner Schmidt wearing a rumpled brown suit that was at least twenty years out of date. His eyeglasses, too, were old-fashioned, thick plastic affairs. His eyebrows, outsized, twisted brambles with John L. Lewis horns at the edges, needed trimming, as did his runaway nostril and ear hair.

Templeton had been reading polygraph charts for thirty-two years; the procedure was part science, part art, which was why civil libertarians had successfully fought against the introduction of polygraph results as evidence in court.

He first studied the transcript of McAllen's interview with Schmidt. Then he talked over the essential questions with McAllen. Then he fastened the leads to Schmidt's fingertips to measure how much the man sweated and attached other leads to measure his pulse and blood pressure.

When he was finished with this task, and he was assured that Schmidt was comfortable, Templeton began the examination. "Herr Schmidt, I want you to give me truthful answers to the following questions. Okay?"

"I understand, and I will."

"What is your name?"

"Reiner Schmidt."

"When were you born?"

"October seventeenth, 1951."

"Where were you born?"

"Rosenheim, Germany."

"What was your father's name?"

"Jurgen Schmidt."

"What was your mother's name?"

"Anna."

"Are you married or single?"

"Married. My wife is named Erika. I have a teenage son, Jurgen, named for my father."

"What is your occupation?"

"I own a bakery. I'm also a football referee."

"Tell me how you felt about the accident that ended your soccer future."

"I was bitter for several years. I felt there was nothing wrong with me, and the insurance companies were being unreasonably cautious. But I got over it."

"I want you to lie about the next two questions. Have you ever had sex with a cow?"

Schmidt grinned. "Yes, of course. Every Sunday afternoon in my neighbor's field."

"Have you ever played in the American baseball World Series?"

"Yes. I was an outfielder for the Oakland Athletics."

"I'm going to ask you a few questions to which I want a yes or no answer. Do you own a gun?"

"Yes."

"What kind of gun?"

"An antique shotgun."

"Did you shoot Peter Tarchalski or Willi Gochnauer?"

"No."

"Do you know of any plot to kill German soccer players?"

"No."

"Now, Herr Schmidt, tell me the truth, did you leave the Cotton Bowl immediately after the Germany–South Korea game?"

"Yes, I did."

"Where did you go?"

"I went to a place called the Apollo Theater. I had discovered it that morning when I went for a walk."

"That morning. You mean the day of the game?"

"Yes. It's open twenty-four hours a day."

"What is it they do at the Apollo Theater?"

"They, uh . . ." Schmidt looked foolish. "They have live sex on stage. Well, as it turns out, 'simulated,' I believe the word is in English. I . . . there are places like that in Hamburg and Frankfurt. You know . . ."

Templeton, watching the needles that recorded Schmidt's physiological reaction to the questions, pursed his lips. He said, "Why did you decline to answer that question earlier?"

Schmidt took a deep breath and let it out through puffed cheeks. "FIFA is quite concerned about the reputation of both players and officials. All it takes is for a minor FIFA official to get upset. One has to remember, their word is law. One doesn't argue with them and win."

Templeton said, "We've got one run of unusual squiggles, but I think we can conclude that he's telling the truth."

McAllen said, "Which unusual squiggles?"

Templeton studied the chart. "Where he told us about going to the Apollo Theater, but there's good reason for him to show a little emotion there."

Schmidt cleared his throat. "I want to get this business over with. Do you understand? I don't want my name and indiscretion to show up in newspaper reports connected with this investigation."

McAllen said, "As far as we're concerned, it's not the business of the media or FIFA where you went after the game, Herr Schmidt."

Rothman said, "Thank you very much, Mr. McAllen."

McAllen smiled. "No need to thank me. It's American law. We're doing our best to catch a murderer. As I said earlier, it's not our job to harass people for the fun of it, but we've got a real, real big problem here."

Templeton said, "By the way, I went to one of those places once, in Amsterdam."

"Really?" Rothman said.

"It was something else, I have to say. No simulation there, believe me."

Schmidt said, "I thought I'd misplaced my cards. I had no idea."

PALO ALTO, 11:00 P.M.

The Germans would play the Bolivians on the Fourth of July. James Burlane had often thought Americans should call this Lafayette Day because without the help of the Marquis de Lafayette, George Washington would have been just another one of history's nerds, a man with false teeth who liked camping in the snow.

Burlane agreed with the Brits that it had been a war for independence, not a revolutionary war. It was possible, at least American historians were fond of doing it, to credit Washington with having won one battle in the War of Independence: the Battle of Trenton against Hessian mercenaries. But what kind of victory was it when the British had already withdrawn from most of their positions before the heroic Washington and his men ever arrived?

Burlane always thought the most accurate reading of history was that the colonists were expensive pains in the ass and the Brits finally did the smart thing and pretended not to care what they did one way or the other.

George III and the British imperialists were at least enemies the American colonists could defeat with perseverance and heart. The Red Card killer was a lethal loner with a limited agenda. He might be finished; he might not. He might be predictable; he might not. He might make a demand; he might not. If he made a demand it might make sense; it might not.

For an advance celebration of Independence Day, Burlane had bought himself a six-pack of Henry Weinhard beer, a pint of potato salad, a kosher dill pickle bigger than a rabbi's dick, a quarter of a barbecued chicken, and two hot dogs piled high with chopped raw onions and bright yellow French's mustard.

French's, a ballpark classic, was no doubt scorned by connoisseurs of civilized food, and it was true, Burlane did like full-flavored German and English mustards, but this was the eve of July Fourth. The occasion called for beer and hot dogs with chopped raw onions and Everyman's Mustard, which is what French's had become. The hot dog, while advertised as all beef, was said to be a tube of ground eyeballs and anuses mixed with fat, garlic, and salt. Wretched fare, yes, but on the day celebrating American independence, it was ritual wretched fare.

He gave a silent toast to his dead father, who had liked his onions, mustard, and beer. His dad could eat Walla Walla sweets like apples.

Burlane opened himself a beer and sampled the potato salad. His mother's had been a better concoction, but this wasn't bad. Proper potato salad, in his opinion, ought to have lots of junk in it: diced boiled egg, cucumber, sweet onion, celery, and dill pickle. Burlane felt the best way to make it was to first marinate cubes of hot boiled potato in French dressing and let them cool before proceeding, but few people went to that effort. Also, the mayonnaise should contain just a tad of yucky French's mustard.

For Burlane, July Fourth was the most important holiday on the American calendar. The parades and picnics and fireworks were all sweet and proper in their way. But Burlane liked to celebrate the occasion alone, away from crowds and speechifying and noise, so he could appreciate the democratic experiment that had somehow managed to muddle through the crapola of history. Burlane gave his earnest countrymen a silent toast with his bottle of Henry Weinhard, hoping most fervently that the penalty-card man would leave them alone on their special day.

15

PALO ALTO, CALIFORNIA, 10:00 A.M., MONDAY, JULY 4
Years earlier, when James Burlane had heard a happy band of travelers speaking Portuguese on a ferry crossing the mouth of the Guadiana River, it occurred to him that the French gave the language strings, while the Spanish played the brass. In the mouths of women calling out instructions over a railyard loudspeaker, Russian was unaccountably sexy. The Chinese barked and jabbered.

It was a pleasure listening to the German soccer players as they wolfed down their breakfast. Their masculine language, with those wonderful guttural vowels, came from the chest and the throat, and when the throats were those of athletes in their prime, the effect was especially grand. A roomful of Dutchmen sounded good, too.

Proud speakers of one babble against equally proud speakers of another; that was what the World Cup was all about.

With a match coming up at two o'clock, the German trainers didn't want to load their players down with grease-laden sausage and eggs, so they had kept them going with coffee and platters of rolls and croissants until their game-day energy fix.

Now, the loading up of carbohydrates and sugar began in earnest. The trainers skipped the salad; they weren't interested in vitamins and water. They began instead with a German dumpling soup, followed quickly by mashed potatoes and heaping mounds of chicken noodles.

The table was heaped with plates of brown bread accompanied by bowls of butter and jams, and the waiters at the Gifford Hotel scurried about keeping them full.

The players had their choice of lingonberry, blackberry, loganberry, and strawberry jam, or orange marmalade. *You like jam, Fritz, try this. How about a little of that? Have some more, Hans. A little sugar never hurt a hard-working midfielder. Isn't this good bread, Jens? It was custom-baked for us by a bakery in Palo Alto. We brought our own recipe. Have some more food. Good old carbohydrates. Fullback food.*

Burlane sat near the head of the table with Sir Roger Dusenberry, seated opposite Elizabeth Gunderson. Jens Steiner, the German manager, had offered the head of the table to Dusenberry, but Dusenberry declined. Steiner was the manager of the German side on the eve of World Cup battle. The head of the table was correctly his.

If the players knew who Dusenberry was, they didn't show it, and Burlane was a complete stranger.

Despite all the hearty German food, Burlane didn't have the appetite he'd had in New York when he had accepted FIFA's offer.

Ladd McAllen thought they had found their man in Juan Carlos

Rodriguez; McAllen had half the cops in southern California working on a covert surveillance of him. But McAllen didn't think Rodriguez had pulled the trigger himself. Somebody else had done that.

Burlane agreed that if Rodriguez was involved he almost certainly did not do the shooting himself. Despite the elaborate security perimeters devised to protect the German side, Burlane had an uneasy feeling in the pit of his stomach. When they were finished and the table was cleared of everything except coffee cups, Steiner rose to address his players. They knew from his manner that this was serious business, and they gave him their immediate and full attention.

Steiner introduced Sir Roger, who rose to speak on behalf of FIFA's Emergency Committee. Elizabeth Gunderson rose as well. Although most of the players knew a little English, there were a few who did not. Gunderson would translate for the players; she was better at German than Steiner was at English.

Dusenberry said, "The American FBI has located a man whom they believe is behind the murders. They are at this moment watching everything he does and listening to every word he speaks. But the man who actually shot Peter and Willi remains unknown. Therefore, the FBI, the California Highway Patrol, and the Palo Alto Police Department have undertaken every possible precaution for your safety. That's in addition to Ms. Gunderson's security people." Dusenberry paused for a drink of water. He cleared his throat before continuing.

"But we can't guarantee your safety one hundred percent. Ultimately, you will have to decide whether or not you want to take the pitch. Herr Steiner tells me that he doesn't want a player on the pitch who is nursing second thoughts, and I can understand that, Herr Steiner, perhaps you would like to put in a word here."

Steiner rose to address the solemn players in their language. When he finished, Gunderson told Burlane, "He told them they will have a secret ballot. If they choose not to play the match, he will so inform FIFA."

2:14 P.M.

James Burlane, dressed as a German trainer and affecting a limp, accompanied the German players to the tunnel where they waited to be introduced. As defending champions, they were the last to take the field.

They could hear the Bolivians being introduced by a mellow-voiced man on the stadium's public-address system.

When Jens Steiner admired Burlane's ivory-handled cane, Burlane unfolded it into a rifle so Steiner could see how it worked.

"Clever! A beauty," Steiner said. He started shifting from foot to foot to ease the tension.

Burlane said, "Must be a little nerve-racking, waiting to take the field in a game like this. You have to win them all if you can. No letting down."

Steiner grinned. "It gets you pumped, that's so."

"When I was in college, the Stanford Indians played here, but they later changed their name to the Stanford Cardinals."

"Oh? Why is that?"

"The Native Americans complained that it was demeaning. The students thought being birds rather than warriors would soften their guilt."

"Guilt?" Steiner looked surprised. "About what?"

"Being smart enough to be admitted to Stanford and rich enough to afford the tab. By the way, every other year, the Cardinals host the Golden Bears of the University of California at Berkeley, to the northeast across San Francisco Bay. *The Game.*"

"To determine who is best in the area, I take it."

"The local equivalent of Liverpool versus Manchester United in England. Passions run high, although they probably don't drink as much beer here on the afternoon of the contest. They might think they do."

Steiner said, "Do you suppose you'll have an opportunity to use your lethal cane this afternoon, Major Khartoum?"

"I hope not," Burlane said.

"Do you think the killer will try again?"

"I don't have any idea. He may be finished with his work. He may not. It depends on his motives."

"Which are, in your opinion?"

Burlane shrugged. "I can't figure them. That's the problem. A terrorist's motives can be so screwed, it's impossible to anticipate what he'll do next."

"Do you think you'll catch him?"

"We'll get him."

"What will you do then?"

"You mean, if I'm given a shot on goal?" Burlane tapped his shoe with his weapon.

"Yes."

Burlane said, "I'll shoot the motherfucker square between the eyes."

"I don't suppose one can reason with them."

"Reason?" Burlane laughed.

"Arabs, you think?"

"Iraqis. Serbs. Kurds. Wheys. Who knows? Some pissed-off chickenshit. In soccer, the offense can't match the defense. Here, it's the other way around. With all the weapons and explosives floating around, every scumbag malcontent and his cousin is a potential goal scorer. They blend into the crowd, so it's nearly impossible to guard them."

6:30 P.M.

The four six-passenger Bell Jet Ranger helicopters rose one at a time from the field of Stanford Stadium and flew over Palo Alto, heading north up the peninsula toward San Francisco.

The German footballers were buoyant. They had beaten Bolivia two to nothing, with Peter Tarchalski's replacement, Dieter Bauer, scoring both goals, and there had been no incidents. They were in the quarterfinal round. One match at a time. They would face their challengers one match at a time.

They followed the Montara mountains that formed the spine of the peninsula, then turned northeast across Interstate 280, with San Mateo and the San Mateo toll bridge on their right and the San Francisco International Airport to their left. They turned north again, with the San Francisco–Oakland Bay Bridge dead ahead.

The pilot pointed out the sights as they proceeded: Below them the San Francisco Bay area—the cooling sun low on the horizon— was spread before them like an extraordinary woman, sensuous in her beauty. They passed between Candlestick Park on their left and Oakland Coliseum on their right. They crossed over the San Francisco–Oakland Bay Bridge and Treasure Island below that. Then, it was Alcatraz below them, and to their left and ahead, due west, the Golden Gate Bridge framed the reddening summer sun.

Steiner, who was elated about the German victory but uncertain about the danger remaining to his players, had taken the seat next to Burlane for the ride back.

After enjoying the sunset beyond Golden Gate Bridge, the formation of four helicopters headed due east. Steiner, who until now had spoken only of the beauty below them, said, "What are you thinking, Major Khartoum? Did the killer give up? Is he going to let us play in peace?"

"That's the University of California, at Berkeley, below us now. I think he deliberately gave us a week off to set us up."

"Why do you say that?"

"He's an exceptional marksman, which means he's practiced a lot. He had the discipline to practice because he likes both the play and the game. He knows we were tense for this one and ready. It's difficult to maintain that degree of vigilance when nothing happens. He knows that."

"So what does he do now?"

Burlane said, "You're an experienced and skilled manager. Your side has the opposition's defense relaxed, thinking the danger is passed. You answer the question. You tell me."

"We hit them again, quickly."

"What if you Germans are still too closely marked, and the killer knows it?"

"He hits somebody else."

"If I were to bet money, that's what I'd say he's going to do. But it would still depend on his motive, which we don't know yet."

"You disagree with the FBI then. You don't think the Argentinian is responsible."

"I don't know. I find it hard to believe, but you have to remember that disputed soccer matches have literally caused wars in Latin

America. Knocking off a couple of kraut footballers as compensation for the ejections in Rome might seem just the ticket to a crazy enough Argie."

They passed high above a mountainous ridge just east of the Cal Berkeley campus. Then they turned to the southwest and in a few minutes settled safely onto a high school grid-football field in Orinda, California, where their hotel and a meal awaited them. All the sausage and Wiener schnitzel and beer they could handle. Afterwards, they would be treated to Fourth of July fireworks in celebration of American independence.

The German players had looked forward to an evening of walking around watching the famous screwballs of San Francisco; now this, a place called Orinda, on the backside of a mountain far from all the storied action. But they didn't complain. North Beach and the drag queens of Polk Street could wait; they had a World Cup championship to defend for their fallen comrades.

After James Burlane got the Germans safely into their new quarters, it was back across the bay to San Francisco for the five-hour flight to New York, so he could be on hand Sunday to help with the security for the Round of 16 knockout game between the United States and the Netherlands. Being the last remaining superpower made the United States an obvious target for an ambitious screwball.

TEWES, NEW YORK, 9:30 P.M.

From the darkness, Edson watched. He had night glasses and a parabolic.

He watched them on the patio, joking and laughing as they collected blankets, folding chairs, and thermoses of hot coffee.

Edson listened to their chatter.

The host was an executive with the New York Mets baseball team, possibly one of the owners. Edson found the stick-thin wife annoying as she glided serenely about attending to the needs of her guests. She told Sven Torberg that this was to be one of the most spectacular private fireworks displays in the country, owing to the patriotism and largesse of one of the lakeshore residents, who was big on Wall Street.

She said of course they would be able see the rockets at the far end of the lake from their patio, but they were going to walk down a ways to join some of their friends. The serene woman was sure Torberg would enjoy meeting the Andersons, of Swedish ancestry, who, in honor of Torberg, would almost certainly bring pickled herring for a snack.

An advance party of Princeton University sophomores, including the son of the serene glider's friends, had gone early to save a spot. Their own daughter and friend, both freshmen at Mt. Holyoke, would join them later.

Torberg, accepting another splash of Absolut from his host, said he was looking forward to the fun.

Then a single yellow rocket popped at the far end of the lake. The Mets executive said that was a signal—a half hour to go. A green rocket would pop when there were fifteen minutes left. The serene woman locked up the house, and, jabbering happily, they all set off on the trail around the lake to join the show.

We hold these truths to be self evident, that all men are created equal . . .

Edson grinned. He picked up his bag of tools and headed for the house. Edson the cobbler. Edson with shoes to fix.

At the far end of the lake, the green rocket burst.

16

NEW YORK, 9:00 A.M., TUESDAY, JULY 5

In Manhattan, there was little demand for nonlunatic clothes at noncrazy prices, and so Reiner Schmidt found that buying a pair of khaki chinos, a light cotton shirt, and a summerweight sports jacket was no small chore. And shoes. A simple pair of shoes, good for walking.

Schmidt learned that if he wanted, in Greenwich Village he could buy form-fitting trousers with an exterior metal jock strap in the shape of a clutching hand. Or he could go to Brooks Brothers, in midtown near Rockefeller Center, and buy himself a power suit for nine hundred dollars or a pair of Cole-Haan shoes for four hundred bucks. There seemed to be running shoes, cameras, and watches for sale on every block on the island. He wondered what the scam was. Were these all fakes?

He knew FBI agents were out there and all around him watching him buy the clothes, but let them. He had once read that the FBI had literally blanketed Manhattan with agents to covertly follow the Soviet master spy Rudolph Abel. Let them jabber back and forth with their little radios. Let them make notes. Scribble, scribble, scribble. Let them speculate. The American taxpayers were springing for it, not him.

Either the FBI had believed the old man's reading of the polygraph and there were only few of them following him around, or they knew that he had told a teensie lie, and they would be everywhere, like lice. Ditching them for even a few minutes would be a formidable task.

Finally, he found a place on Lexington Avenue and bought the clothes. He took the subway back to his room in the Sheraton Park Avenue, which FIFA had rented for him. There, he changed into his new clothes. Thus assured that there was not some miniature tailing device clinging like an invisible burr, he filled both pockets with small balls of paper and left the hotel. He started down Park Avenue with a brisk stride.

At the first corner, he dumped a wad in a metal receptacle and kept walking.

He repeated this at the end of the second block, and then went for a series of lefts and rights, depositing more wads of paper in trash receptacles.

This was a simple enough tactic. The Americans didn't know whether they were facing a lone killer or a conspiracy of unknown number. Since any single wad was a possible drop-off, better for the FBI agents to stay clear and see if anybody picked it up. Thus each receptacle became a magnet, demanding the attention of one or more agents. The more bodies riveted to trash containers, the fewer to follow him around. The fewer the better.

Having worn out the drop-off gambit, Schmidt entered Union Square's subway station, whose physical ambience and sampling of New York reminded him of the filthy, violent future world of Mad Max. Somehow, in European undergrounds, civility still obtained.

As Schmidt went down the stairs, he was treated with a freshly painted exhortation, *Eat my dick, Mayor Giuliani, you dork*. This was followed by older witticisms and adolescent exhortations, a compendium of street wisdom: *cunts, cunts, cunts; Kut Koch's Krotch; thrill kill; fuck the bitches; drink piss; acid in their assholes; scumbags; Ralph does it; Bobbye + Lou; hot lead & big dicks; luv needles; we've all got AIDS; eat McShit and die; scream baby*.

Such sentiments, together with jagged and violent splotches, circles, triangles, swastikas, and crucifixes, were spray-painted on the tiles in just about every color imaginable: Day-Glo green, orange, and yellow; black; purple; blood red. One frustrated Picasso had painted an erect African penis. Another had spray-painted huge eyeballs, complete with comic book lines indicating motion, tumbling down the tiled underground entrance like huge, veined basketballs. Schmidt imagined that Dante might have made much of New York's subway were he alive. Among the wayfarers, Schmidt surmised, were a sprinkling of distant grandsons and granddaughters of such textbook Americans as Thomas Jefferson and Davy Crockett. Into the garden they had stepped; now, in New York, at least, they were waist deep in garbage, human and otherwise.

While there were ordinary, sane-looking people entering and emerging from the Union Square Station, there were curious types everywhere, it seemed, their costumes and the looks on their faces saying, variously: *I like to show off and might kill to get on television; I'm on speed and might kill for the fun of it; I lost my job and might kill to demonstrate my frustration; I have disturbing visions and might kill to appease the phantoms; I'm pissed off at my wife and might kill to show her how I feel; I'm a Christian fanatic and might begin killing people in order to save them from the devil; I'm a Muslim fanatic and might blow the train up in the name of the only true god; I'm the victim of an unfathomable obsession, better to keep your distance from me*.

Schmidt remembered the lyrics from the American national anthem he had heard sung the day before:

O'er, the land of the free.
And the home of the brave.

Schmidt avoided all eye contact. He had been told that to make eye contact with the wrong New Yorker was like throwing meat to a mad dog. In New York, subway cars were Satan's toys, electric coffins with wheels that lurched, clanging and banging, *ka-wump-a-wump-a-wump* through the darkness of the subterranean night.

He bought a subway token for a buck and a quarter and slipped the coin into the slot at one of the revolving turnstiles. Keeping his eye on the green signs directing him to the Lexington Avenue line north, he walked quickly across a wire-enclosed overpass above a subway lane. Below him, a train rumbled out of the tunnel. With much clattering and banging and *eeeeeeeeEEEEEEEE!* of squealing brakes, it came to a stop below him. The squealing of metal on metal made him shudder. Such were the burdens of the Big Apple that there was no money to reline the subway brakes. So on they squealed, grinding nerves along with metal, and getting worse year after year.

Let the citizens grind their teeth.

As Schmidt went down the stairs to the waiting platform, he watched the passengers leaving the train that had just stopped. One of them, a middle-aged, fat man wearing eyeglasses, wore his hair in a Mohawk. He was dressed like an Indian, wearing moccasins and leather breeches, in the manner, Schmidt supposed, of the movie *The Last of the Mohicans.* Schmidt was relieved that he did not have a bow and quiver of arrows.

Schmidt waited. A Lexington Avenue #4 squealed *eeeeeeee-EEEEEEEE!* to a stop. It was worse than chalk on a blackboard. He got quickly aboard and walked to the next door. As the door started to shut, he leapt off, just as *eeeeeeeeEEEEEEEE!* on the next platform over a train going south, downtown toward Wall Street, squealed to an obnoxious stop. He ran across the overpass to the south-bound train and darted onto it. He didn't want to go to Wall Street, so he'd get off at the next stop and see if he could flag a quick taxi. Or maybe he'd cross back over and take the Lexington Avenue north. The possibilities were nearly limitless.

Schmidt was lucky enough to find a seat, and as the train lurched, rumbling through the blackness, he read the advertising placards above the windows, which were given over to education in one form or another. Remedial English was touted; so was the ability to run a computer. One placard admonished passengers not to share needles. Another, urging the use of rubbers, featured young men embracing.

Some kind of education was called for in New York, although Schmidt wasn't sure what it was, exactly. He had heard Americans in Europe claim that New York was not really part of the United States. Through accident of history, they said, New York had become the American center of finance and mass media; these much coveted bones of commerce were the city's most important source of protein, so the rest of the country was stuck with Big Apple bullshit.

Schmidt had spent three days in Atlanta after refereeing the Nigeria versus Bulgaria match in Orlando. Atlanta was getting more than its share of attention owing to its being the headquarters of Ted Turner's CNN. Schmidt had found it a beautiful city, a place that seemed to work. And its citizens laid off the spray paint; a person might actually want to live there. New York had the attraction of a zoo. Some people loved zoos; others, like himself, were content with an occasional visit.

Birds of prey were commonplace in New York, including numerous varieties of hawks, but true eagles were rare. The storied, reclusive eagles nested in the tops of cliffs high above the streets. When one did see an eagle, dressed in a power suit and flanked by an adoring entourage, he was floating in the wind of opportunity, eyes alert, watching for moving meat. Schmidt was told that the owls, the smart ones, were almost never seen.

Were the FBI agents still with him, he wondered?

Were they still watching? Jabbering on their transceivers? Speculating?

He'd soon find out.

10:00 A.M.

Federal Express arrived with the two boxes of soccer balls. After looking inside the boxes the American equipment manager, Bob Knowles, accepted delivery and signed the receipt.

The twenty-four all-leather Adidas Galaxy balls, made specially for World Cup 1994 in Lendershien, France, were magnificent. The note inside was written on the stationery of Finance Committee chairman Hans Schwartz, who Knowles knew was a Swiss.

Dear Mr. Knowles,
These balls, which are ready for play, are delivered as per FIFA agreement with Adidas. If you have any questions, please call before 11 o'clock, when I'm off to watch the match myself.
Cordially,
Hans Schwartz, chairman, Finance Committee

Knowles bounced one of the balls. It seemed to have the proper spring. He fished a gauge out of his gear and stabbed it into the small rubber hole that served as the ball's valve. The air pressure was 9.75 pounds per square inch, which at sea level was just about right on the money. The rules said it should be inflated from .6 to .7 atmosphere, which meant from 9 to 10.5 pounds per square inch or from 600 to 700 grams per square centimeter. He weighed it. Fifteen ounces. The rules said from 14 to 16 ounces. The ball was 27.5 inches in circumference, exactly halfway between FIFA's 27- to 28-inch standard. It was a quick ball. A beauty.

He dialed the Finance Committee number.

A woman answered. "FIFA Finance Committee. May I help you?"

"I'd like to speak to Herr Schwartz, please."

"Who do I say is calling?"

"Bob Knowles, the equipment manager of the American side."

"One moment."

"*Ja,* Mr. Knowles? This is Hans Schwartz."

"Fed Ex just came with twenty-four Adidas Galaxy balls. But we just received an equal batch last week, Herr Schwartz. What happens to the old ones? If this keeps up we'll be inundated with fine balls."

Schwartz laughed. "Our contract with Adidas says they will provide correctly pumped, new game balls and warm-up balls for selected matches televised in their European and Latin American markets, and all matches from the quarterfinals on. Their balls are supposed to be the best in the world, and they want them to look white and new on television and when they appear in magazine and newspaper photographs. So Adidas pays us a fee and provides the balls. I don't think anybody cares what you do with the old ones. Give them away to Boy Scouts or get the players to autograph them if they will, make yourself a few bucks on the side." He hesitated. "Don't tell anybody I said that."

"Ahh," Knowles said. Those balls were worth about a hundred fifty dollars each, or thirty-six hundred dollars in all. And with players' signatures? He said, "I was wondering was all. Didn't want to get myself in a pickle with FIFA. A goal with a sandlot ball would look pretty good to us today."

"They're good balls, I take it. Did you check them out?"

"Oh yes, they're first-rate."

"I suppose the least you can expect is to kick a decent ball in a World Cup quarterfinal. Good luck today."

"Thank you," Knowles said. "The odds are we'll need it."

"The Cinderella Americans, who would have thought?"

"We've got some hustlers and a couple of kids who can kick a soccerball. We'll do our best. Thank you for your trouble, Herr Schwartz."

"No problem."

Jan Vanderkellen, equipment manager of the Dutch national side, also received a shipment of Adidas Galaxys for the second straight week. Vanderkellen was also chary of getting into a quarrel with FIFA bureaucrats. Like Knowles, he called Herr Schwartz of the Finance Committee to see what he should do with the old balls.

18

10:30 A.M.
A lie detector was, first of all, scientific, that is, sort of scientific, because it was based on measured physical response. People did exhibit physical changes when they lied. They had been taught not to lie, and when they lied, their pulse quickened, and they began to sweat a little.

Also, the response to all lies was not the same. A big, dramatic lie was more likely to result in a big, obvious physical reaction than a little lie mixed in with the truth. A computer could scan the blips and tell the operator where the anomalies had occurred. But how was a computer to properly crunch the numbers of the human context, that is, the nature and motivation of the liar?

As Miles Templeton had learned from long personal and professional experience, there were liars, people who found it convenient to fudge with the truth, and then again, there were *liiiaaars*, as in Charles Laughton lashing out at Marlene Dietrich with those baggy, furious, accusing eyes of his, full lips bunched with passion. Templeton had the 1957 movie *Witness for the Prosecution* on tape, and when he'd had a couple too many, he loved to pull it out for friends. He loved to waggle his face as the bewigged Laughton had done, and point an accusing finger; "And you, madame, are a *liiiaaarrrrrr!*"

There were psychopaths who lurched from reality to fantasy without knowing the difference; the world, for them, was a collage of images of what was, what might have been, or what could be. Psychopaths of this sort really didn't lie, they just dipped into the stuff of dreams and nightmares, emerging as Dwight Eisenhower one minute and Captain Kangaroo the next, forget logical transitions. And forget the polygraph.

There were creative, entertaining liars who everybody knew were full of it to their eyeballs. These liars felt compelled to embellish their past with unusual adventures and were ordinarily skilled at mixing pounds of horseshit with soupçons of truth— entertaining their friends with on-the-spot invention. Templeton had personally known several of these liars over the years, including a college acquaintance who had once played poker with Harry Truman and pitched to Mickey Mantle in a pickup game, in which the Mick, who had been drinking too much Blatz beer, slugged four straight home runs over a grove of elm trees. These liars were often skilled at throwing in the odd detail, like the Mick drinking Blatz beer, to make their stories more believable.

There were liars who were so locked onto themselves, so inherently and unstoppably, cancerously selfish, that they thought any claim or statement that was to their benefit was entirely justified and so not really a lie. Whatever issued forth from their hysterical lips was truth. They were right. They were good. Lies were wrong. Lies were bad. They didn't lie.

These liars, fueled by emotion, had never progressed beyond childhood; their psychic record was stuck in a single groove: me, me, me, me. Templeton's hysterical ex-wife had been one of these. On the eve of their divorce, she had told a judge that Templeton had beaten her and had threatened more physical violence. He was dangerous. On the basis of this abominable, outrageous lie— taking a shrew's word for it and demanding no other evidence— the judge had issued a restraining order. The poor, abused woman, beaten by this brute! She was forced to seek the help of the courts!

Templeton could not go down to the judge and say, hey, this hysterical bitch is a fucking liar of the worst order. He was stuck.

This lie was an embarrassing stain on his honor, and it had made him furious. He was not a man who hit women; he would never forgive or forget this lie. There was no punishment imagined by the Grand Inquisitor or Lucifer that was good enough for anyone who indulged in such posturing at somebody else's expense, neither skinning her alive, pulping her with a baseball bat, choking her with crazed bees, nor even forcing her to spend eternity apologizing to people. This type of liar could sometimes beat an unskilled polygraph operator but not Miles Templeton. Never. He saw right through the gilt of bitter sugar they wore like armor. It was one of the reasons that he had wound up running lie detectors for the FBI.

Then there were calculating liars who knew all about polygraphs and their limitations and so calculated their lies well in advance. They knew that certain kinds of powerful, emotional truths—an embarrassment, say—produced a result similar to a lie, so they mixed and matched truth and fiction to get the desired ambiguous reaction.

Sometimes an omission, that is, what wasn't said, was just as much a lie as what was; unless the interrogator asked all the questions and was patient, a good liar could sometimes squeak through.

These liars were tough cases, and Miles Templeton suspected that he had been duped more than once. Once again, Templeton went over the squiggles.

He had run the results through the computer several times. Each time the computer said there was an anomaly, that is, a potential lie, when Reiner Schmidt said he had watched a live sex act at the Apollo Theater.

Had Schmidt not gone to the Apollo Theater? Or was there something else, something that Schmidt was holding back that had made him react so to that question?

Suddenly, to his horror, Templeton was convinced that, yes, Reiner Schmidt had lied to that question. What a time to screw up. Shit!

He quickly called Ladd McAllen.

12:30 P.M.

Bora Milutinovic's mouth turned dry when he opened the envelope and saw the yellow card and the newspaper headline letters, all capitals, pasted neatly on it:

CANCEL THE MATCH OR I WILL EJECT BOTH SIDES. RED CARDS ALL AROUND.

Milutinovic immediately called Elizabeth Gunderson and Ladd McAllen.

Gunderson phoned Sir Roger Dusenberry. Dusenberry told her he would need a few minutes for his staff to inform members of the Emergency Committee, who had beepers.

While his secretaries set to work, Dusenberry punched up the president of the Executive Committee, Italo Fasi of Italy, who contacted Senior Vice President Diego Sanchez of Spain, plus the committee's seven vice presidents and twelve members.

Dusenberry told Fasi he would go directly to Essex House, 160 Central Park South, where the American side was billeted. Elizabeth Gunderson and Ladd McAllen would brief him further at the Essex. From there, Dusenberry would poll the Emergency Committee by telephone and call Anderson back to get a sense of the Executive Committee.

1:00 P.M.

Sir Roger Dusenberry, watching Elizabeth Gunderson, Ladd McAllen, and Coach Bora Milutinovic, compressed his lips as he set the receiver back in its cradle. He closed his eyes. He bit his lower lip. He opened his eyes, staring at the floor. "They say we play the match . . ."

"Well!" Gunderson said.

". . . if I'm convinced it's safe. The vice presidents of the Executive Committee all agree with Fasi, this is properly the decision of the Emergency Committee. The members of the Emergency Committee all say I'm the chairman, chosen partly because I'm supposed to know about stadium security, plus I'm on the scene. They defer to me. The decision is properly mine. They have a taste for power, you see, but none for responsibility. Titles, they like. Perks, they adore. Responsibility?" Dusenberry shook his head.

Gunderson said, "What did you say?"

"I told them I haven't made up my mind yet, and I haven't, really." Dusenberry grimaced. "Can it really be said that I'm qualified to make this decision on my own? Our chief problem in the FA is drunks, not terrorists, although we have to be aware of IRA nitwits. If the rest of my committee is going to lay all responsibility on me, the least I can do is make them sweat it out for a while, don't you think?"

"That's what I'd do."

"Ms. Gunderson, how would you like to cancel a semifinal match because of a yellow card and have it turn out the card and note were sent by some pimpled juvenile?"

"If you could guarantee lives would be saved, cancelling the game would be an easy decision, I suppose. But there's no way of knowing, is there?"

"A titled Englishman making such a decision on behalf of working men and women? For all its pretentions, football remains a working man's game, doesn't it? The great leveler. Chaps from all races and nearly all sizes can play it well. If I say 'play on' and we're dealing with a killer and he's successful, I'll be blamed for wasting lives out of sheer ego; if we find the card was sent as a practical joke, I'll be a laughing stock, an object of ridicule. They'd etch an asterisk on my tombstone."

Gunderson said, "I see what you mean. Some choice."

"Yes, isn't it? I get to take my pick. Mind you, if anything goes wrong, there won't be a member of either FIFA committee who will admit they lacked the spine to do anything except foist the decision off on me. They'll politely roast me."

"And your druthers?" McAllen asked.

"I think if he were alive, my cousin Sir Winnie—a distant cousin perhaps, but still there—would say the World Cup is symbolic of something far more valuable than the whim of ignoble swine, and one should never let pigs have their way without putting up a fight. Our adversary flashes a yellow card and takes our name, informing us that we're not to play the match. I say let him show us the red if he thinks he can, but we hold the match as scheduled." Dusenberry raised an eyebrow. "If you Americans have no objections. It remains your stadium, after all."

1:12 P.M.

They met in the home-team locker room, ordinarily used by the New York Giants of the National Football League. A grid football team, given as it is to both defensive and offensive players, as well as specialists in punts and kickoffs, requires metal lockers and bench space to accommodate nearly fifty players. An adjoining area had tables where trainers could massage, tape, and otherwise prepare players for the contest before them.

Next to the rubdown and taping room was an area with whirl-pool baths, which in turn adjoined a labyrinthine room with all manner of barbells and muscle-building equipment so the combatants could produce by hard work what was otherwise denied them by recent concern over the use of anabolic steroids—more strength for the spectacle of the contest.

Ladd McAllen and his colleagues had managed to stuff both sides into these rooms, plus the entire Giants Stadium security staff—nearly 200 people in all. The security people were herded into the main locker-room area, while the players listened from the adjoining training and weight rooms.

It was a solemn gathering with much nervous swallowing and licking of lips. Some were uniformed cops from the New Jersey State Police and Centurion Inc., the security force at the Meadowlands sports complex near Rutherford, New Jersey; others were FBI agents, who had received special antiterrorist training, and people in Elizabeth Gunderson's FIFA security force.

The facilities in Giants Stadium were among the most modern available anywhere, yet no matter how well or how often the place was cleaned, the smell of sweat persisted.

James Burlane watched the meeting from the corner of the locker room, wanting to remain as inconspicuous as possible. Whereas the previous day he had been with the German side at their bench, today he was to be with the Dutch.

McAllen said, "I want dogs at the entrances. They're supposed to be able to smell shit that blows up, aren't they? That's how they're supposed to earn their Friskies. Well, let's see if they're for real or if they're all hype. I want every swinging dick and his girlfriend to have to walk by a properly trained nose. I don't care if they're little kids or old ladies, they get sniffed. Jolly the dogs up so people won't get all freaked out. They're sniffers, not eaters. If you screw up, it's your job.

"The same with metal detectors. I want every human being in Giants Stadium to have to walk by a metal detector. Nobody is exempt. Not the media people. Not people selling beer and hot dogs. Not FIFA pooh-bahs or grand high muckamucks. Not your grandmother. Nobody. Not even Hillary Rodham Clinton.

"I want everything from jock straps to soccer balls to pass by a metal detector. There will be no thermos bottles in the stadium. Let 'em take us to the Supreme Court if they want to, but the answer is no. Today, if they want to watch the game, they do as we say. Every camera will be opened for inspection or it doesn't go inside, no fucking if's, and's, or but's. If they're dumb enough to have film inside, tough."

Gunderson said, "That includes ladies' handbags." The issue of women's handbags was no joking matter. Females somehow thought their handbags, even if they seemed hardly smaller than suitcases, were by sexual prerogative, if not divine right, off-limits to inspection. For reasons perhaps unconnected to this conceit, more women than men were shoplifters.

McAllen said, "Thank you, Elizabeth. Ladies' handbags get opened too. We don't know the sex of this screwball or who he might be working with. And if you let just one body past uninspected, just one, it's your ass. I don't give a flying fuck who you're working for or what your rank is, I'll see to it!" McAllen wound up nearly shouting. He stopped. He licked his lips. He sighed. He lowered his voice.

"You understand, I gotta shout like this and make threats. It's the drill. If I don't demonstrate proper resolve, it's my buns if anything goes wrong, and I got a wife and two teenage daughters who like to talk on the telephone. We've got choppers coming in to lift the players out of here after the game. There will be no human being remaining in Giants Stadium other than us when that occurs. Not one. For any reason. I want the place checked out with dogs to make sure. We'll keep the players in the locker rooms until we know it's safe. If necessary we'll feed them in the rooms and even bring in concubines if that will keep them pacified. But we will not risk lives. The taxpayers are paying for us to defend them, so we provide them with the best protection we can under the circumstances."

Gunderson said, "We're all on the same radio frequency. If you hear your name, pay attention, because something's likely happening in your sector."

McAllen said, "Do what you're told, and do it immediately. If you see anything at all that strikes you as odd or out of the way, speak up. If you see some motherfucker pull a weapon out, shoot him dead and ask questions later. Better we shoot one another than let him get his way."

Sir Roger Dusenberry turned to Burlane and said, "Just like a football manager getting his chaps pumped for the big match, eh, Major Khartoum?"

"Laying out the game plan," Burlane said. "He gave it to 'em Vince Lombardi style, which is how you're making your decision."

"Oh?"

"The Green Bay Packers are taking on the Dallas Cowboys in the playoffs in 1967. It's late December, minus-thirteen-degrees-Fahrenheit below zero, and there's a cold, lazy wind swirling snow across Lambeau Field. The Packers are down by three with fourth down and goal to go with sixteen seconds remaining. They're twelve inches from the end zone. They take their final time out. Do they kick a field goal and go for a win in overtime, or do they gamble and go for a touchdown? If they go for it and fail, they lose."

"A memorable moment in grid football, I take it."

"It certainly was. The field was terrible and the Packers faced an incredible wall of Texas beef. The Packer quarterback Bart Starr, hands under his armpits to keep them warm, conferred with Coach Lombardi. 'What do we do?' he asked Lombardi."

"What did Lombardi say?"

" 'Go for the touchdown, fuckface.' "

Dusenberry smiled. "An eloquent gentleman. What happened?"

"The Packer right guard, Jerry Kramer, pushed his way through a behemoth Cowboy defensive tackle named Jethro Pugh, and Bart Starr, right behind him, twisted into the end zone. It was a remarkable moment because it was a genuine gamble, however debatable."

2:45 P.M.

Pat Duffy felt loose and good. One step at a time, Coach Milutinovic had said. And one step at a time they had taken it. A cliché, yes. But it was also the truth. Duffy felt a surge of pride at representing his countrymen and he knew from the swelling hub-bub and roar in Giants Stadium that his countrymen were solidly behind them and then some.

The World Cup had a history of home sides making the finals. In 1990, the Italians were extremely disappointed that their side didn't make the finals. In this tournament that factor was discounted out of hand.

The Dutch no doubt expected the Americans to sit back and defend. Well, Coach Milutinovic said they wouldn't do that; they were solid enough in the rear so that they could play a little loose in the beginning to see if they couldn't get a quick goal. If they didn't score first, the obvious Dutch tactic would be to wear them down with their passing and ball-handling skills. That's what Milutinovic would do if he were them. Make the Dutch play defense too, he said.

That was perhaps easier said than done, but the Americans were game. When the tournament began, they would have been satisfied with proving they belonged on the same field with everybody else. Getting this far had been an impossible dream. But then, after their amazing upset over Brazil, their confidence had swelled.

Pat Duffy and Luis Garcia and several of their teammates formed a circle and passed the ball lazily back and forth, savoring the moment. After all their hard work and dreams, they were just three matches away from the Big Dream. Just three matches.

If they made the finals, well, hey . . .

Garcia looped Duffy a pass from across the circle. The ball, which had been lively enough in the beginning, seemed to have lost some of its zip.

He gave the flaccid football a whack with his foot, disgusted that the American hosts to the World Cup were unable to do such a simple thing as provide decent warm-up balls.

Then came the call. It was time for the game, time for Pat Duffy to grab some pine. He wasn't scheduled to start this match because of a sprained ankle that had cost him some speed, but if Coach Milutinovic needed a defender who could push forward or one who could fill in at midfield, then Duffy would get his call, bad ankle or not.

He looped a ball toward the bench and trotted to the side of the pitch to join his teammates for their final talk with Coach M.

As the ball boy stowed the balls under the bench behind them, Duffy thought he smelled black pepper. Perhaps not black pepper exactly, but a chemical smell that was close, an odor like black pepper with perhaps a soupçon of gasoline.

He heard Teddy Lee, a midfielder who played with a Scottish side in Aberdeen, say, "Jesus, who farted?"

They all laughed nervously. They all smelled it. Somebody had let a real bloozer.

Coach M made a face. He said, "Hey, hey, it's only a soccer match."

Luis Garcia said, "Somebody ate a skunk, ay!"

Behind Duffy, another ball boy said, "What's happening to these balls? Shit!"

The odor of black pepper or whatever was more pronounced. What was that smell?

Coach M said, "Remember: concentrate; move to space; pass the ball; shoot when you've got a shot. We will score the first goal. We will protect our lead. We will win the game. They may be good, but they're not superhuman. This is our turf. This is our day. We will not let out countrymen down. Let's go now."

The American players gathered in a circle and put their hands in the center, chanting: "Let's go. Let's go. Let's go."

Duffy took his seat on the bench as his teammates took their places on the field where the referee waited.

The smell was getting stronger.

What was going on?

Duffy felt mildly dizzy.

He pitched forward off the bench onto the grass. Suddenly, he could hardly breathe. He couldn't move his arms or legs. He couldn't move anything. He willed himself to move, but he could not.

He was conscious, but Giants Stadium and everything in it turned slowly.

He saw a teammate beside him on the grass too.

Hard to focus his eyes.

Black pepper.

It was the black pepper smell. Had to be.

Soft balls.

Black pepper.

Duffy struggled to breathe. He could hardly breathe.

Shouting. He heard shouting. It took all the energy he could muster to expand his lungs. He wanted to, but he couldn't.

He managed to move his head slightly and look up. Above them, Giants Stadium was being evacuated.

He managed to take another breath.

He had inhaled something that smelled like black pepper. Where had it come from?

Soft balls and black pepper.

Pat Duffy remembered his mother cooking breakfast. She put lots of black pepper on the eggs because she knew he liked it.

The smell of pepper was coming from the balls.

The balls under the bench.

The pepper was poison.

The balls were leaking poison.

2:46 P.M.

James Burlane understood without knowing why.

The balls.

He yelled, "Run from the footballs. Run from the balls. Run from the footballs. Footballs, footballs, footballs. No, no, no. Nay, nay, nay! Don't breathe! Don't breathe! Get away! Get away!"

20

10:00 P.M.

Whether James Burlane worked for FIFA or not, he found it hard to believe Elizabeth Gunderson or Ladd McAllen wanted him hanging around while they dealt with the media circus.

Burlane knew Gunderson would share with him the nitty gritty of what the FBI had found out, if anything. He expected it would be *nada;* the Red Card terrorist had swung from the Germans to the Americans and Dutch without a hint as to why.

So Burlane, beeper in his jacket pocket, went for a hike and a think. He went to The Bald Eagle's modern-style sports bar just half a block from the Royalton hotel on West Forty-fourth street, where FIFA had reserved a room for him. If he was needed, which he doubted, they could beep him.

The Bald Eagle's got its name from the New York Giants' great 1960s quarterback Yelberton Abraham "Y.A." Tittle. A photograph of Tittle, one hand holding his helmet, the other on the top of his hairless head, was on the wall, as were pictures of the all-purpose halfback Frank Gifford, the famed linebacker Sam Huff, the outsized tackle Roosevelt Greer, the big defensive end Andy Robustelli, the placekicker Pat Summerall, quarterback Phil Simms, fullback John Riggens, and the rest of the Giants of yesterday if not yore.

On his way in Burlane studied the photographs, thinking that his countrymen were a curious people to have invented such a game as grid football. He went inside and found an empty booth. The talk in the bar was of the disaster in Giants Stadium, and on the main screen was a replay of players collapsing onto the turf earlier in the day. The Germans had suffered the lunatic Arabs at Munich. Now, it was America's turn.

Three American and two Dutch athletes were dead, and seven others hospitalized. The dead Americans included Jeff Trumpey, an all-American defender from the University of Michigan, Denton Gierde, a midfielder from the University of Massachusetts, and Luis Garcia, who had scored the winning goal against Brazil. The dead Dutch players were Jan Vandenberg, a midfielder with Ajax, and Teo de Leuw, a defender with Feyenoord.

The warm-up balls, twenty-four stashed under each bench, had been inflated with a nerve gas and with a form of gaseous acid that ate through the rubber valve and leaked the nerve gas into the air. The balls had simultaneously deflated on both sides of the field. Some gases are heavier than air, some are lighter. The light gases rise to the ozone; the heavier gases hang and linger. The gas in the balls was heavy and hung in a deadly pall; there was not a hint of breeze in the enclosed Giants Stadium to clear it out.

FIFA president Dr. Antonio Coelho, of Brazil, and Sir Roger Dusenberry, chairman of the Emergency Committee, jointly announced that a decision on the tournament's future would be made on Monday, after FIFA officials had a chance to confer with American law enforcement agencies.

The television monitors in the corners said international sports trivia was due up in ten minutes. Burlane ordered a beer and a game remote.

In an emergency like this, reporters barked questions like irritable dogs—as though the truth, a succulent bone, was deliberately being withheld from their agitated and deserving snouts. They were the People's Interrogators, and they were being deliberately starved. Their growling and gnashing of teeth was righteous. They were hungry. Also, they ultimately got paid according to how many viewers and readers they delivered.

The celebrity journalists took turns singing lead: *What if?* barked one. *What might be?* snarled a second. *What could be?* bayed a third.

Followed by the refrain from all, a form of chant:

Who is to blame? Who is to blame? Who is to blame?

Those watching from the safety of their living rooms would presumably be amazed and thrilled at the unfolding of the profitable drama. Officialdom would toss the People's Snouts such succulent tidbits and morsels as they were able to uncover, but the pious barkers would not be placated.

Television journalists were like modern Greek gods: they looked human—they were inevitably handsome or beautiful physical specimens and had sincere faces and good voices—but they had canine brains. As Sisyphus was doomed never to get the rock to the top of the mountain, so they were sentenced to permanent hunger for the elusive truth.

The man issuing red cards had yet to make a demand or issue a threat. Mush-brained zealots, operating in a zone of stupidity, ordinarily went for the gratification of having their "demands" aired over the media. The man issuing red cards understood that if one wants results, as opposed to air time, one first establishes a position of power, then makes clear satisfaction that can actually be met, preferably in private and certainly without public discussion. Such demands as "eliminate Israel by tomorrow afternoon," or "turn Northern Ireland over to Catholics yesterday" just didn't cut it.

On The Bald Eagle's monitors, NTN began scrolling the names of top scorers to date, together with when and where they played their high-scoring game. EDSON led in both categories: he had the top single game and led the race for best three scores combined with a game in Delaney's, Chicago, on June 27 and Hurrying Hugh's, San Francisco, on July 4 and 5. ESYMY was second, with strong games in the Austin Hotel, Vancouver, B.C., on June 5, June 18, and June 21.

EDSON logged on.

Edson Arantes do Nascimento was Pelé. Was Pelé EDSON's inspiration?

Four minutes until game time.

Burlane noticed other players begin looking about. Unless the person logging on as EDSON was a joker, the NTN champ was in the house. Mr. Know Everything. Who was he? Unfortunately for the curious, The Bald Eagle's had as many nests as swallows had holes in a chalk bank, and EDSON could be playing in any one of five or six rooms.

But then perhaps it was a joke. Some drunk who thought he'd be cute had logged in as EDSON.

Three minutes.

In the spirit of the World Cup, Burlane entered as GBANKS; Gordon Banks was the English goalkeeper when England beat Germany 4–2 for the 1966 World Cup title, held in London's Wembley Stadium.

Then, NOGOAL entered the contest.

Burlane wondered if NOGOAL might not be EDSON, a form of challenge to whoever it was calling himself GBANKS. The 1966 Cup final had been marred when England's Geoff Hurst made a shot that hit the bar and bounced back onto the field, never once crossing the line. The referee attempted to placate the howl of English fans in Wembley by making a show of consulting a Russian linesman, who, off his nut, imperiously waved his flag, signaling that a goal had been scored. The game, which England won 4–2, was reputed to be the best World Cup final ever played, but Burlane had yet to meet a German who, when the subject was mentioned, didn't wonder aloud what might have happened if England hadn't been handed a freebie goal in the early going. If ever there was a dispiriting home-field call, it was Hurst's goal.

Had GBANKS been challenged? With seconds left before the list closed, Burlane, feeling goofy, entered RDCDFY.

WHAT COUNTRY WON THREE OLYMPIC FOUR-MAN BOBSLED COMPETITIONS BETWEEN 1976 AND 1988?

SWITZERLAND

AUSTRIA

SOVIET UNION

ITALY

EAST GERMANY

Burlane tapped East Germany. He waited. The game was up. The monitor said, FAST HANDS, NOGOAL, then scrolled players' scores; both NOGOAL and RDCDFY had scored a thousand points.

The next question was up. The monitor asked: EMIL ZATOPEK, A CZECHOSLOVAKIAN, WAS WHICH OF THE FOLLOWING?

A THREE-TIME WORLD CHAMPION IN SNOOKERS.

WON THE OLYMPIC FENCING CHAMPIONSHIP IN 1954.

WON THE OLYMPIC 10,000-METER RUN IN LONDON IN 1948.

CONSIDERED THE BEST RAPID-FIRE PISTOL MARKSMAN WHO EVER LIVED.

WAS A TWO-TIME WORLD CHAMPION ARCHER.

Burlane hit 10,000 meters in a flash and waited for the results. The monitor said, CONGRATULATIONS, RDCDFY.

Although he'd been first, Burlane noted that NOGOAL also scored a thousand points.

NADIA COMANECI SCORED THE FIRST PERFECT 10 IN OLYMPIC HISTORY ON THE:

BALANCE BEAM

COMPULSORY EXERCISES

INDIVIDUAL ALL-AROUND

HORSE VAULT

Burlane hesitated, then went for balance beam.

NADIA COMANECI, A RUMANIAN, SCORED A PERFECT TEN ON THE BALANCE BEAM IN THE 1976 OLYMPICS IN MONTREAL. FAST HANDS AGAIN, NOGOAL.

WHAT WAS THE NAME OF THE 12-METER YACHT IN WHICH TED TURNER WON THE AMERICA'S CUP IN 1977?

COURAGEOUS

ENTERPRISE

COLUMBIA

BAD NEWS

AMERICA

Burlane zapped Courageous.

TED TURNER'S COURAGEOUS, RACING FOR THE NEW YORK YACHT CLUB, BEAT AUSTRALIA IN THE QUADRENNIAL RACE, HELD THAT YEAR OFF NEWPORT, RHODE ISLAND. GBANKS REPEATS.

* * *

Edson wondered who was the smart-ass GBANKS/RDCDFY? Did RDCDFY stand for Red Card For You? It could be read that way. RDCDFY apparently knew a little about international sports. A visiting European, perhaps.

The next question appeared. BILLY JOHNSON, THE ONLY AMERICAN EVER TO WIN A GOLD MEDAL IN THE OLYMPIC MEN'S DOWNHILL, LEARNED TO SKI AT:

ASPEN, COLORADO

SQUAW VALLEY, IDAHO

MT. HOOD, OREGON

STOWE MOUNTAIN, VERMONT

SNOQUALMIE, WASHINGTON

Edson, wanting to beat RDCDFY, dove for Mt. Hood.

BILLY JOHNSON, OF GRESHAM, OREGON, LEARNED TO SKI AT NEARBY MT. HOOD. RDCDFY SAYS 'IN YOUR FACE.'

Edson was annoyed. How could anyone have answered that any quicker than he had? Edson and RDCDFY were tied for a perfect score, but RDCDFY was one up in first strikes.

Edson had watched Billy Johnson win the gold at Sarajevo. Johnson had been such a luck-out. If the old lady's slope there hadn't been tailor-made for a glider, he wouldn't have finished in the top twenty. He was able to maintain a tight tuck for the length of the run and that was about it. He had thighs that didn't cramp. Big deal! Who cared where he had learned to ski?

WHO WAS THE ATHLETE WHO SET A WORLD RECORD IN THE DECATHLON IN WINNING THE OLYMPIC GOLD?

BOB RICHARDS

RAFER JOHNSON

DALEY THOMPSON

BRUCE JENNER

C. K. YANG

Edson popped Daley Thompson, cursing himself for not spotting Thompson's name quicker.

BRITISH DECATHLETE DALEY THOMPSON SET A WORLD RECORD OF 8,495 POINTS IN THE 1980 OLYMPICS IN MOSCOW. CONGRATULATIONS, RDCDFY, YOU DID IT AGAIN.

Edson waved for another beer and shook his head to clear the cobwebs. He had to get serious. He came back very quickly on the next question. FROM WHICH COUNTRY WAS FORMER WORLD HEAVY-WEIGHT CHAMPION PRIMO CARNERA? Argentina. Primo Carnera was the Wild Bull of the Pampas.

In the end NOGOAL, with 28,500 points, edged out RDCDFY with 28,250, but it was dicey at the finish. Still, Edson was pleased that he had once again topped all players in North America. It was easy enough to beat North Americans at a silly quiz; all they cared about was grid football, basketball, and baseball. Okay, so the Canadians knew about hockey as well, what with all that ice around them in the winter. Then what was there? Well, the Canadians also had lacrosse, which, as Edson understood it, originally was played by native Americans, Edson could think of no more underrated team sport than lacrosse.

Edson wished Mueller were with him. Mueller would have had a good time watching NOGOAL's duel with RDCDFY for first place. While RDCDFY was an obvious internationalist, it was clear that the great majority of the customers in The Bald Eagle's didn't have the foggiest idea about sport in other parts of the world, and Edson suspected they couldn't care less.

Edson felt sympathetic to the feelings of Europeans and Latin Americans who didn't give a screw if the Americans ever warmed up to proper football. Perhaps there were some things that were far better off without Americans around. Americans, Americans, Americans. Edson had long since tired of hearing about them. It was getting difficult to breathe without securing the approval of Americans, who resolutely stood by the dubious principle that whatever was good for them was good for everybody else. The very word *American* was beginning to grate.

If the Americans ever decided to take proper football seriously, they'd be marketing foam rubber soccer balls for the cribs of the next generation of males. They wouldn't stop until they'd moved FIFA's headquarters from Zurich to Salt Lake City. The Americans were difficult to control once they put their mind to something. One had to be careful of the bauble one dangled before their eyes.

Edson caught the attention of the waitress. He didn't want to linger in the same bar as RDCDFY. He didn't trust him.

Know when to be careful, Mueller always said.

1:00 A.M., WEDNESDAY, JULY 6

Reiner Schmidt knew that the FBI's polygraph operator had been uncertain about his reaction to the question of where Schmidt had gone after the Germany–South Korea match. He'd said he'd watched live sex at the Apollo Theater. They didn't ask if it had been boy–girl or boy–boy, and he'd seen no reason to volunteer.

No wonder he had reacted as he did. So now, they probably thought he had lied because he was a terrorist, that he went around pumping up footballs with acid and nerve gas. When he'd ditched them in the morning and the players were gassed in the afternoon, they probably went unhinged and beat the poor polygraph operator with rubber hoses.

The way Schmidt saw it, if the FBI had bothered to check out the Apollo Theater, they'd have known it was for gays. And if they'd thought about it a little, they'd have understood his reaction to their question. It was no doubt politically incorrect of them to note that he had been watching cocks and not pussies, and so nobody had figured it out. America!

Well, Schmidt was tired of playing their game.

Let them watch him if they wanted. Let them follow him. In fact, let them tell FIFA if they wanted. Schmidt was tired of the hassle of keeping secret the fact that naked men gave him an erection. It was not as if Schmidt, in perverse defiance of the norm, had deliberately instructed his cock to misbehave. Researchers were now saying there were differences in the brains of homosexual and heterosexual men. Oh, really, doctor? Talk about the obvious.

Naked men gave him an erection. Heterosexual men liked to watch naked women. Why shouldn't homosexual men be allowed the same pleasure? The truth was that heterosexuals were hormonal elitists. Heterosexuals were born with their heads on straight. Gay men's heads were slightly crooked. Crooked, crooked, crooked. Look at the freaky faggot. Freakie, freakie, freakie. He, ha, ha. Ho, ho, ho.

Just what was he supposed to do about it? He hadn't deliberately chosen to afflict himself with a passion that made his life miserable and over which he had no control. A person is entitled to a little freedom. A little release. No harm done. Being a closet homosexual certainly didn't affect Schmidt's ability to referee World Cup soccer. He was one of the best in Europe, and everybody knew it. He had reason to be proud.

If the FBI hauled him in again, Schmidt would tell them the whole truth and get it over with. Ladd McAllen had said his personal life was one of the American government's business, and Schmidt thought McAllen was sincere. For whatever their faults, Schmidt believed the keepers of the dubious American zoo did their best to accommodate as much ambiguity and as many kinds of animals as possible. They had no choice.

2:30 A.M.

"Earl?"

The man named Earl, his eye on the door of the Gotham hotel, punched the button on his radio. "Here and wide awake. My people are all in place."

"Any action since our friend came home?"

"He's still watching *Picnic* on television. He might have fallen asleep, but I doubt it what with What's-her-name and those tits of hers." Earl sucked air between his two front teeth.

"Kim Novak. Kim Novak and William Holden."

"That's right," Earl said. "Kim Novak. God, wasn't she hot! In addition to her tits, she had those eyes. Remember, in the beginning William Holden rides into town on a freight train, broke but handsome and charming. A man with a past. Temptation for Kim Novak, who's engaged to the owner of the town grain elevators or something like that."

"Other than him watching *Picnic*, is there any action?"

Earl said, "About ten minutes ago a Sikh arrived in a cab from a night on the town. He's on the guest list, Mr. R. Singh."

"Don't Sikhs carry knives in those turbans of theirs? Isn't that part of their religion?"

"Awwwww." Earl shifted on the car seat.

"I thought I read that somewhere."

"In a comic book maybe. You're going to have to lay off reading so much *Spider Man*. He's a Sikh, asshole, a religious man."

"I'll let you go back to playing with yourself."

"Where'd you get shit like that? Jesus!" Earl was disgusted.
"Let us know soonest if anything happens."

4:40 A.M.
Sir Roger Dusenberry awoke without knowing why.

There was somebody in his room. He turned on the lamp at his bedside. "You!" He rubbed his eyes. He glanced at the door.

The blond said, "It was easy. I bet you didn't breathe a word about me, did you? Not a word. They had no reason to protect you, so . . . open goal. Just waiting. Foolish." He shook his head.

Dusenberry licked his lips.

The blond man smiled. "I see you're wondering about this." He tapped his pistol in the palm of his hand.

"Yes, I was, as a matter of fact."

"This is a .22 automatic pistol. A German-made Walther P-38. This thing on the end here is a silencer. It's really not needed on a .22, but it looks evil, doesn't it? A .22 makes a loud snap. This is more like a loud spit." The blond man imitated the report of the silenced Walther, spit, spit, spit.

Dusenberry jerked back. "I . . . please."

The blond man grinned. "I bet this is all driving you FIFA assholes crazy, isn't it?"

"Listen . . . if only . . ."

"If only what? You didn't expect me? After all this? No wonder you British lost your empire. Really, Sir Roger. I'm embarrassed for you."

6:12 A.M.
The phone rang just as the last of the hot water disappeared through the stainless steel filter on the bottom of the Vietnamese coffeemaker James Burlane had bought in Ho Chi Minh City and now carried around with him everywhere, together with his Hong Kong rolled-steel wok, a properly blackened beauty.

Elizabeth Gunderson said, "Have a good night's sleep?"

"I had crab cakes and beer at a sports bar down the street. Played a game of sports trivia and then went home."

"You win?"

"I had some fun," Burlane said. "You got more?" he asked.

"You haven't been watching television or listening to the radio, I take it."

"At this hour of the morning? Please, Ms. Gunderson. Give me credit."

"He struck twice last night."

"What?"

"At a quarter after five, the FBI got the cheery news that somebody had slipped into Sir Roger Dusenberry's hotel room and shot him three times at close range with a .22-caliber pistol."

"Oof!"

"He's still alive. Two bullets entered his stomach, and the third hit a rib and lodged in his heart, but fortunately Sir Roger had asked for a five A.M. wake-up call and hot coffee to give him time to prepare for his seven-thirty FIFA breakfast. The hotel desk actually did something when Dusenberry didn't respond to the wake-up. In New York? Can you imagine? Talk about miracles!"

"The FBI must have put them on some kind of alert."

"Well, yes, but even so."

"Can he talk?"

"The doctors have him hooked up to an artificial heart until he can handle a regular transplant. Right now he's in a coma, and they don't know if he'll come round or not. Our second oopsie has to do with Herr Reiner Schmidt. He returned to his hotel a little after midnight last night. The FBI didn't have the foggiest idea where he'd been all day. He could have been soaking it up in Irish bars or dispatching lethal soccer balls. Ladd says a few minutes ago they went to pick him up for another round of questioning, and they found him with his throat cut."

"What?"

"Ear to ear."

"Do they have any idea who did it?"

"Ladd says they've got the entire hotel hostage and are putting everybody through the drill. But it's all show for the press. The truth is they're just hoping."

"They don't have any suspects at all, then."

"They think it may have been a Sikh, a guest named R. Singh, who returned to the hotel at two-thirty A.M. and left again a half hour later."

"By the way, were there prints on the death balls?"

"What do you think?"

"*Mmmmmm.* How about the gas itself? What do McAllen's people say about that?"

"Not much. The nerve gas could have come from several places. Iraq maybe. North Korea. Even China. Or it could have been old Soviet stock that found its way onto the black market. It's of a common type that killed several hundred sheep near Dugway Proving Ground in Utah twenty-five years ago. You remember that?"

"Yes, I do. From the sheeps' standpoint, it was an ill wind that blew at Dugway that day."

"All the Red Card man had to do was figure out how long it would take the acid to eat its way through the rubber valve and then *ssssssst,* whoosh, the gas was released into the air. If the gas had escaped on the field, the gambit might not have worked. But as it was, the gas rushed out of the balls with players sitting right above them. They caught a hint of odor when Coach Milutinovic was giving them their pregame instructions, but just as the reserves sat down, the rubber valves collapsed completely."

"A crude but effective bomb made out of a soccer ball. And what's the word from FIFA? Are they going to replay the game?"

"The Executive and Emergency committees are gathering for breakfast at seven-thirty. That's the meeting Sir Roger was anticipating."

"Who will replace him as chairman of the Emergency Committee?"

"The committee's vice chairman, Sven Torberg, of Sweden, will stand in as acting chairman. He's been following Ladd's progress along with Dusenberry, so he knows what the situation is. But Dr. Coelho and the Executive Committee will have the final word. They may say play on. They may cancel the entire tournament. They may dither. We won't know until they meet."

"They'll dither," Burlane said.

"That's my bet."

SANTA BARBARA, 9:00 A.M.

In California, Juan Carlos Rodriguez was exploring Anna Maria Varga's succulent nether parts with his hand when he received his call. He paused in his earnest ministrations. The phone kept ringing.

Annoyed, he gave Anna Maria's *mons veneris* a squeeze and picked up the receiver. *"Dígame! Dígame!"*

The man spoke Argentinian Spanish with a German accent. "Tony Artes has a computer in his office. Do you know how to run a computer?"

"This is nine o'clock in the morning!" Rodriguez was still sore at being disturbed.

"I have physical evidence that would get the FBI off your back once and for all. If you don't watch it, they'll try to nail your ass for the gassing at Giants Stadium yesterday in addition to murdering Tarchalski and Gochnauer. Are you interested?"

Rodriguez said, "I'd like to see what you have, yes."

"Do you know how to use a computer?"

"I use one to follow my investments, and so I can tell if my managers are being sticky-fingered."

"Your host is using Microsoft Word with a mouse. Have Ms. Varga get you a pen and paper, I'll tell you what to do."

Rodriguez looked at Anna Maria and made a writing motion with his hand. She popped off the bed to get him a pen.

When he had pen in hand, Rodriguez said, "Ready."

The man told him how to link Artes's computer to his own via the telephone modem. He then gave him instructions on how to open file MARTHA12.DOC, which had been filled with a note to one of Tony Artes's ladyfriends. Then, he told him how to open a utility program, PCSHELL, and use its DELETE function.

"The first thing you do is link our computers. If I'm not on-line within one minute after we hang up, the deal is off. The MOS.DOS in Artes's computer has been modified so the telephone modem will transmit the commands you give the word processing software, but not the contents of any of the working files. I'll watch you open MARTHA12. When you're finished reading, I'll watch you use PCSHELL to delete it. I'll also watch you delete its backup, MARTHA12.BAK. But I will not see the file itself, nor will the people who are eavesdropping on this conversation. If you try to copy MARTHA12 or fail to delete both it and its backup, I'll know immediately and the deal is off."

10:14 A.M.

The special agent in charge of the surveillance of Juan Carlos Rodriguez and Anna Maria Varga used a cellular telephone to relay the substance of this call from Santa Cruz island to FBI headquarters in Washington. The agent waited for instructions.

Two minutes later his recorder indicated it was receiving digital information from Tony Artes's computer. This too was relayed to Washington.

10:26 A.M.

MARTHA12.DOC was in written in Spanish:

Dear Sr. Rodriguez,

As you know, Tony Artes has two entire walls of tapes in the room where he keeps his music collection. On Side A of Artes's own collection of songs, Ojos de Argentina, *you'll find a couple of sentences from a recorded conversation.*

Play the edited version.

If you want the whole, unedited tape, which will put these quotes into context and exonerate you, go to Los Angeles and find a telephone booth. Don't use a credit card. Feed the machine with coins. Call your man Terry Herman at Kensington Ltd. Give him a Tango Delta for $250,000 in account number RobART-o/OJ4-34R, also at Kensington Ltd. No conditions on the Tango Delta. When the money is in RobArt-o/OJ4-34R, Condition Foxtrot Able, the unedited tape will be delivered to you in The Brown Bear Bar on Hollywood Boulevard within the hour.

Kensington Ltd. was Rodriguez's bank in the Cayman Islands. Tango Delta was the current code for the simple movement of fluid assets. Kensington had codes that covered a combination of conditions that might be attached to Tango Delta. An automatic delay was one. A requirement for callback and confirmation was another.

Foxtrot Able would enable the owner of account RobArt-o/OJ4-34R to move the money any time he saw fit, within or outside Kensington Ltd. There were fewer restrictions on moving money within Kensington than to another bank; bankers didn't mind switching numbers in their own accounts, but surrendered deposits to other banks with reluctance.

10:44 A.M.

Side A of *Ojos de Argentina* had two voices on it; both were fuzzed electronically to foil voiceprinting and so sounded like computers talking or robots in science fiction movies. That is, the timbre of their voices, the elusive quality that distinguished them from other sounds of the same pitch and volume, had been electronically altered. The listener understood that these were real people, but just who would remain a mystery.

Voice A: ". . . Tarchalski and one other?"

Voice B: "Yes, two, in order to avenge the ejections in Rome."
Silence.

Voice B: "You can do that? Shoot that well?"

Voice A: "I'm competitive."

22

SANTA BARBARA, 2:30 P.M.

Juan Carlos Rodriguez hired a private plane to fly him and Anna Maria Varga from the Santa Barbara airport to Los Angeles, where he used an airport pay phone to call Terry Herman.

Some Caribbean islands catered to the tourism industry, opening casinos and free ports. Others, like the Bahamas, had casual tax codes. The Cayman Islands, aware of their closeness to Latin America and the drug trade, advertised no-questions-asked banking laws. Switzerland accommodated the treasure of dictators and white collar bandits; the Cayman Islands got cocaine dealers and tax evaders. Kensington's officers, including Terry Herman, spoke fluent Spanish.

Rodriguez gave Herman his account number plus code Tango Delta—transfer of deposits—the order for cash to be moved from his account. He said he wished to move $250,000 into RobART-o/OJ4-34R at the same bank. The move and deposit codes were correct, and his voiceprint was valid.

"Condiciones, señor?"

Rodriguez said, *"Nada. Solo Tango Delta."*

The odds were that the transaction had to do with cocaine, weapons, or theft in one form or another, but Herman was a professional at not caring about such matters. *"Buena suerte,"* he said.

"Gracias, señor," Rodriguez said.

3:00 P.M.

The Brown Bear Bar was familiar territory to Juan Carlos Rodriguez and Anna Maria Varga. On an earlier adventure, they had discovered that The Brown Bear, an unpretentious cafe with sidewalk windows, was great for people watching.

In Argentina, the beautiful woman who played the long-suffering Annabella in *La Vida* could not sit down for a casual sandwich in an ordinary café without instantly becoming the center of adulatory craziness. But Hollywood was another matter. This was New Babylon, and beautiful women were everywhere; wannabe actresses trolled themselves as bait in hormonal waters, each hoping a line of thigh or curve of tit would catch the eye of a passing director or producer.

Juan Carlos Rodriguez was a celebrity in Buenos Aires, although he was nowhere close to Anna Maria's league. He was good-looking in a robust, square-jawed, Cesar Romero sort of way. He had a handsome Roman beak. He exuded Y chromosomes. On Hollywood Boulevard, he could have been a middle-aged gigolo, easy. Or a wannabe movie producer. Or a wealthy nightclub operator escaped from the soupy puke that choked Mexico City.

So Anna Maria got to sit and watch and enjoy in relative

anonymity. She was so good-looking that people couldn't help but watch her. That was a fact she had long ago accepted. Here, her extraordinary beauty meant she did something in the entertainment business, even if it was nothing more than spread her legs in porn films, but at least she was Anna Maria Varga, stunner, the watched one, not beautiful Annabella, the Weeper of *La Vida*.

Juan Carlos and Anna Maria watched a tall African-American man in a white fedora, white double-breasted suit, and red shoes walking with his hand on the small of his lady's back, she being black as well, or perhaps half-black, but with her frizzy hair colored Bozo-the-Clown red and sticking straight out, like she'd been electrocuted.

They saw an elderly woman with a substantial nose and solid blue shoes towing three black miniature poodles with jeweled collars and tailored jackets. Their names were written in zircons on their jackets. One jacket identified its neutered owner as Abe. The second canine was Looie, also a castrate. Abe and Looie had blue collars. The third, Dovie, was female with a plump look about her, suggesting she had been spayed. Dovie's collar was pink.

They saw two tall blondes with outstanding tits in the manner of Parton's pair. They were sisters or possibly twins.

Seeing them, Juan Carlos Rodriguez said, "*Que tetas! Dos y dos son quatro. Ay! Caramba!*"

For which he received an elbow from Anna Maria. "*Alta su boca!*"

"*Dios mío!*" He made kissing sounds, smothering the four tits with affection.

"*Ay!*" Anna Maria elbowed him again.

Rodriguez checked his watch. An hour and a half had passed since he moved the money. No tapes.

7:00 P.M.

Juan Carlos and Anna Maria, lingering over their coffee, watched the parade of drag queens, teenyboppers, and tourists pass by the window of The Brown Bear.

A squadron of large-bellied bikers with beards and Los Angeles Dodgers T-shirts gurgled down the boulevard with Harley-Davidsons rumbling between their thighs. A gaggle of Hare Krishna followers in saffron robes and high-topped Nike running shoes strolled down the sidewalk.

Eavesdropping on the Mexican-American couple in the booth next to them, they learned that Sir Roger Dusenberry remained in a coma following emergency surgery to install a temporary mechanical heart. FIFA had postponed until Tuesday its decision on the future of the World Cup.

A few minutes later, another Mexican-American couple walked in. The woman's eyes widened instantly at the sight of Anna Maria Varga.

Anna Maria glanced at Juan Carlos. Was this it, then? Was the woman bringing them their tape?

The woman hesitated, then came forward. "Annabella?" she said.

A fan. "*Sí,*" Anna Maria said, suppressing her disappointment. "*Cómo se llama?*"

"Luisa."

Anna Maria scrawled *Vaya con Dios, Luisa, Annabella,* on a napkin and put her finger to her lips, a signal she wanted her privacy.

The woman understood. "*Por supuesto, y muchas gracias.*"

Rodriguez checked his watch again. Two hours had now passed. "*Mierda.*"

Anna Maria's face turned tight. "*Cabrón!*" She was referring to the gringo who had just swindled Rodriguez out of a quarter of a million U.S. dollars. Ay!

"What do we do now?"

"We give him one more day, in case something went wrong that he couldn't help. Then we protect ourselves. We take what we have to the FBI."

23

The walls of Pancho Villa's in Greenwich Village were festooned with outsized sombreros wide enough to provide shade for an entire Mexican village, and from the ceiling hung colorful papier-mâché fighting bulls, big-eared donkeys, strutting roosters, and screw-tailed pigs.

The male waiters, Puerto Ricans with handlebar mustaches, wore *bandito* outfits, complete with sombreros, pistols, and bandoliers of ammunition. The *señoritas*, also Puerto Rican, wore full skirts and peasant blouses inadequate for their outsized boobs.

Harry Beauchamp surveyed the room, looking vaguely amused. "I do hope those pistols are props and not intended for crowd control."

David Byrne, the latest editor of the *New York Post*, a nine-month veteran of Beauchampism, cleared his throat.

"And thank God," Beauchamp went on, "they're not carrying those big Mexican knives. You know those things, cane knives or whatever they are. In Manhattan, can you imagine? I would have taken you to Cucumber's, but the concept is probably too basic for you. Do you have any idea why I take you to places like this?" Beauchamp cocked his head, waiting for an answer.

Byrne eyed the pool of refried beans on his plate without enthusiasm. "Good food, I thought."

"I want you to observe the jackass imagination of your readers firsthand, and to eat something that will make you fart."

"I beg your pardon?"

"Like real people with juices and urges. Your readers fart, don't they? If they didn't, they'd explode. I like giving you the experience. Do you good."

Byrne laughed, chewing.

"I grew up eating beans, did you know that?"

"I . . . uh, no I didn't."

"You'd have preferred going to some pretentious hole and socking it to me for a few hundred dollars. I know that. Beans give you protein and fiber. That's why they go right through you. Farts are fun if you let them. You know, I got hooked on Mexican food when I bought a magazine in Mexico City a few years ago. The *molé* sauce. *Mmmmmm*. And the *chiles rellenos*. Tell me, Mr. Byrne, can you remember the last time you pissed out of a window?"

"Well, I . . ."

"I want a feature this Sunday on the adventures of emergency pissing. Not just out of windows, but any amusing place. A closet. Someone's shoes. I know a beer-drinking chap who pulls over to the side of the road as though he has motor problems. He yanks up the bonnet and bends over the radiator looking concerned, which he is, and, while he 'fixes' the motor, sod the traffic, he unloads used ale in front of the bumper. Nobody's the wiser."

Byrne grinned. "Good thinking."

"See! I want some amusing anecdotes from men with painful, full bladders who said sod Ms. Manners and found a way to relieve themselves. I want one telling how Ronald Reagan once soaked his thigh trying to aim Little Dutch into a Coke bottle. I want John Kennedy, shielded to his shoulders by a brick wall, smiling at Boston schoolchildren while he soaks a patch of violets with his bigosh. And give me Colin Powell furtively unfolding the chairman's yardage for a quick leak. We all have to deal with the sodding things. We need them to reproduce ourselves and drain unwanted fluids. Do we have to be so serious about them? There's a story people will read."

Byrne hesitated. "Yes, I suppose they will."

"Reader identification. You just tell me how many people have spent a lifetime without having to piss like a Prussian stud with no loo within ten kilometers. A writer who can't do something on full bladders, I don't want on my newspaper."

Byrne pulled out a notepad from a jacket pocket and scrawled a quick note.

Beauchamp bunched his face in frustration. "Throw a couple of women in there as well, one actress and one politician. Have one of them allegedly poke her bum out of a window at a party. You choose the women. No, better, I want the pretty actress Roberta Roberts and Hillary Rodham Clinton. Don't tell me Ms. Clinton doesn't pee? But not, I repeat not, Madonna. She is so tot-ally borrr-ing. Readers are long past caring what she does. She could piss on an electric fence and people would yawn."

Byrne blinked.

"I can find all kinds of people who wanna be the editor, Mr. Byrne. You're putting your readers to sleep, man." He shook his head. "God, how long does it take for you people to learn how to publish a newspaper? It's no bloody wonder you lose money every year."

"I'm sure we can get the hang of things on this side of the Atlantic."

Beauchamp narrowed his eyes. "It's been two hundred years since you told us to bugger off, and I don't see a lot of progress judging from the *Post* the last couple of weeks."

Byrne cleared his throat.

Beauchamp said, "I want a feature on constipation. Everybody's had it hung up there one time or another, and the American boomers are getting older; their bowels have to be changing. I want some wicked stories of hard stool gotten out of hand, maybe a man who fired brown bullets after an entire month of tight sphincter. Tell your writer to use his imagination. I want unusual remedies from exotic places, Borneo, Tibet, or wherever. Boise. I want a primer on masturbation with the headline: 'The Very Last Word On Loping Your Goat.' Take notes, if you value your job, Mr. Byrne."

Byrne readied his notebook. He jotted a quick line.

Beauchamp said, "I want that masturbation piece to have a decked headline. The subhead should read: 'Teen Males Ever Inventive, Come Up With New Ideas Every Year.'" Beauchamp looked amused. "Throw in some fun euphemisms. 'Beat the meat.' 'Trot the turkey.' 'Polish the knob.' Don't looked so alarmed, Mr. Byrne. Everybody knows teenage boys pound their puds every chance they get. They can't help themselves. Portnoy did. You did. I did. Loosen up a little."

The waiter was suddenly at their side, saying, "I have a telephone call for Mr. Harry Beauchamp."

Beauchamp looked surprised. "A telephone call?"

"Yes, sir, the gentleman said it was most urgent. He's on hold. If you'd like I can bring you a cellular phone."

"Yes, please, if you could."

The waiter nodded and went for the phone.

"Throw some women in there too. Women read papers, don't they? You see what I'm driving at?"

"Identification," Byrne said.

"I want a number written called 'At Last: All Your Sexual Problems Solved.' " Beauchamp looked triumphant.

Byrne, looking thoughtful, took a sip of beer.

"Tell them the two-word solution is Eliminate Boredom. They eliminate boredom by imagining they're screwing somebody else. It's that simple. Complain, complain, complain. The silly ninnies don't have any imagination. No wonder they read trash! They pay us to think for them."

The waiter was back with the cellular phone.

"This is Harry Beauchamp."

"There is a package waiting for you in your hotel lobby, Mr. Beauchamp. It contains a videotape and an audiotape. Play the videotape, then the audiotape. If you want the full unedited audiotape for your protection, take a taxi uptown, and from a telephone booth call your financial manager in Zurich. Have Herr Mann deposit one million American dollars in the Banque de Crédit Suisse Internationale. Would you like a moment to get a pen and pad? I'll give you the number you'll need."

Beauchamp, making writing motions to Byrne, said, "Yes, I would." Then, pen in hand, he said, "Okay."

The man gave him the code. "Remember. No money, no exoneration. Move the money, and I'll have the complete tape delivered to you at your hotel tonight." He hung up.

Beauchamp, alarmed that the imprint of his handwriting might show through the paper, ripped several pages from Byrne's notebook before he handed it back. "I hate to cut off our good chat, Mr. Byrne, but I'm afraid I have some pressing business to attend to. Shall we pick up our conversation tomorrow? Same time?"

"Certainly."

"No place to piss. Can't shit. Mind filled with sex. Frustration in all three cases, and they cover the economic and racial spread. Nobody's spared. Who gives a sod what Serbs and Croats do to one another? There's nothing in those mountains anybody wants. Let them have their grisly fun if they want. And no stories about starving Africans. What a bore! I want you to have a list of story ideas ready for me tomorrow. I want to see what you can come up with."

Byrne made another note. "Got it, Mr. Beauchamp."

NOON

Harry Beauchamp returned to his hotel to find that, indeed, a package was waiting for him in the lobby. He returned to his room and started the videotape. No sooner had the tape begun rolling and the images appeared on the screen than he quickly shut it off, yelling, "Sodding kraut!"

Shaken, Beauchamp poured himself a stiff bourbon and knocked it back. He quickly poured himself another.

His hands trembled as he slid the audiocassette into the machine. His face was tight. He licked his lips. He turned it on.

Silence.

Then two male voices whose voices had been altered . . .

Voice A: ". . . Tarchalski and one other?"

Voice B: "Yes, two, in order to avenge the ejections in Rome. Everybody down there knows about Rodriguez's *macho* posturing and his famous pledge to Anna Maria. We blame it on Rodriguez."

Silence.

Voice B: "How about the business of planting incriminating evidence on Rodriguez? That would be more difficult, would it not?"

Voice A: "I'm a professional. If that's part of my job, I'll see to it that it's done and done correctly. I know what I'm doing and how to do it."

9:00 P.M.

Harry Beauchamp drank whiskey and watched television. He didn't want pizza sent up. He didn't want a massage. He didn't want jugglers or acrobats or hashish or dancing girls or a thousand-dollar-a-night call girl peeling down for the old in-out.

He wanted to be left alone, with the door solidly locked and chained, to watch the telly and wait for the tape, sifting through the facts as he knew them, trying to deduce the identity of his adversary.

The telly in the United States was a form of keyhole through which the foreigner could peer in at Americans literally and figuratively groping one another. Most Americans believed passionately in the perfectability of man, which had led to all manner of quasi-official half-truths and agreed-upon lies, and absurd and doomed assaults on this or that outrage of the day. But the news of the disaster at Giants Stadium overwhelmed everything on this summer night, being not only outrageous but also having occurred just across the Hudson River. This was the home of the Giants grid football team, associated in the public mind with New York, qualifying it as being sort of in the navel of the universe, which was centered on Manhattan island. Ordinarily, New Yorkers regarded New Jersey as having all the class and romance of used motor oil.

Beauchamp had a remote to flip from channel to channel, sampling the fare. On one, serious-looking chaps studied a chess match diagrammed on the wall. Smart Semitic types, he imagined. White threatened a pin on black's knight. All that furious mental activity! He punched up the Teenage Mutant Ninja Turtles battling Japanese samurai. He found a channel where one could watch surgeons remove a tumor from a man's anus. On another channel, the Mets were getting ready to play the Padres in San Diego.

He paused on a news bulletin long enough to learn that Sir Roger Dusenberry had survived a second day on a mechanical heart but was still in a coma; FIFA had postponed until Wednesday their decision on the future of the 1994 World Cup.

He flipped to the next channel. An elderly man showed his viewers the proper way to thin and weed gardens. On the next, a cameraman followed running, shouting cops through Detroit slums. Such a place!

He settled on the beginning of Sean Connery in *Goldfinger*, an early James Bond. Shirley Bassey's baaaaaaad, brassy vibrato echoed through his mind:

Gold-finger,
He's a man . . .

Beauchamp checked his watch: ten o'clock. How long would he be made to wait, he wondered?

24

NEW YORK, 8:30 A.M., FRIDAY, JULY 8

"Hello?"

"Ms. Elizabeth Gunderson, please."

"Speaking."

"Ms. Gunderson, this is Harry Beauchamp. Yesterday afternoon, I purchased two tapes for one million dollars American. I think you should know about them."

"One million dollars?"

"For a videotape and a few sentences of altered male voices on a cassette tape. I perhaps acted precipitously, but I got them. I was foolish enough, perhaps desperate enough, to pay for the full tape in advance, then didn't get it. I got buggered, is what happened. A solid poke."

"No chance of getting your money back, I take it?"

"None. It's the Red Card terrorist, Ms. Gunderson. Has to be."

"You think so?"

"Who else? The problem is, put together, the two tapes make me look sodding guilty of conspiring to murder Peter Tarchalski and Willi Gochnauer. If I adopt the killer's MO and send them to you by commercial delivery service, will you agree to put me in touch with Major Khartoum? I would like to talk to him before your Mr. McAllen and his friends have another go at me. Major Khartoum is after the truth, is he not? Same as you? The truth is what matters."

"Absolutely. If we know the truth, we can proceed with the soccer tournament. Please do send me the tapes, Mr. Beauchamp. I will have Major Khartoum call you as soon as possible. Are you at your hotel now?"

"Yes, I am."

"Have you called Ladd McAllen?"

"Next on my list. I thought I should first tell you people at FIFA."

"Do call him. Under the circumstances, he may find it prudent to place you under protective custody, perhaps even move you to a safe house somewhere."

Beauchamp laughed. "I'd ordinarily tell him to take a sodding leap in the Hudson River, I'll do as I bloody well please. But in this case, Ms. Gunderson, with this idiot on the loose, I'll let your Mr. McAllen do as he sees fit."

"Tell me, why do you suppose the terrorist tried to murder Sir Roger?"

"That's a real puzzler, I have to admit, Ms. Gunderson. Why, I ask myself? I haven't found an answer. Dusenberry really is an okay chap, I suppose, beneath all that royalty manure."

9:00 A.M.

"Ms. Gunderson?"

"Yes, it is."

"Ms. Gunderson, this is Mon Fernandez. I have Juan Carlos Rodriguez on hold on another line. He says as owner of FC Independiente and a member of FIFA, he has some evidence on his behalf that would rebut allegations made by the FBI that he would like you to hear. I told him you would be obligated to share it with us. He doesn't care. He just wants to jerk us around."

"Evidence?"

"Bearing on the World Cup murders. He says he has evidence that he's been framed. Ladd, who is on hold on another line, says not to argue with him and to let you take care of it."

"Did you ask him if he's talked to his lawyer about this? Brilliante?"

"Yes, I did. But he doesn't care whether Señor Brilliante sees this or not. He wants to give it to FIFA's chief of security. That's you."

"What kind of evidence is this?"

"Evidence that cost him a quarter of a million bucks on Monday, he says. It's a cassette tape of two men talking. Their voices have been altered, he says, but there's no mistaking what they were up to, which was to frame him for the murders of Peter Tarchalski and Willi Gochnauer. Maybe you will know what to make of it."

"Anything to do with the business at Giants Stadium?"

"Not that he can figure, he says."

"Is it a long tape?"

"It's quite short."

"Did you ask him if he would play it to you over the phone?"

"Yes, I did, and yes, he will."

"Do it then and give me a dupe, okay, Mon? You Latins and your egos, ay!"

Fernandez laughed. "Will do, Elizabeth."

9:22 A.M.

The tapes from Harry Beauchamp came in a padded envelope. Elizabeth Gunderson signed the receipt, made herself a cup of coffee, and retrieved the tape from the envelope. She popped it into the VCR, took a sip of coffee, and hit the play button.

The tape rolled.

A naked man.

A second naked man.

She blinked, stunned.

She turned off the VCR and popped the audiotape into her cassette deck and listened to it.

Then she dialed Ladd McAllen. "Are you sitting?" she asked.

"I'm sitting."

"I just watched a most unusual videotape that may interest you."

"Oh?"

"Two naked males, Peter Tarchalski and Reiner Schmidt."

"Say again, please, Elizabeth?"

"Big as life. Homosexuals. Naked as jaybirds, doing their unusual thing. I hesitate to add that I didn't watch the whole performance. Once I saw what was happening, I turned it off. Watching boys cavorting together truly isn't my usual interest. Boy-girl maybe, where I can identify with one of the partners, but not this. There is absolutely no doubt as to who they are and what they're doing."

"Are you serious?"

"Of course, I'm serious. Do you think I'd make up something like this? Some kind of sick joke? And no, I'm not smoking marijuana or eating mushrooms. I've also got fragments of two men talking. Their voices have been altered, but it sounds for all the world like Harry Beauchamp is our man."

"Where on earth did you . . . ?"

"Beauchamp sent them to me. He said he paid a cool one million for them to a person or persons unknown. He says he was contacted while he was having lunch with one of his editors at his usual restaurant in New York, a Mexican place near the village." She named it.

"Is he a regular there?"

"Whenever he goes to New York, he says."

"Did you ask him why anybody would want to murder Roger Dusenberry?"

"Yes, I did. He says he has no idea. I suppose you have to say this puts a new light on things."

"Yes, I guess you'd have to say that. Just what new light, I'm not sure. I suppose we should put him in a safe house in case he's innocent as he claims. If he's guilty, he'll at least be where we can keep an eye on him. The last thing we need is a repeat of Schmidt or Dusenberry."

"I already suggested a safe house."

"You did? Good for you. What did he say?"

"He agrees. Is Dusenberry going to come around?"

"Still hard to tell, they say. Maybe. Maybe not."

10:13 A.M.

"The one thing we don't do is assume anything," Burlane said. "That's what he's counting on. With ordinary players we can assume. Not with him. He was just plain unlucky in his shot at Dusenberry. He was unmarked in front of the goal mouth. Impossible to miss, a person would have thought."

"Point-blank range."

"Remember what happened in our game with Brazil? Rubio and Antonio are without a doubt the best tandem of goal scorers in the world. And yet, against us, they missed shots they could ordinarily make in their sleep."

Gunderson said, "Major Khartoum, will you call Harry Beauchamp and talk to him? He wants to talk to you before he talks to Ladd McAllen. I don't see anything wrong with that."

"Beauchamp? Sure, I'll give him a ring and see if I can't learn something."

5:00 P.M.

"Did you see it?" Harry Beauchamp's voice was tight.

James Burlane said, "Elizabeth Gunderson told me what was on it. This has to be an untoward turn of events from your perspective."

"Homo. A bleeding homo. Why did I have to wind up with him? Buggering referees! Why me? Did you listen to the cassette tape?"

"Ms. Gunderson played it for me over the phone, and I recorded it. I've listened to it several times."

"What do you think?"

"I'm not sure. There are all kinds of possibilities, I suppose."

"Like what?"

"Like you had Peter Tarchalski murdered and are lying through your teeth. No offense, Mr. Beauchamp, but looking at it from my perspective, that's a distinct possibility. Say this is a ruse to put the villain into protective custody while his hired hand keeps circling the goal mouth. A nice sleight of hand."

"Tripe!"

"You had a nine-million-dollar transfer on the line. I know you must be very wealthy, but hey . . ."

"If you don't believe I moved the money, I'll give you my account number. You can check it for yourself."

"All those numbers and no legit names. You could have moved that money to yourself, Harry. Give me a break, please. I wasn't born yesterday."

"I'm telling you, this is a frame. Some hateful sod is bloody well trying to frame me. Judging from poor Dusenberry, who knows what he'll do next?"

"If you *are* innocent, our adversary has obviously studied the logic of motive. What does Sir Roger have to do with this, do you think?"

"I don't have any idea."

"Did you know Tarchalski was homosexual?"

"Peter Tarchalski? Queer? Are you mad? Of course not. That's foolish."

"Yet there he is, Ms. Gunderson tells me. He and Herr Schmidt."

"He always had women clinging to his elbow. Arsenal's striker. The top goal scorer in the FA. And don't tell me that was all show and no action. They all wanted to ride his German sausage, and for all I could see, Peter was doing his best to accommodate as many as possible. The favors of admiring females are a player's bennies in the FA, face it. They don't want to be hosed by some buck-toothed sod who drives a bleeding lorry. It's a wonder Tarchalski had enough energy left to play football."

"You had absolutely no idea or suspicion that he was gay? None at all?"

"Why, no! Not the foggiest idea. I was stunned by that tape, I can tell you. Putting it to a referee is just unthinkable! It's suicidal. Why on earth would he do something like that? Wonder he didn't wind up with AIDS, indulging in such tastes. My word! And allowing it to be taped. It's as bad as . . ." Beauchamp fell silent.

"Anna Maria Varga?"

"The bitch!"

"See there. You've got plenty of reason to put it to Rodriguez. Until we get this figured out, you're hip deep in hot shit, bub."

"I didn't do it. I'm innocent."

"They all say that."

"But you believe me, don't you, Major Khartoum? You may not admire everything about me, but you know I'm no murderer."

"Maybe. I don't know," Burlane said.

"What do I say when Elizabeth Gunderson and her people show up to talk to me?"

"You get yourself a lawyer, and you tell them the truth, the whole truth, and nothing but the truth."

"I already have. I've told you everything I can think of that's relevant. There's nothing more to tell. I was in the restaurant. I got the call. And here I am."

"Then my advice to you is to make sure your lawyer is real, real good. If you can remember anything at all that might help me figure this out, call me immediately, any time, day or night."

"This is the same guy who murdered Tarchalski and Gochnauer, isn't it? He gassed the football players and murdered Schmidt in bed and tried to do the same thing to Roger Dusenberry. The same sodding maniac. A bleeding madman."

"Could be the same person. Might not be a bleeding maniac."

"Major Khartoum, if you can get to the truth of all this with me still alive, I'll do anything. I mean that."

"Really?"

"Absolutely."

"If I bail you out, Mr. Beauchamp, I'll want you to find a civilized buyer and sell him the *New York Post*."

"Good luck finding anybody who'll buy it."

"You said anything."

"Easy to say because I didn't do anything wrong. I'm innocent. Find the truth. You'll see then. You do care about the truth, don't you, Major Khartoum?"

"Yes, I care about the truth."

"Khartoum! What kind of name is that? A town of boogie-woogs. Jesus!"

Burlane sighed and gave him his telephone number.

"I didn't mean anything, really. If you had something like this happen to you, you'd get excited too. A queer! How was I supposed to know?"

Burlane said, "I meant it about the *Post*." He hung up.

25

10:00 P.M.

Watching grim-faced men on television discuss the consequences of alternative actions in the World Cup crisis, James Burlane cooked the rice.

Burlane liked to listen to such discussions with the sound up just loud enough to hear what the officials and purported experts were saying. Lacking numbered jerseys, they used costumes, manner, and political codes to affix various labels and tags to themselves so that the viewers—most of whom were content to remain passionately ignorant—would know who was on what side. They wanted the viewers to know when it was safe to hoot and jeer and when they should pay attention.

Burlane liked to guess the sides by studying the performance rather than the program, although the players' names were often shown at the bottom of the screen. Burlane supposed this was to accommodate the deaf, who were furiously reading lips, and to force people like himself to turn up the sound.

Later, the participants, from newsmen to FIFA officials, would say how horrible the disaster was, a nightmare, but Burlane suspected they were secretly pleased to be in on the horror. One of the biggie zits of the decade and they were a part of it, a wonderful break in the boredom.

No announcement or decision, no matter how petit or benign, was outside the vortex of controversy. The facts of the case, as released by FIFA and the FBI, were few; something had to consume the airtime and newspaper space a tragedy of this magnitude demanded. The vacuum was filled with drivel and manufactured contention; such facts as were known were breathlessly repeated with the syntax altered to make them sound sort-of-new.

The dramatic issue of the hour was whether or not Prince Charles should fly to New York to be at Sir Roger Dusenberry's bedside. None of the talk could prevent him from going, because he was already above the Atlantic on a Concorde flight. If there was a chance Dusenberry might come round, Charles wanted to be there.

From London, a howl of protest went up that the Americans had demonstrated themselves incapable of protecting World Cup players. A terrorist was stalking the tournament. It was folly for the heir to the British throne to subject himself to such danger. Didn't Charles understand his responsibilities to the United Kingdom?

Others said stout fellow, good chap, courageous, and the rest of it. That Charles wanted to be at his friend's side spoke well of the future king, they said. Which one of Her Majesty's subjects wanted to argue with that? Who wanted a king who would ignore a friend who lay close to death?

Burlane used his Swiss army knife to shred a knob of ginger twice the size of his thumb, plus a half dozen green onions, separating the white from the green.

Then he put his wok on the portable burner, plus the wire rack on the inside that turned it into a steamer. This was his travel wok, so he had to cut his sea bass in half to make it fit.

He watched the mouths move on the tube, producing a grave and agitated murmur. Everybody had an opinion, it seemed. They all looked so very solemn, he wondered if their faces might not ache from maintaining the proper gravity. Nobody wanted to cancel the World Cup. Nobody wanted to give in to a terrorist. And yet . . . Nobody wanted to be blamed later for any loss of life if FIFA decided to replay the aborted U.S.–Netherlands game.

A spokesman for Prince Charles said that although the Prince had no idea if the shooting of Sir Roger was connected with the murder of the German players or the gassing at Giants Stadium, for the moment, he assumed it was. Charles considered it a matter of British honor that the killer not achieve his apparent goal of causing the tournament to be cancelled. The British people had been through the grinder before; they were not the type of people to capitulate before a barbarian. Charles was confident that Sir Roger, if he were to come out of his coma, would say the same thing: The matches should, eventually, be played. The terrorist might cause delay, but no more.

The Brazilian president of FIFA, Dr. Antonio Coelho, announced an indefinite postponement of play until the danger to human life was past. FIFA would reschedule the matches, but when—and where—remained undecided. Coelho said FIFA was in constant contact with the FBI and international police agencies, which had put all possible resources into the investigation. When FIFA was given the all clear, play would resume to determine the 1994 champion.

Then, Henry Kissinger was on the screen, giving his opinion with solemn gurgling and murmuring. He was only the honorary chairman of FIFA, but he was still Henry Kissinger. Shaking his head in anger at the terrorist, he agreed with the decision to postpone play, but said he passionately believed that the tournament should not be cancelled.

When eight minutes were up, Burlane removed the fish and put it on the plastic plate that was part of his travel kit. He poured the water out of the wok and began heating a good squirt of corn oil—a couple of tablespoonsful—from a plastic bottle that held no more than half a cup total. While the oil was heating, he arranged threads of ginger on top of the fish, followed by the dark green silken onion threads, then the white threads.

When the oil started to smoke, he quickly poured it over the fish; the oil cooked the ginger and onion slightly and carried their flavor down over the steamed fish. Over this he sloshed some soy sauce.

His late supper ready, he opened his bottle of Rolling Rock beer, added rice to his plate, then rubbed a Granny Smith on his thigh, a combination salad and desert to top off the meal.

On the tube, a pretty CNN reporter thrust a microphone in front of two well-appointed but perhaps inebriated gentlemen in a pub. They were being watched all over the world. They looked expansive. They were in a mood to express themselves.

Honest proles, well lubed. Burlane quickly popped on the sound.

The first said, "Why shouldn't Charles go to America if he bloody well wants? Shows he's got a pair there at least, going to help his mate. Besides, looks like the old Queenie Weenie's going to hang on to the crown till she croaks, doesn't it? Probably wears it sitting on the loo."

His friend added, "They're saying the poor sod got cuckolded, aren't they? Maybe he'll knock off an American piece on the sly. Where's the harm? They say those American women will recharge your batteries."

"But watch your wallet."

They both laughed.

The first man said, "And don't forget to wear a condom."

They laughed louder.

The second man said, "Just make sure it isn't made in Great Britain."

Which brought on a booming, knee-slapping round of guffaws. Haw, haw, haw!

"EC standards," said the first, hardly able to control his mirth.

26

NEW YORK, 9:32 A.M., SATURDAY, JULY 9

The ultraposh Emmanuel Greenblatt Hospital on New York's upper East Side did not cater to proletarian patients, and to accommodate VIPs in critical condition, the hospital provided special apartments for concerned relatives or attending physicians and, in this case, FBI agents and FIFA investigator James Burlane.

For a patient unfortunate enough to be confined to the bed, there was a large-screen Sony on the wall opposite the bed. Merely by flicking on the remote and selecting the right channel, one could select compact discs or movies; there were four stuffed leather chairs for guests to enjoy the music or movies. If the patient wanted to use the screen for computer games, he could do that as well.

A patient who could move about had even more options. The window of Sir Roger Dusenberry's sixteenth-floor room looked out on a gardened balcony that contained a white Italian table with a marble top and four chairs with padded seats and backs, from which ambulatory patients and their guests could enjoy the New York skyline at night. If they wanted a closer look at a particular room or detail on the street, they were provided with a tripod-mounted Swarovski 40 × 75 power spotting telescope.

Refreshments for the balcony talkers or optically assisted voyeurs had to be fetched from an outsized refrigerator built into the wall, which contained hospital-approved snacks and drinks, but the patient, never wanting, was given a remote to call for help in fetching food or drinks.

It wasn't enough to have the bedside nurse tape whatever came to Sir Roger Dusenberry's mind when, or if, he regained consciousness; Ladd McAllen wanted an FBI agent on hand who knew what questions needed answering. McAllen took the 7:00 A.M. to 3:00 P.M. day watch. Elizabeth Gunderson drew the 3:00 P.M. to 11:00 P.M. swing shift, to be replaced by Mon Fernandez from 11:00 P.M. to 7:00 A.M.

If the hoo-ha and blather in the media were correct, Dr. Avi Abramowitz was just about the best cardiologist in the business, close to being precisely the right surgeon to install and monitor the artificial heart in Dusenberry's chest until he was strong enough to accept a transplant.

At 9:35 A.M., with McAllen on duty in Dusenberry's room, the nurse rang for Abramowitz and Burlane, whose hospital apartment adjoined Abramowitz's.

A minute later, Abramowitz entered the room, followed closely by Burlane.

Dusenberry, who had clear plastic tubes running into both arms and up his nostrils, blinked. What he saw was a slightly rotund man in a pale green surgical gown and matching green sanitary bags over his shoes. Abramowitz had pale skin and piercing green eyes. His black hair was curly and he wore a short, neatly trimmed full beard. He was in his late thirties.

"So!" Abramowitz said. "Oy!"

Dusenberry, his voice a bare whisper, eyed McAllen. "I need to talk."

Abramowitz interrupted. "Whoah, there, cowboy. Maybe we ought to take this one step at a time, don't you think? My name is Dr. Abramowitz, and I put an artificial pumper in you yesterday. Don't you want to hear about that?"

McAllen adjusted the voice-activated tape recorder to make sure it was picking up Dusenberry's barely audible voice.

"A baboon's heart?" Dusenberry asked.

Abramowitz shook his head. "Plastic. Latest model."

To McAllen, Dusenberry said, "I can help you find him."

McAllen glanced at Abramowitz.

Abramowitz bunched his lips. "It's also extremely important that you rest, Sir Roger. How long will it take?"

"More lives may be at stake."

Abramowitz sighed. "Okay, a few minutes, depending on how your vital signs are doing and whether or not you can stay awake."

"We have to stop him."

Abramowitz said, "I hate to be overly blunt, but too much talk can kill you; the facts are the facts, and it doesn't do any good to dodge them."

"My life to risk, don't you think?"

Abramowitz said, "I have to be honest."

Dusenberry said, "Thank you. This talk is tiring. Perhaps if I just took a nap now." Dusenberry closed his eyes.

To the nurse, Abramowitz said, "You call me when he wakes up. I want to be here to make the call on how long he talks."

Dusenberry opened his eyes again. Looking at McAllen, he whispered. "If I don't make it. Joke. Frame. Dmitri Rassileva. German accent. Spanish. *La Prensa*. TV-PORTI. He knew." He closed his eyes again and fell asleep.

McAllen said, "What do you think, Major Khartoum?"

Burlane said, "Hard to tell. We've got what sounds like a Russian and maybe the Rodriguez connection."

10:00 A.M.

On the phone from his Maryland digs, Ara Schott said, "As near as the people at the Company can figure, the Dmitri Rassileva that Dusenberry was talking about is most likely an old-line Stalinist who was once in charge of athletic competition among the Warsaw Pact countries before the curtain went down.

"Where Dusenberry likely met him."

"It's possible. He accompanied English FA teams to matches on the Continent. Now, Rassileva's turned capitalist with a passion."

"He learned the single most important question, I take it?"

"Which is?"

"Who stays up to take care of the sick cow. Only the Bolsheviks never did get it, dumb peckers."

Schott laughed. "I don't know if you've read about the Moscow outfit that's been using a help-a-plucky-Russian-company pitch to sell running shoes. Lenin's."

Burlane laughed. "I bought a pair, Ara. Figured Nike doesn't need more of my business. It was like buying Girl Scout cookies, only more expensive. You give, but at least you get something for your money."

"That's Rassileva's company."

"I see. Good for him! Does he have a German accent?"

"No," Schott said. "He speaks some German, but his English has a Russian accent."

"Travel in Argentina?"

"The KGB says no. Foreign travel yes, to Africa, Europe, and North America, but no Argentina noted in his dossier."

"Then Dusenberry was talking about Rassileva and somebody else, somebody who speaks English with a German accent and possibly Spanish as well."

Schott said, "It sounds that way. Someone who knows about Argentina."

"An Argentinian or a German emigrant to Argentina. The Russians are trying to find Rassileva, I take it."

"For once, it's good to have them on our side. They say they'll run him down soonest, and if he doesn't cooperate, they'll see to it that he will. How are your Lenin's?"

"They're fine. They're probably off the same Chinese assembly line as Reeboks or Adidas, though, so it won't give unemployed Russians much to do. I really like the abstract Lenin on the side. Bright red. He looks good there with his beard and everything. They're hip shoes. I just hope they weren't made in a Chinese prison."

"Do you suppose a hundred years from now Lenin'll be associated with running shoes instead of nutball politics?"

Burlane said, "After we learn the shoes are made in China, we'll discover Rassileva is just a front for an American advertising agency."

"Owned by a Japanese electronics company," Schott said.

"Itself the pawn of the yakuza. See there. The wonderful world of free trade."

11:15 A.M.

Ladd McAllen put on his surgical face mask and leaned close to Sir Roger Dusenberry. "Take your time, Sir Roger. No need to hurry." The nurse rang for Abramowitz and Burlane.

"It's a long story."

"Easy, easy," McAllen said.

"Harry Beauchamp . . ."

"Pick up with your story, but easy. Take it easy."

"We got the idea at the club, you see, my friend Reg James and me. That is I got the idea. Harry Beauchamp had been publicly quarreling and bickering with Peter Tarchalski, which wasn't unusual; Harry was always quarreling with somebody or other. We had been hearing stories about his so-called phenom in Costa Rica, which we knew was why he was being so casual about Tarchalski's feelings."

Dusenberry closed his eyes.

McAllen leaned forward.

Dusenberry looked up again. "The more we heard about the Costa Rican, about how it was impossible to mark him and the rest of it, the more harsh and strident Harry became in his comments about Tarchalski. That's the way Harry was. Nobody seemed able to meet his standards. I think he resented having to pay his players for their work. Anyway, Reg has a nephew Ron . . ." Dusenberry grimaced.

Abramowitz and Burlane arrived simultaneously.

McAllen glanced at Abramowitz, seeking permission to continue.

Abramowitz, his eyes on the life-support monitors, nodded his head yes. Abramowitz said, "Your friend Charles has come to see you. He's on his way over."

Dusenberry smiled. "Charles. Stout fellow."

McAllen said, "Is Dmitri Rassileva a former Russian sports official?"

"Yes."

"The killer speaks English with a German accent and perhaps Spanish."

"Yes."

"He is familiar with Argentina."

"He seemed to be."

"Argentine or German."

"I don't know."

"You were telling me about Ron James."

Dusenberry nodded. "A special effects technician at Nottingham Ltd., one of Harry's employees."

"Take your time."

"James has a few quid to throw around, and he felt like drinking. So . . . I . . . we . . ."

"Easy, easy, Sir Roger."

"Reg and I went to school together, you see, at Eton. We got thoroughly potted and one of us came up with the joke. It was only a joke, Mr. McAllen. You have to believe me. Practical jokes were part of our lives, and we had some wonderful memories of them. For example, the headmaster used to ride his bicycle home to have lunch with his wife every day, so one day Reg and I put a thin layer of epoxy glue on the seat before he butted up." Dusenberry managed a weak smile. "We risked a terrible hiding, but he never figured out who did it. A practical joke. You understand, don't you?" He closed his eyes, saying. "An adolescent form of humor, I suppose."

McAllen caught Abramowitz's eyes.

Abramowitz nodded yes. "His signs are holding."

Dusenberry took a deep breath. "Well, the James family had footed the bill for young Ron to go to America to study computer-enhanced special effects. He attended UCLA and landed a job in Hollywood. He worked on *Terminator II* among other movies. We had nearly killed our film industry in England because of our tax system, but we've amended the laws in recent years, and movie-making has been making a comeback. When Harry established a studio at Nottingham with all the equipment he'd had in Hollywood, Ron James came home to work for him. Unfortunately, Harry treated his Nottingham people just as he did the footballers at Arsenal, so they all hated him."

McAllen said, "Including Ron James."

"Ron was thinking of going to work for an Italian film company in Milan. He'd been offered a handsome raise."

"Tell me about the practical joke."

"Well, the details of Tarchalski's sale to Cologne had just been released in the press. Good old predictable Harry. He wanted fast cash, but didn't want to miss the big party in America."

"The World Cup."

"Yes, I . . . This is quite difficult. I think I would like another nap now, Mr. McAllen."

"What was the joke?"

Roger Dusenberry nodded off to sleep.

1:10 P.M.

James Burlane and Dr. Abramowitz were playing cribbage and eating popcorn in Abramowitz's sitting room when the people downstairs used the hospital intercom to tell them Prince Charles and his retinue were on their way up.

Burlane continued counting his hand. By the time he finished with the crib and pegged across the finish line, the doorbell rang.

Abramowitz, dismayed at getting trounced after having beaten Burlane twice in a row, answered the door with a mug of beer in hand. There stood Charles, Prince of Wales, Duke of Cornwall, surrounded by a retinue of aides and security guards.

Burlane had never been a royals buff, but like everybody else he was curious about the private person, divorced from the mythical persona. He was thankful Americans had decided against titles and the rest of it, but he didn't begrudge the English their royal family. There was something to be said for having a family to which proles devoted their passion for gossip while the prime minister was allowed to get on with the business of running the government in relative peace.

In person, Charles seemed not at all royal, but fairly ordinary. He was, in keeping with his position, immaculately dressed. He wore gray trousers with razor-sharp creases, a blue broadcloth cotton shirt, a muted red tie, and a dark blue summer jacket with gold buttons, whose neat seams spoke of a proper tailor and thus expense. Burlane suspected that the central problem of Charles's life, besides his predictable costume, was that he couldn't get his end in on the sly without it becoming an affair of empire and grist for the Fleet Street rags. It was as though no male prole in the entire British Commonwealth had ever succumbed to sexual lure and the excitement of a little strange once in a while, a break from the old lady. There was no free lunch, even for a future King of the United Kingdom.

Burlane couldn't imagine anyone getting his rocks off on perpetual deference. "Yes, Your Majesty." "Of course, Your Majesty." "Good point, Your Majesty." "Right away, Your Majesty." Never, but never, ever, a friendly "Fuck you Charles, you dumb twit!" Never! Poor bastard.

Charles's immaculately manicured hands and perfect haircut gave him a boiled, sterile look, if not exactly anal compulsive. In China during the cultural revolution, the Red Guards dispatched people with such hands and haircuts to work on pig farms. But Charles was not to be held personally responsible for looking so perfect, Burlane knew. It was expected of him. He was not allowed to get dirty or ruffled except, perhaps, on the polo field; only in pursuit of sport, where manly oozing was appropriate, was Prince Charles allowed to sweat. No wonder Charles and his father, Prince Philip, were such avid sportsmen! Burlane could understand why; he had a fleeting fantasy of plopping a wig on Charles's head and giving him a new nose for a night on the town.

If Abramowitz was impressed by the fact that it was Prince Charles who had arrived to be with his stricken mate, he didn't show it. He was the captain of this ship, and his forever enemy, the Odious Pirate, Death, was standing just off the bow. It was Abramowitz's challenge to see Sir Roger through the hour, and nobody outranked him, not even the once but maybe no longer future King Charles.

In deference to the prince, Abramowitz wiped his mouth with the back of his hand to take care of any residual beer foam.

2:00 P.M.
Prince Charles, glancing at Ladd McAllen, looked down at Sir Roger on the bed, took a deep breath and let it out slowly. "Will he live?"

Abramowitz considered the question. "I don't know. If Sir Roger were younger and we had the right donor heart, I'd feel better about it. But as it stands now, with his stomach also shot up, it's difficult. Even if we did have a good heart to transplant, it would be dangerous to put it in until he's stronger. He needs to rest."

Charles didn't look satisfied.

"You want odds?"

"Yes, please."

"Right now is a critical period. Sir Roger needs all the rest he can get. Is his body capable of rallying the energy necessary to survive? That's the question. He's got maybe a forty percent chance of getting strong enough for us to insert a biological pumper. Then he'll go through another cycle of recovery. All this is extremely hard on his system. He's gotta want it. It's part physical, part mental."

"Did you talk to him?" Charles asked.

"Yes, we have. I told him it could kill him, but he said he doesn't care. He's weak so there's no telling when he'll come around again—if he'll come around. And when he does, there's no telling how long he'll be able to stay awake. You'll have a few minutes at best. If his vital signs weaken, I'll have to kick you out."

McAllen said, "We'll take what we can get."

Charles said, "They tell me if it weren't for you, Roger would be dead, Dr. Abramowitz."

Abramowitz colored. "All I or anybody else can do is our best based on what we know and the quality of our equipment. Fifty years from now something like this will probably be no sweat. But as it stands now . . ." He shrugged his shoulders.

Charles said, "I still want to thank you. It can properly be said you didn't choke in the clutch, can't it? You did what you had to do. They've got me ensconced in fancy digs just down the street. Do you suppose you could have someone ring me the next time he comes round? I'll pop over as quickly as I can."

4:30 P.M.

Sir Roger Dusenberry, looking up at Elizabeth Gunderson, licked his lips.

Gunderson said, "You were telling us about a practical joke, Sir Roger, and a special effects technician who worked at Nottingham Ltd."

"Yes, he did. I asked my friend Reg if his nephew Ron had the skill to put Peter Tarchalski's head on another man's body. He said he thought so, of course. I said well, what if Ron made a tape of Peter having a homosexual encounter with Reiner Schmidt, an Austrian referee whom we all suspected of being a closet gay?"

"A referee of international matches?"

"A FIFA veteran and a likely choice for the World Cup. You see, if it was ever revealed that Tarchalski had been having a homosexual relationship with a referee, it would scuttle Harry's deal."

Gunderson said, "Along with Tarchalski's career."

"Certainly it would have, but we never expected things to go that far. It was a joke; you see. A stupid practical joke. It took Ron four months of working nights and weekends in the studio. He produced quite a creditable job, but it never occurred to us that Harry wouldn't figure out that the scene had been faked in his own studio."

Gunderson said, "All Harry knew was that if the tape was made public Tarchalski was worthless on the international market."

"Nine million dollars. Evaporated. We know that he had some kind of confrontation with Tarchalski. I kept wondering when Harry was going to discover the fakery, but he never did."

Burlane, who until now had deferred to McAllen and Gunderson, said, "Harry told me he popped the tape into the VCR in his hotel suite, and as soon as he realized who was on it doing what, he hit the eject button. He didn't need to watch any more to know that he stood to lose a nine-million-dollar transfer fee."

Dusenberry closed his eyes and opened them again. He said, "Peter went over FA's head, went straight to FIFA, requesting a meeting of FIFA's Executive Committee after the World Cup. He said it was urgent, and the Executive Committee agreed. He no doubt didn't want to get into a public quarrel on the eve of the World Cup.

"Hamburg also wanted Peter. Hamburg was his hometown, and that was where Peter wanted to play. Peter probably thought Beauchamp had his studio fake the tape to stifle any objections he might have to the Cologne deal." Dusenberry moistened his lips. "If I . . . I'm feeling . . ."

Abramowitz said quickly, "I think that has to be it, for this session, folks. It looks like he's starting to work, and we don't need that."

Without opening his eyes, Dusenberry said, "A little nap would be nice."

Sir Roger fell asleep just as Prince Charles entered the room.

27

Prince Charles, determined to remain at Dusenberry's bedside until he woke up, returned that evening with the current American bestseller, a book about science's new understanding of the ecosystems. No more dashing from hotel to hospital to arrive just as Sir Roger was falling asleep. The Prince settled in for a good read. However long it took, Charles was determined to be present when his friend awakened.

Elizabeth Gunderson was still on duty when Dusenberry awoke and Abramowitz, Burlane on his heels as usual, arrived within half a minute to monitor his patient's vital signs.

When Dusenberry saw that Charles was in the room, he seemed to surge with energy. "Your Highness!"

Charles said, "Thought I'd pop by. Does that thing vibrate down there or what? A mechanical heart? My word, Roger! Although preferable to a baboon's, I suppose."

"It's so very good to see you, Charles." Dusenberry looked pleased. "Would a baboon's heart propel me around eighteen, do you suppose?"

"I know what you have to say to this lady is very important. The two of us can talk later."

"I hate so very much for you to hear this, Your Highness. It's so embarrassing. So stupid."

"Now, now, don't overdo it, Roger. You're telling us now. That's what counts."

Gunderson said, "You said your friend Reg James's nephew Ron faked a tape of Peter Tarchalski having sex with the FIFA referee Reiner Schmidt. Harry Beauchamp confronted Tarchalski, and Tarchalski asked FIFA for a meeting after the World Cup. Then what? Then what did you do?"

"I had no idea what might transpire at the FIFA meeting. But I did know the odds were good that if a Scotland Yard wizard was shown the tape, he'd have it checked. If they ever traced it to Reg and me, I would be disgraced and drummed out of FA, if not worse. I had to do something before Tarchalski talked to FIFA."

Gunderson said, "But if Tarchalski went to FIFA it would be exposed as a fake, so your problem became how to blame the tape on Harry."

"Correct. You Americans don't have a monopoly on the equipment needed to do that kind of work. What you have is the money and the distribution systems needed to produce and market expensive feature-length films. The scene could have been faked at Nottingham, but it could just as well have been made at any of several places in the United States and Europe, or in Japan."

Gunderson said, "So you thought, well, what if you were to arrange a dramatic, but fake attempt on Tarchalski's life and lay a trail to Beauchamp."

"Precisely. Beauchamp's motive was clear: a dead Tarchalski meant Lloyd's of London would lose the nine million, not him. You see what I mean? An attempted murder was all I needed. Scotland Yard would figure Harry screwed up and hired a bum shot. Tarchalski's reputation is defended. Everybody is happy."

"Except for Harry Beauchamp," Gunderson said.

"Well, there's that. But with all his money and power, he'd squirm off, we all know that. In retrospect, here is where things went very wrong indeed."

Dusenberry, who obviously had more on his mind, struggled to continue, but Abramowitz cut him short. Dusenberry didn't argue and was asleep within seconds.

28

New York, 6:30 a.m., Sunday, July 10

Sir Roger Dusenberry, obviously buoyed by Charles's visit, was exceptionally strong for the penultimate episode of his misadventure. This session was conducted by Mon Fernandez and witnessed by Dr. Abramowitz, Burlane, and the duty nurse.

Fernandez said, "You were telling us how things went wrong the moment you got the idea for the practical joke."

"I did not want to kill Tarchalski. You must understand that. I repeat, I did not. No, no, no. I didn't want to see Harry Beauchamp in jail. My motive was simply to get Harry out of English football into some line of work more suited to his talents and personality. He had become an unbelievable pain-in-the-rear. I wanted him out of FA. Nothing more. And I certainly didn't bear Peter Tarchalski any ill will. I'm as appalled as anybody about what happened to him."

"So what did you do next?" Fernandez said.

"I had to get somebody to do the job, didn't I? A professional. I didn't want him to be from the U.K. If I could, I wanted to get someone from out of the country. In the twelve years I'd been FA's chief of security, I'd met a lot of people abroad. During the cold war, the Soviet bloc athletic programs were run by the state, and they used professionals to see to it that members of their overseas contingents didn't defect. I wondered if there might not be someone available with the skills I needed, so I called Dmitri Rassileva and put a 'what if' kind of proposition to him. I said I was making the request on behalf of a friend."

Fernandez cleared his throat.

"Yes, I know. In retrospect, what I did was unbelievably stupid. Rassileva said he knew of a professional living in Argentina who might be able to help my acquaintance. He would call the man with the gist of my request. If the man was not interested, Rassileva would tell me. If he was, he himself would get in touch. Rassileva didn't call back, and a week later I had a visitor, a tall, blond, middle-aged man, who gave his name as Fritz, which I assumed was bogus. He gave no other name or hint of his identity. He looked fit and athletic. He spoke American English with a German accent. But he tossed in a Spanish word here and there. I assumed that he lived in Argentina, which he seemed to know all about.

"We went for a walk and had a chat in the park. I learned from him, for the first time, what had happened to Beauchamp in Argentina. There had been rumors that he had gotten involved in some sort of fiasco, but nothing about the incident appeared in the papers here.

"He said Harry Beauchamp had every reason to knock Peter Tarchalski off, and he had to be furious with Anna Maria Varga and Juan Carlos Rodriguez in Buenos Aires. Why not nick Tarchalski's bum—wad of fat there, no harm done—and blame it on

Rodriguez? That way folks in the U.K. would get to enjoy the juicy details of Beauchamp's humiliation in Argentina."

"And his terms?" Fernandez asked.

"He wanted fifty thousand pounds sterling, which was half his ordinary fee, but he wanted the money up front, not after nicking Tarchalski's bum. I had to trust him. He said he would fulfill his contract before or during the World Cup to make the Rodriguez frame credible, but before Tarchalski testified before FIFA's Executive Committee, in order to protect Reg and me."

Fernandez said, "Did you have fifty thousand pounds in a savings account? Or did you have to borrow it?"

"I borrowed it."

"From?"

"A friend."

Fernandez made a note. "A friend? Who?"

"Does it matter? A well-placed friend. He didn't know what it was for."

Fernandez said, "Tall chap with a firm jaw and regal beak?"

Dusenberry said nothing.

Fernandez said, "He also said he would frame Juan Carlos Rodriguez. Is that correct?"

"Yes, he did. He was to fire wide of a second player, which was also necessary, you see, in line with the business of revenge for two ejections."

"The logic of the frame thus looping back to Harry Beauchamp."

"With all signs pointing to Harry. Yes. The German sounded believable and reasonable. I trusted him. All I had to do was pay him his fifty thousand pounds and wait for the fun."

Here again, Abramowitz called a halt to Dusenberry's story, and Dusenberry went back to sleep.

10:00 A.M.

Ladd McAllen took the final installment of Sir Roger Dusenberry's tale when Sir Roger awoke later in the morning, once again strong and eager to finish his story. The session was again witnessed by the duty nurse and by Dr. Abramowitz, who arrived with James Burlane in tow.

McAllen said, "You were telling about your joke with the fake videotape and how it backfired. A blond man recommended by Dmitri Rassileva asked fifty thousand pounds to nick Tarchalski on the butt as part of a frame. What happened then?"

"I borrowed the money and gave it to him a week later. Then I waited. The World Cup approached. Nothing happened. I didn't worry about being bilked. I knew he would do the job. Then, I woke up one morning to read that Ron James and two other chaps had died in a terrible fire at Nottingham Ltd. On account of a girlfriend, Ron was still sitting on the Italian offer. I swear to you that killing Ron James was not part of the deal. I told him Ron had made the tape, yes, but he made no mention of having to kill him. Reg was heartbroken, but he didn't know anything about my deal with Fritz. I told no one."

McAllen said, "Oof!"

"He did everything I wanted, then just blew me off when it came to pulling the trigger. Flat murdered two German athletes. I just don't understand."

Burlane said, "Who suggested the Juan Carlos Rodriguez gambit as part of framing Harry?"

"Uh, he did, as a matter of fact. Looking back, I think he saw in me an opportunity of which I was unaware, and I think he got the idea right then and there, in the park while I was talking to him."

"Really?" Burlane said. "How was that?"

"When I told him the story, he got this odd, bemused look on his face."

Burlane said, "Don't you think a lot of people would give you an odd bemused look for proposing what you just did?"

"No, it was more than that. He thought about my story for a moment, then asked me to repeat it. He listened very attentively, apparently sympathetic to my plight. I also think he suddenly saw a possibility of some kind, a larger goal of which I was unaware."

McAllen said, "He must have been familiar with the workings of FA and FIFA."

"He knew all about them. And he knew his sports, I'll give him that. Also, when I first saw him, I thought I had seen him before, but I don't know where. He had, what do I say, a competitive look about him."

McAllen said, "Is it possible that you saw him in your capacity as FA's director of security? It's your job to accompany English sides on international travel, isn't it?"

"Yes, I do. And yes. It's entirely possible."

"Is it possible you could have seen the killer as a part of your duties in a former Soviet bloc country?"

"Entirely possible."

"East Germany?" McAllen said. "Stasi?" He glanced at Burlane. Stasi was East Germany's dreaded state security agency.

"Of course, East Germany," Dusenberry said.

Burlane said, "He also knew his Argentina, you're saying."

Dusenberry said, "He knew it well."

Burlane said, "Knew all about *La Prensa* and TV-PORTI and the rest of it?"

"Knew all about Rodriguez's cattle ranches on the pampas, and about his night clubs and hotels and resorts. He knew about Anna Maria's character on the soap opera. It's called *La Vida,* if I'm not mistaken. When we shook on it, he said he was a *cavazhero* and so would keep his word. What is a *cavazhero?* Or maybe it was *cabazhero.* It was hard to tell which."

Burlane said, "It's Spanish for gentleman, spelled c-a-b-a-l-l-e-r-o, literally 'a horseman'; it's pronounced *cabalyo* in Castilian Spanish and *cabayo* in all of Latin America except Argentina, Uruguay, and Paraguay, where the double *l* is pronounced with a *z* as in the English 'azure.' That makes it *cabazhero* or the *cavazhero* that you heard. You have to remember that the Spanish *b* is not nearly as hard as in English—sort of halfway between our *b* and *v*. We hear *Habana* as 'Havana,' and so it has become in English."

Dusenberry said, "He learned his Spanish in Argentina, then."

"Maybe. Or Paraguay," Burlane said. "Less likely, Uruguay. Both Argentina and Paraguay have large populations of Germans, southern Brazil as well."

"A joke, that's all," Dusenberry said. "It was one of those bloody stupid public school jokes one reads about."

III

CATENACCIO OF ROWAYTON

ABC Sports, ESPN, and the European Broadcasting Union—the host broadcaster due to its experience in televising soccer—sent their signals around the globe from the International Broadcast Center in Dallas, Texas.

The broadcasters entered the 1994 World Cup finals with hopes of a cumulative audience for the 52-game tournament of 31 billion people in 180 countries, expecting 2 billion fans would watch the championship match. They based this estimate on the 13.5 billion who had watched the 1986 tournament in Mexico, and the 26.7 billion who had watched the 1990 tournament in Italy. More than a billion people watched the Germany versus Argentina final in Rome; by comparison, the 1993 NFL Super Bowl in the United States attracted 253.4 million viewers.

Twenty-eight of the 52 matches had been played in the 1994 tournament when the Red Card terrorist first struck at the Germany–South Korea match on June 28 in the Cotton Bowl, Dallas, Texas.

1

James Burlane, pinning the telephone receiver against his neck with his shoulder, peeled a banana as he talked. "You've talked to your friends in Virginia, I take it."

"Oh, sure," Ara Schott said. "The FBI has already got them on the case, but they're sharing everything with us as well. They know we're working for FIFA, and they want to help. There are still people over there who remember you, Jimmy. They regard you as one of them. You're their Main Man in all this."

Burlane took another bite of banana.

"Remember Jack Hart in research?"

"He's the guy who helped me create Sid Khartoum."

"Right. He said when he spotted in the *Washington Post* that FIFA had hired a Major Sid Khartoum as its investigator, he about shit bricks. He wanted to know how you're doing, and I said other than horniness, disappointment in the Chicago White Sox, and an occasional outbreak of psoriasis, you were doing okay."

"I remember I had originally thought of plain Sid Khartoum, but Hart said no, I should give it a touch of the outlandish to make it sound real. A good legend had to have a signature kink here and there. He said how about Major M. Sidarius Khartoum? Bingo, that was it. I loved it."

"Hart is pleased that Major Khartoum is still in business. They may have sacked your ass, but everybody knows that came from the top."

"From anal-compulsive dickheads."

"Anyway, they're thrilled to be able to do what they can to help. The way they see it, they're ordinarily scorned by the tax-payers as the odious ones. A sinkhole for tax dollars. Now, they have exactly what we need."

"They're doing what?"

"They're feeding their computers details of the profile Ladd McAllen gave them, hoping to come up with a shortlist of possibilities."

"How long will that take?"

"I don't know. Ten minutes maybe. A half hour. The computers are quick, but everything has to be properly keyed in. They have thousands of dossiers entered into their computers, a lot of blond-haired East-bloc marksmen in their files. They have to cull out those who are disqualified for other reasons. An obvious scar that Dusenberry would have noted. Something."

"What did McAllen give them? You never know, I might have spotted something he overlooked."

Schott said, "Okay, McAllen told them we're dealing with a fair-skinned, blond Caucasian male in his mid- to late-forties, who is apparently of Western or Northern European ancestry. He is six feet to six feet two inches tall and has an athletic build. He is a skilled marksman. He knows how the FA works in England and how FIFA controls the game. He speaks American English with a German accent. He speaks some Spanish, possibly with an Argentinian accent. He is meticulous and careful. He plans everything in advance. He appears familiar with Argentina. He may live in Argentina. He was recommended by Dmitri Rassileva, a Soviet sports bureaucrat. He has contacts in the international arms market."

"A deduction based on the gas in the soccerballs."

"Right. He is good with computers. He knows how banks operate in Switzerland and the Cayman Islands. He has possibly been to Hollywood."

"Because he sent Juan Carlos and Anna Maria to The Brown Bear."

"Correct."

"I don't know what I'd add to that. Maybe McAllen should suggest they start with assholes who baby-sat Soviet bloc athletes."

"That was at the top of his list."

"He had a point-blank shot on goal at Roger Dusenberry and

missed. He was unlucky, as the Brits would say. If it hadn't been for that . . ."

"Breaks of the game, James. Did you rent your machine?"

"Got it." Burlane gave him a fax number.

"Stand by. We'll see what they come up with."

11:03 A.M.

The machine clicked on with a hum, and James Burlane popped to his feet to watch the list of biographical summaries begin to fax from the Central Intelligence Agency in Langley, Virginia.

Burlane read the first entry on Langley's offered best-bet list as the printer extruded the summaries line-by-line.

SUBJECT, East German Volkspolizei captain Ernst Karl HEIN, assigned to the state security agency, Stasi. HEIN, height 6' 2", 180 pounds, brown hair, blue eyes, no distinguishing marks or scars, was born on 24 Oct 1948, in Dresden. HEIN is the adopted son of East German diplomat Willy Hein. His adopted mother, Bettina Kohl Hein, was the sister of Jurgen Kohl, a major player in the East German Communist party.

HEIN went to high school in Reston, Virginia, and is a graduate of George Mason University in Virginia. For sixteen years, HEIN, a protégé of Stasi security officer Fredrich Peter Mueller, was the chief baby-sitter for East German athletes competing in foreign countries. Mueller is now serving a life sentence in Stuttgart Stammheim for torture and multiple murders. HEIN, an alleged accomplice on several of the charges on which Mueller was convicted, escaped German authorities and is believed to have fled to Argentina.

A pilot and skilled marksman, HEIN won a bronze medal in three-position small-bore rifle shooting in the 1968 Olympics in Mexico City.

The People's Police. American English with a German accent. Marksman. Argentina. That was it. Their man. Burlane read the remaining candidates, but no one came close.

11:08 A.M.

"Ahh," Elizabeth Gunderson said. "I bet you're calling about Ernst Hein."

James Burlane laughed. "Yes, I am."

"You want to know if FIFA's trying to find former East German football players. Major Khartoum, really. I'm embarrassed for you. Think."

Burlane, puzzled, bunched his eyebrows, thinking. Then, he said, "Jens Steiner!" The German manager, Jens Steiner, was a celebrated defector from the East German side.

"That's right. Herr Steiner was a star forward at Leipzig, and the most skilled goal scorer for East Germany. In 1979, he slipped out of the locker room moments before a match with Czechoslovakia in Prague, and was not seen for three weeks. Then he showed up in West Germany and signed on with Borussia Mönchengladbach."

"Was Ernst Hein his watchdog then?"

"Yes, he was."

"Defected on Hein's shift. Oof! Somebody better hustle Steiner's buns off the street for his own good."

"We've got him stashed safely away in a safe house in Los Angeles. Would you like to join me in talking to him via a conference call? We can set it up in a few minutes."

11:35 A.M.

"How well do I know Ernst Hein?" Jens Steiner laughed bitterly. "Where do I start? Ask me how well I know Satan, and I'll describe Hein. But I haven't seen him since the day before I defected. From what I read in the papers, I thought he lived in South America."

Elizabeth Gunderson said, "What kind of person was he?"

Steiner fell momentarily silent, then said, "Let me put it this way, Ernst Hein never let a transgression go unpunished, never, ever. We either did as we were told or suffered the consequences. He was a committed, disciplined Stasi officer. He said anybody who attempted to defect would get the red card. Before me, two other athletes had attempted to take off, and he killed them both."

"He was a *Volkspriest*," Burlane said.

"Huh?"

"A People's Priest. God's Will or Allah's Way. Substitute idiots, as in Idiot's Will or Idiot's Way. It was the Way of Idiots to plant a bomb under the World Trade Center in New York. The People's Will? The People's Way?" Burlane sounded disgusted. "What happened after you defected? Did the West Germans protect you?"

"For three years. When they thought Hein had probably cooled down, they stopped, but it was an expensive gesture, so I understood. I didn't argue."

Gunderson said, "But you always looked over your shoulder for the Vopos, nevertheless."

"Not just Vopos. For Stasi. Ernst Hein. As far as I know, I'm the only one who ever gave him the slip without winding up dead. But after reunification, I calmed down. We all wanted to put that crap behind us. But when Ernst Hein says he'll give you a red card for a particular infraction, and you go ahead and do it, then you do tend to think about it, I admit. His devotion to duty is unreal. It's been like living under a permanent yellow."

11:50 A.M.

Elizabeth Gunderson said, "Tell me more about Hein's relationship to Fredrich Mueller."

Steiner said, "Mueller is probably how he got to be that way."

"Got to be a fanatic?"

"Yes. Mueller assumed the role of mentor, I suppose, or teacher, something like that. A guru. That's the word. Hein was smart and seemed to be able to do anything he set his mind to. He was Mueller's prize student. It was obvious Hein wanted to be just like him."

"A Mueller clone."

"Mueller was a linguist with an interest in sports trivia. So was Hein. Mueller was interested in rifles and marksmanship. Hein won a bronze medal in the 1968 Olympics in Mexico City. See what I mean?"

Burlane said, "Tell me about the sports trivia."

"Mueller and Hein accompanied the athletes everywhere, and they were always talking about competition and sports and champions and what made champions and so on. If they weren't with us, they were with the ski team or swim team or somebody. So I suppose it was natural that they talked about sports. They were with us all the time. In the bus. On the plane. It was impossible not to hear them jabbering away. Talk, talk, talk. Sports, sports, sports."

"Competition." Burlane said.

"Competition and winning," Steiner said. "Who are winners and why? What does it take to win consistently? Listening to them was a form of education for me, I admit, and I've put a lot of their ideas to work as a manager. But I look at football as an apolitical game. Mueller believed it was ritual warfare. Champion athletes were like great warriors, and, just as individuals demonstrated their prowess by winning, East Germany demonstrated the superiority of socialism by fielding winning athletes. I was one of them."

"And the key to winning, in Mueller's opinion?"

"Discipline. Concentration. Perseverance. Mueller was always talking about concentration and perseverance. One never quit, ever."

"And a good game plan, I take it."

"Oh yes. We never played an international match without knowing everything imaginable about the players who would be marking or attacking us. We were thoroughly coached and prepared. If we lost, it was not because we were not fit or were casual about preparing. We were socialist warriors."

"In short, the East German side conformed to Mueller's vision."

"Yes, it did," Steiner said. "He used to tell us it took seven years for a Roman legionnaire to learn how to use a short sword properly. Did we think learning to play football was easier than that? I've often thought I've become a successful manager partly because I was indoctrinated with Mueller's philosophy. What if it's true? What if I was named manager of the German side and have brought it this far because of what I learned from Fredrich Mueller, a man who kept me imprisoned? Isn't that something?"

Gunderson said, "I take it the idea that any one of you would want to bolt to the West was unthinkable to Mueller."

"To Mueller or Hein. It was outrageous, not to be tolerated. That's why Mueller was so furious at Hein after I defected."

"You say Mueller was sore," Gunderson said. "Tell us about that."

"Word got back to me through friends on the East German side that Mueller dressed Hein down in front of the side. My friends said they had never seen Mueller as livid. He stalked back and forth kicking footballs at lockers. He screamed at Hein and threatened to sack him. I had just strolled out of the locker room never to be seen again, he shouted. Hein had failed. He was with Stasi. How had he allowed something like that to happen? How? Mueller threw a trash can through a window."

Gunderson said, "Oops!"

"I'm only getting this secondhand, mind you, but I believe every word of it. Only Mueller could have gotten away with it."

"Oh?"

Steiner said, "Hein would have killed anybody else. There's no doubt of it. But Mueller was special to him. He could do anything or say anything to him and get away with it."

"Why was that?"

"I hate to sound like Freud, but Hein was adopted, you know, and he didn't get along with the man who adopted him, but he'd go to extreme lengths to please Mueller. And Mueller had the highest expectations of him. If Mueller chewed him out like that, it was his way of expressing affection."

Gunderson said, "Was there any suggestion that their relationship was homosexual? That might account for his knowing about Reiner Schmidt's secret life."

"A lot of people suspected Schmidt might have different tastes, but nobody really cared. I just think Mueller and Hein were unusually good friends. Mueller was an older man wanting to pass on what he had observed and concluded. Hein was a younger man who recognized an unusual mind and wanted to learn from him. They liked one another's company. Mueller was Hein's guru."

"Also, I suppose Stasi kept lists of people they thought they could blackmail, not to exclude soccer referees."

"Exactly. Herr Schmidt's homosexuality was an open secret. Nobody cared as long as he did his job on the pitch, and he was an outstanding referee."

Gunderson said, "Did you hear what happened to Mueller and Hein after the wall went down?"

Steiner said, "They convicted Mueller of the grisly torture and murder of several political prisoners, and he's still doing time in Stuttgart Stammheim. The two of them had it good for years, you know. They traveled with archers, shooters, skiers, ice skaters, bobsledders, football players, track-and-field athletes, shooters, biathletes, you name it. And when we were abroad, they had far more freedom than us. We got to see the inside of trains and planes and buses, and hotel rooms, but that was about it. Virtually everything we saw was through glass of one sort or another, or through a fence or over a wall. If we got to shop, it was with Hein watching over our shoulders. We were prisoners. Mueller and Hein were trusted Stasi officers. They went where they pleased and did what they pleased."

Burlane said, "Baby-sitters of the People's athletes."

"Correct. They had helpers, of course, but Mueller and Hein were the ones we had to deal with in the end. We all knew that. There were a couple of players who maybe shouldn't have been on the side, and we all suspected they were snitches. But we couldn't prove anything. How? We didn't dare even think defect, much less talk about it. Also, as the People's star athletes, we had decent apartments and other perks. We ate well. We had cars. And although we were on a constant leash, we were able to buy decent clothes and other goodies on our trips and bring them back to our wives and girlfriends. Understand, nobody wanted to lose their perks through foolishness."

12:25 P.M.

James Burlane said, "You say Mueller and Hein were interested in sports, and you mentioned shooting and hunting. What else did they do?"

Steiner said, "They went fishing in Russia with some of their KGB friends. They went into a remote-controlled-airplane phase after they brought a couple back for a party bureaucrat. Then, a year or two before I defected, ultralights came out on the market, and they each brought one back from Canada.

"Early models. Flying wings."

"Right. They looked like model airplanes powered by lawn mower engines. I know I wouldn't want to trust my life in one. But Mueller and Hein just went nuts flying the silly things. They used our practice pitch for a landing field."

"They had a good time zooming around."

"Mueller wasn't bad. Of course, he was older and his reflexes had to be slowing down. But Hein was a real daredevil with his, I have to say. He was truly good. Mueller called him the Golden Turkey."

Gunderson said, "In reference to his blond hair."

"Yes. Mueller was teasing, of course. If Hein was any kind of bird in that machine of his, it was some kind of hawk or eagle. He could do all kinds of stunts in it. Anything his little plane was capable of doing, he could do. You sound like you know something about them."

Burlane said, "My neighbor owns one of the early ultralights, a cheapie wing of canvas stretched over aluminum tubing with a twenty-eight-horsepower Rotax and the pilot slung beneath it with more tubes."

"That's what these were, flying wings," Steiner said.

"Hang gliders with power," Burlane said. "The later models look like real airplanes. But you still shouldn't be trying to land in a wind above twenty miles an hour, that's a fact."

Gunderson said, "How about family and friends? Tell us about Hein's friends."

"His job was his life. Mueller was his family. I don't think he had much to do with his adopted family. His only friends outside Mueller were members of a group of ultralight pilots who had pull in the party."

"To be able to swing such a luxury."

"That's right," Steiner said. "They were almost all of them Stasi officers. They gave little air shows for party functions. Captain Hein was said to be the star performer."

12:38 P.M.

James Burlane said, "Hein no doubt has been following your success with interest."

"I don't imagine it thrills him that the man who stained his record has a good shot at leading Germany to a repeat of its World Cup title. We managers get our recognition too. Franz Beckenbauer won the cup in 1990. I represent Hein's only defeat, and now I'm leading the side of the hated bastards who imprisoned his beloved Mueller."

"Steiner said, "He'll be enraged when he learns that we figured him out and spirited you out of harm's way."

"Oh, he won't quit. He'll press on. It's like Fredrich Mueller is forever watching over Hein's shoulder. Hein thinks he has to be the best. The smartest. The most skilled. The best in every way."

Burlane said, "The perfect son. And he has to prove it."

"He's technically sane, I suppose, but he is lethal beyond belief."

Burlane said, "He intends to give you a red card before he's finished."

Steiner sighed. "Almost certainly, if I know Hein. I don't know why I didn't think of this before, but it just never occurred to me. I didn't make the connection. It was as though I had swept him into the dustbin of my past and forgot him."

"But now, here he is," Gunderson said.

"The way he looks at it, I got away with something at the expense of his perfect record, and he wants his measure of revenge. He just won't stop. That's the way he is. I know it's him out there. There's absolutely no doubt at all."

"He sees himself as the Last Vopo."

"Something like that, I think. Hein is Mueller, but Mueller is not Hein. Ask Mueller what he'll do."

3

1:00 P.M.

James Burlane said, "The ripping off of Beauchamp, Rodriguez, and Dusenberry was all side action. Mueller has trained him to consider all options and prepare a proper game plan. Gotta have a game plan."

"Tell me about Ernst Hein's game plan, Sherlock," Elizabeth Gunderson said.

"Okay. Sir Roger Dusenberry inadvertently laid an opportunity before Ernst Hein that Hein recognized immediately, a chance to spring Mueller from prison, make some money, and nail Jens Steiner at the same time. An extortionist's trifecta."

"So he acted."

"He did his research and began laying the groundwork. He figured how much each of his marks could come up with in an emergency. Then he floated a rumor in Buenos Aires about Rodriguez having hired a killer. He stole the stadium plans that had been handled by Rodriguez. Then he went to the United States and planted the plans in the house where Rodriguez was staying. Then what, Ms. Gunderson?"

"He wasted Tarchalski and Gochnauer in Dallas, pushing FIFA into a corner."

"Correct. He tapped Rodriguez and Beauchamp in the process. He knows we won't want to abandon the tournament, so any time now he'll ask for Mueller's release."

"He'll do this privately."

"He wants results, not his name in the papers or his picture on television. After Mueller is safe in South America, he'll waste Jens Steiner. Someone else can lead the German side if it gets to the championship match."

Elizabeth Gunderson said, "And if we don't release Herr Mueller?"

"He'll hit us again."

Gunderson said, "Under the circumstances we do what, do you think?"

Burlane sounded surprised. "Why we defend! We're the people's defenders."

11:17 P.M.

James Burlane was calm, almost detached, as he watched the media circus on the tube. On all channels, the news was the same. The FBI had identified the Red Card terrorist as Vopo Captain Ernst Hein, formerly in charge of preventing the defection of East German athletes performing out of the country.

Ladd McAllen, chief of the FBI investigation, said Hein was

simultaneously attempting to gain revenge on a defector from the German Democratic Republic and free his friend and surrogate father from prison.

The object of Hein's revenge was Jens Steiner, now manager of the German national side; Steiner was a Leipzig striker when he defected in 1979. However, Hein's father figure and guru, convicted Stasi murderer Fredrich Mueller, had agreed to testify against him in return for early release from Stuttgart Stammheim prison.

To assist the FBI, Mueller would be at the U.S. versus Netherlands quarterfinal game to be played Monday night in Giants Stadium.

McAllen said the FBI suspected Hein of now having murdered twelve people: Russian businessman Dmitri Rassileva; three Nottingham Ltd. film technicians; Austrian referee Reiner Schmidt, and seven soccer players—two German, three American, and two Dutch.

The woman on the screen, who had been murmuring the World Cup news with a grave face, looked concerned at what she was now reading on the monitor. She gave the floor director a nod.

On the tube, a tape of a laughing Sir Roger Dusenberry coming off the golf course with Prince Charles. Burlane punched up the sound.

On voice-over, the woman with the grave face said, ". . . ince Charles was at Sir Roger's bedside when he died. Dr. Avi Abramowitz, the cardiologist who had implanted the artificial heart, said because of his stomach wounds, the odds had been against Sir Dusenberry all along. He said Dusenberry, determined to nail the Cup terrorist, had expended all his energy telling the FBI what he had learned of the murderer. 'He used up the strength he needed to live. He literally gave his life,' Abramowitz said. Through a spokesman, Charles said, quote, 'Sir Roger urged us not to quit. Play on.' "

There was no mention of Dusenberry's practical joke gone wrong, Burlane noted. But then, Burlane saw nothing wrong with that. Abramowitz was probably right. In the end, Sir Roger kept a stiff upper and did the right thing. As the lady said in that wonderful song, everybody needed a hero.

A sorrowful Prince Charles, on the verge of tears, was shown getting into a limousine.

The woman said, "Sir Roger Dusenberry, by FBI count the thirteenth red card issued by the World Cup terrorist, was fifty-eight years old."

A few minutes later Elizabeth Gunderson called, saying, "We're going to play the game."

"I've been watching McAllen on the tube."

"We've got Prince Charles to thank. He pleaded with the Executive and Emergency committees on behalf of Dusenberry. He said Sir Roger surrendered his life so we could identify the killer. Now that we know who he is, we can properly defend. We should go ahead and play."

"Were you there?"

"I was there. Ladd McAllen was there. We gave them our recommendation, which was McAllen's modification of what you had in mind. After Prince Charles made his plea, the committees met in private to make their decision, then we were called back in. The vice chairman of the Emergency Committee, Sven Torberg, has replaced Dusenberry. The game will be held at three P.M. tomorrow afternoon in Rowayton, Connecticut."

"Ro-which?"

"Rowayton, a village on Long Island Sound about forty miles north of New York. Dr. Coelho has a Belgian friend who lives there, a certain Jacques de Beauvoir. Coelho says he has been de Beauvoir's houseguest on several occasions."

"Ah, such is the way the world works."

"De Beauvoir was there, so Ladd and I got a chance to talk to him. He says Rowayton is on the eastern shore of a north–south facing peninsula. By the sudden, unannounced sealing off of the street along the base of the peninsula and banning all boat traffic in the inlets on both sides, the Connecticut National Guard can quickly establish a security zone. The town is small enough that the police chief and his deputies know who's who, and if they don't, they can find someone who does."

4

If James Burlane had had his druthers, he'd have flown the sides out west and bused them into some isolated spot like Ely, Nevada, or Sheridan, Wyoming. But then, he was not Jacques de Beauvoir, a Belgian viscount and an old pal of FIFA president Dr. Antonio Coelho of Brazil.

While Ladd McAllen drove the government sedan north on Interstate 95, a pensive Elizabeth Gunderson sat in the passenger's seat. It was FIFA's tournament, not the FBI's; if Dr. Coelho and his colleagues wanted the United States–Netherlands match replayed in Rowayton, then that's where it would be played.

Burlane, alone in the rear, studied a map of the larger city of Norwalk, of which the village of Rowayton was a part. Norwalk claimed a four-mile stretch of the Long Island Sound coastline that ran southwest to northeast, reckoning from New York to Rhode Island.

Burlane was a lover of maps and liked to study them upside down and sideways, looking for unusual forms. Everybody knew Italy looked like a boot. Well, Japan, viewed from the southeast, looked like a seahorse with Hokkaido as its head. Honduras and Nicaragua looked like the profile of a woman's rump in the presenting position, with breasts of Guatemala, belly of El Salvador, and knees of Costa Rica. And along coastlines, wherever there were bays or mouths of rivers, there was almost always a promontory or point that looked like a nose or snout or beak. The coastline of the British Isles featured several cartographic old geezers who honked and snorted through crazed mouths and nutty noses.

Burlane thought Norwalk, Connecticut, was shaped like the head of a snarling dragon, if one imagined its ten-mile-long border with Westport as the top of its head. The border with New Canaan and Wilton was the back of this Norwalk dragon's head; the triangular intersection of Wilton and Westport in the northeast corner was a nifty ear.

The dragon faced Long Island Sound. Calf's Point, the southeast corner of Norwalk, was the dragon's snout. The curving Norwalk

River was a fire-breathing mouth in which Veterans Memorial Park, Fitch Point, and Gregory Point were teeth on the upper jaw.

On the southern bank, Keyser Point was the beast's evil tongue, poking out beyond Twilight Point. The chin was shaped by a series of landforms: the estuary of Village Creek, Wilson Point, Wilson Cove, and a series of four modest outcroppings, or points, in a one-mile stretch before the mouth of the Five Mile River. The Five Mile served as Norwalk's western boundary with Darien, the base of the dragon's head.

Burlane counted eighteen small islands less than a mile offshore of the angry mouth, and two small puffs of smoke, Calf Pasture Island and Sprite Island, just above the serpent's nostrils.

The village of Rowayton was flanked by the estuary of the Five Mile River on the west and by Wilson Cove on the east, with the four small points—Noroton, Pine, Roton, and Prices—at its southern tip. Prices Point, the extreme southwestern tip of Norwalk, was the effective beginning of Rowayton Avenue, which flanked the river.

Most of the dragon's head was working-class and middle-class. Real estate on the dragon's chin, located on the picturesque coastline of Long Island Sound and therefore much coveted, was where the money lay.

McAllen took Exit 12 off the turnpike and followed Tokeneke Road northeast toward Rowayton. When McAllen parked the Chevrolet in front of Rowayton Pizza, four men, three in uniform, were already there, smoking cigarettes and drinking plastic cups of thermos-bottle coffee.

Burlane was struck, upon first glancing at the group, by how much they resembled those awful light-upon-black velvet paintings of poker-playing dogs he had seen in working-class bars. They were American kitsch, one step removed from the sentimental paintings by Norman Rockwell, he supposed, but there was something about them that made them fascinating. The dogs, some of them with cigarettes drooping from their canine lips, considered their hands with mugs of beer on the corner of the table.

A more sophisticated version of the animals-as-humans theme was Sorel's bestiary, a satiric look at American political figures that was a favorite of *Ramparts* magazine in its late-1960s heyday. Burlane remembered in particular one of Bobby Kennedy as a giant rabbit with those two outsized front teeth of his.

Norwalk mayor Harry Raymond, a smallish, balding man, smoked a pipe; Raymond had thin lips and determined, slightly bulging eyes. A casting director would have made him a librarian or professor of literature. If he had been born an animal, he would have been a Chihuahua.

Norwalk police chief Harold Dobbs had bags under his eyes, and his belly hung ever so slightly over the broad leather belt of his uniform. He had a lethargic look about him. Dobbs, surely, would have been a basset hound.

The bespectacled commander of the Connecticut National Guard, Major General Howard Towson, looked more like an accountant than a military officer. He had an amiable look about him, and large brown eyes—a spaniel. As though to somehow toughen his image, he smoked Marlboros. He was a Marlboro-smoking spaniel.

The square-jawed John Derrick, commander of the Connecticut State Police, was the only one in the group who would have passed muster with a Hollywood casting director. A muscular boxer.

Rather than being alarmed by the canine appearance of this group, Burlane found himself reassured. It had been the American experience to dip into the pot of its disparate citizenry in times of crisis, and, when the clichéd push came to shove, they had more often than not lucked out. The draw had given them James Madison, John Adams, George Washington, and Thomas Jefferson at the beginning of the republic. With civil war bearing down on them, the Americans had pulled a skinny Illinois lawyer, Abraham Lincoln, from the pot. And later, when they had needed men with grit in time of depression followed by world war, they had drawn Franklin Roosevelt, Dwight Eisenhower, and Harry Truman. Roosevelt had been well born, from a wealthy and powerful family, but Truman had been a haberdasher, a hat salesman sent to Congress. He was made vice president because as senator he'd refused to follow the instructions of the Missouri political machine of the time. But when he had a job to do as president, he did it, and he did it well.

No sooner had Gunderson turned off the key than Jacques de Beauvoir and Dr. Antonio Coelho wheeled up in de Beauvoir's immaculately restored 1968 Saab. De Beauvoir, polite and well mannered, was tall and slender, a sleek, elegant greyhound dressed in casual slacks, a simple cotton pullover, and well-used walking shoes. Coelho, large-beaked and brown-eyed, also had a patrician look about him; coarse proles did not wind up as presidents of FIFA. If he was not a poodle trimmed for show, he was close.

As Gunderson and her colleagues introduced themselves, yet another car pulled up, a black Cadillac limousine out of which emerged two more officials: Sven Torberg, the tall, angular, blond Swede who was the new chairman of the Emergency Committee, and the rotund Henry M. Kissinger, honorary chairman of the 1994 World Cup Organizing Committee. They were, respectively, a pointer and a bulldog.

When the introductions were complete, General Towson suggested they split into several parties so that de Beauvoir and those officers familiar with the community could give them a quick tour of the area to be defended. Afterwards they would meet on a private beach on the neighboring peninsula, Wilson Point, where Elaine de Beauvoir and a neighbor would have coffee and hot croissants waiting. There, with the morning sun rising above Long Island Sound, they would discuss their strategy.

Burlane was quick to volunteer to ride in de Beauvoir's Saab. It was a two-door coupe and there wasn't a lot of room, but he squeezed into the back seat, joined quickly by Sven Torberg. Henry Kissinger, perhaps not as quick as he once was, yet respected enough to claim the right-of-way, squeezed into the passenger's seat.

The elegant and urbane Jacques de Beauvoir was six feet four inches tall, so the driver's seat, immediately in front of Burlane, was pushed back as far as it would go. Looking concerned, twisting in the seat, he said, "Are you going to have enough room back there, Major Khartoum? Mr. Torberg? It has to be cramped quarters."

Burlane said, "I'll survive. Anything for a ride in this car."

Torberg grinned. "Me too. It's a Saab, after all."

"I confess. I wanted to ride in it," said Kissinger.

"If I ever go to heaven, I expect it'll be in a car like this," Burlane said.

Kissinger grinned. "Limousines are so boring and pretentious!" They all laughed.

Torberg said, "But heaven won't be Swedish made, Major Khartoum. The taxes are too high there."

They laughed again.

4:45 A.M.

Rowayton's main drag, if such it could be called, was the north–south running Rowayton Avenue that flanked the sailboat-lined estuary of the Five Mile River.

They passed the Upper Crust Deli and the Five Mile River Grill, but Burlane was pleased to note that there was not a Shakey's or a Pizza Hut to be seen. There were no Taco Belles, McDonald'ses, or Burger Kings. It was an old-fashioned village. There was a drugstore if one wanted aspirin or digitalis, a wine store, and a gear shop if one wanted to buy a set of new sails or a wholesome cooler of Stroh's.

The east–west running McKinley Street, lined by trees on both sides, formed a T with Rowayton Avenue. De Beauvoir drove slowly east on McKinley, explaining that Rowayton's history, originally based on oysters, was filled with stories of the comings and goings of the wealthy who moored their yachts in Five Mile River; also, from the late nineteenth century through the 1930s, a fashionable amusement park had flourished at Roton Point.

De Beauvoir said, "By the way, this won't be the first time the residents of Rowayton have had to defend themselves; their Revolutionary War ancestors were forced to contend with marauding British loyalists in whaleboats. One of the most famous whaleboat encounters took place a year after the British surrendered at Yorktown, when Tory Captain Joseph Hoyt, in an eight-oared boat accompanied by a five-oared boat, was met by patriot defenders of Rowayton in an eight-oared boat and a ten-oared boat. Hoyt was like Ernst Hein in a way. He was a refugee from Rowayton who had been displaced by the patriots who won the war, and he refused to yield to the new order. The battle took place off the islands you'll be seeing in a few minutes."

"And the outcome of that encounter?" Kissinger asked.

De Beauvoir grimaced. "Hoyt and his companions engaged the eight-oared boat with bayonets, swords, and hand-to-hand combat, and were about to win when their boat was broadsided by a swivel gun mounted on the bow of the ten-oared patriot boat. Every combatant in both boats was wounded or killed."

It was obvious that militant multiculturalists and professional victims had yet to throw their intrusive weight around in Rowayton. In his polite way, the cultured and diplomatic de Beauvoir told them that creepie-weeps and druggie-wugs with glazed brains could be found in abundance in proletarian northern or eastern Norwalk, but one did not shoplift and defecate in parks and throw plastic wrappers on the sidewalks in Rowayton.

Rowayton was an American flower of a classic Anglo-European variety, nurtured, in the beginning, by Puritan values of thrift and hard work. In more recent years, it had matured as a form of tidy parasite on the sinkhole that was New York; it was a two-minute drive to the Rowayton stop on the Metro North rail line, and every twenty minutes, a commuter train picked up passengers for the forty-minute run to Manhattan, rolling through the horror of the Bronx toward more civilized and lucrative Wall Street and Madison Avenue. To some, Rowayton remained a pretty daisy on the Connecticut coastline; to others, less sanguine, it was a cute little toadstool popped out of Big Apple manure.

Burlane imagined that on the Fourth of July, the townspeople who gathered downtown to celebrate Independence Day had a wholesome, well-scrubbed, American look about them of a sort now widely held to be mythical or a thing of the past or irrelevant. Rowayton truly was picturesque in a sweet, New England village sort of way—a perfect setting for a Stephen King movie, say, in which evil inserts its unwelcome nastiness into the garden. No, no, Mr. Author, please, no serpents here. Spare Rowayton. It is where we think we want to live. If we lived in Rowayton, we would have picturesque personal lives too; we're convinced of it. Look at the residents of Rowayton, responsible, courteous to one another; that's the way we want to be.

After 500 yards, de Beauvoir pulled to the side of the road, and gestured across the road with his long arm out of the open window.

McKinley Street was at the southern end of an 800-foot-wide by 1,000-foot-long expanse of splendid green, featuring two softball fields, one with homeplate in the southwest corner, the second with the homeplate to the far northwest. The Rowayton library was to the right of the two softball fields, and north of it were public tennis and squash courts. Rowayton's redbrick elementary school was at the top of the rectangle.

De Beauvoir said, "It's good, solid turf. It's quick and was mowed just two days ago. It has been well cared for. I know, I'm a member of an advisory committee that oversees the maintenance problems. We have room enough to make the field one hundred twenty yards long and eighty yards wide. All we have to do is lay down some turf over part of the far infield or leave it the way it is and just chalk the touchlines and goal lines. We'll borrow goals from the high school. That won't take more than a couple of hours if we put our backs into it. The people running the pool cameras can run cables from the back of the library for their electrical hookups. We can provide construction cranes to give the television cameramen good shooting angles. All they have to do is tell us how many cranes, where they want them, and how high the cameramen want to be, and we'll take care of it. We check to make sure the balls are filled with air and not something lethal, and we're set. We play a soccer game. We could play it in the street if we had to, or somebody's pasture. The simplicity of the game is part of its beauty."

Kissinger said, "Mr. de Beauvoir is right. The play is the thing. If a stranger comes into the Rowayton area and inquires about soccer fields, he'll be directed to schools, parks, and community centers. Nobody will know of any soccer field in Rowayton."

De Beauvoir was pleased. "Precisely, Dr. Kissinger. We chalk the lines and play ball. Let Hein find us if he can."

De Beauvoir put the Saab into gear and continued to the end of McKinley, where he took a left north onto Highland Avenue. They were now east of the proposed site of the match. They passed the library. They passed the tennis and squash courts.

De Beauvoir turned onto a broad curve in Wilson Avenue as it turned east along the cattails and marsh grass along Wilson Cove, itself the refuge for more sailboats.

Burlane did his best not to be a consumerist; he coveted neither his neighbor's belongings nor his neighbor's wife's ass—well, once in a while his neighbor's wife's ass, however covertly—but he did dream about owning a sailboat. They were beautiful, in his opinion, and he liked the feeling of slicing through the water to the brisk thump of a good wind. In a storm, lacking the power to face the wind directly, a sailboat could be dangerous. Sailboats were like women, he supposed. The sleeker and more beautiful they were, the more unpredictable, and the more costly to own and maintain. Burlane felt this logic was as tight as clockwork, yet a sailboat with her sheets full of wind still turned his eye and stirred his imagination, as did the stride of a good-looking woman with a blouseful of breast.

De Beauvoir turned east again, past a security guard, to enter Wilson Point, the small peninsula just east of Rowayton. Most of the houses here were made of stone and had gabled windows and steep-pitched roofs with wooden shakes. Several of the estates had multiple wings, while more modest houses settled for a stone servant's cottage to the side. The driveways were curved, a form of conspicuous consumption of expensive real estate. A few of the lawns were large enough to qualify as fairways. There were no picket fences; there were walls, made of proper stone. Proletarian brick would be in poor form here; Burlane understood that. All this had the look of real, not pretend, money, and the money was not all new; a fortune here and there had roots beyond the previous decade.

The exception to the prevailing architecture was a splendid, dazzling white house in the international style, all angles and cubes à la Piet Mondrian, with large expanses of glass. This eye-catching house, sitting atop a rounded hillock, belonged to the congenial Jacques de Beauvoir.

They continued down the road for their rendezvous at a private beach for the use of the residents of Wilson Point. De Beauvoir's wife and a neighbor awaited them with coffee and croissants, and within a space of five minutes the participants had all gathered. The tide was out and the sun was rising over Long Island Sound.

Only hours earlier, General Howard Towson, awakened from a sound sleep by Governor Lowell Weicker, found himself the designated General Schwartzkopf for the day. The taxpayers of the state of Connecticut expected the commander of their national guard to be a take-charge kind of guy when the occasion called for it. Now, it was time to earn his pay. Towson glanced at Henry Kissinger. He cleared his throat.

5:30 A.M.

General Howard Towson spread a map on top of one of the picnic tables used on the private beach and the party gathered round, studying the dragon's chin.

He thought for a moment, then said, "I obviously haven't had time to think through any kind of strategy, so I suggest we talk our problem through, with each of you offering suggestions as you please, as though you were my staff officers. As we all know, Mr. Kissinger here has been on the hot spot a few times. Mayor Raymond, Chief Dobbs, and Mr. de Beauvoir know the neighborhood intimately. Please interrupt any time you see fit. Mr. McAllen, you say we're dealing with a professional who might well have his way of monitoring our every movement. Secrecy is not guaranteed."

"No, it isn't," McAllen said.

Kissinger, bunching his famous eyebrows, said, "I like the business of having Mueller watch the game. It forces Hein to pick his targets. Or at least exercise some discrimination. No more killing people with nerve gas while he watches on television."

"That was Major Khartoum's idea," Gunderson said, glancing at Burlane.

Towson adjusted his eyeglasses and retrieved a Marlboro, which he considered, but did not light. "We have water on three sides, which is good, but I think we would be irresponsible not to have both primary and backup perimeters across the approach by land. Commander Derrick, if your state police can seal off Witches Lane from the Five Mile River to the base of Wilson Point, my guardsmen can seal off Wilson Avenue from the banks of the Five Mile to Wilson Cove. The guardsmen have the Stingers, so they should man the inside perimeter."

Towson, the Marlboro still unlit, put a ruler by the scale and measured the proposed barriers. "Witches Lane is a one-mile assignment with three through-streets: Rowayton, Highland, and Wilson avenues. The Wilson Lane perimeter is five-eighths of a mile with the same streets to watch, plus Roton Avenue."

"Fair enough," Derrick said.

Towson lit his Marlboro and took a drag. "Chief Dobbs, since your police officers know the area residents, I think it would make sense if you assist Commander Derrick's people and my officers on the perimeters."

"Of course," Dobbs said. He pulled at his belt as if to give some relief for his belly.

Kissinger, his voice low and gravelly, grave, said, "This is the problem we faced in Vietnam. The enemy was everywhere and nowhere at once. The terrorist has replaced the bomb as our principal national security problem. How does one defend against the terrorist? Tamil separatists used a human bomb to get India's Prime Minister Rajiv Gandhi, and their own prime minister. How does one defend against human bombs? It may be that Dulles and Dean Rusk and I had it easy compared to the secretaries of state in the next century." Kissinger paused.

"Do you have a suggestion, Dr. Kissinger?" Towson cocked his head, smoke trailing from his nose.

Kissinger said, "Why don't we ape General Giap's tactics in the Tet offensive of 1968? Put our guardsmen and police officers in civilian clothing. Have the guardsmen and our FBI agents and SWAT squad members begin filtering into Rowayton several hours before the match. Have them slowly fill the shops, bars, eateries, and the library, plus the homes of Rowayton policemen. An innocent telephone call by an excited teenager can have us on the radio in minutes, so we have to be careful.

"Say we reschedule the match for three-thirty P.M. And, what if, say at two P.M., ABC or ESPN cameras begin showing the warm-ups to the pending three P.M. match at Newport. We put some young men on a field in Newport in American and Dutch uniforms. Surely, ABC or ESPN will lend us some sportscasters to help out in the ruse. By the time Ernst Hein goes to Newport to investigate, we'll have established our security perimeters down here."

Towson, thinking, bit his lower lip. "A feint! Good idea, Mr. Kissinger. I can order my guardsmen to go through the motions of securing Newport. Dr. Coelho, do you think FIFA has the weight to mount such a ruse at this late an hour? Athletes will have to be recruited. Someone will have to talk to the people at ESPN and ABC Sports."

Coelho, speaking with a slight Portuguese accent, said, "I can do that."

"Objections to the Kissinger fake to the north? No? Mayor Raymond, you and Chief Dobbs will have your work cut out for you if this is to work." Towson flipped the spent cigarette onto the beach and ground it out with the heel of his foot.

"We'll take care of it," Raymond said. His pipe was empty. He tapped the ashes on the sand, and began repacking it with tobacco.

Towson, retrieving another Marlboro, looked around. "Done, then. Dr. Coelho, we will leave the responsibility for contacting ESPN and ABC up to you. Major Khartoum?"

Khartoum pursed his lips, thinking. "We've forced Hein to show himself if he wants a shot on goal. We know he's a long-time, skilled pilot of ultralights. I say that's what he'll turn to come show time. But we have to remember, he has the advantage of surprise. We'll likely hear him before we see him."

Kissinger narrowed his eyes. "And he knows we'll be reluctant to fire dangerous ground-level shotgun blasts in a residential neighborhood. Our moral integrity is the terrorist's tactical advantage."

Towson sighed and took a drag on his new cigarette. "And your proposal, Major Khartoum?"

Burlane shrugged. "I can fly one of those toys. My neighbor owns one, an early, dumb-looking thing. I bet there are plenty of enthusiasts in this part of the world that would loan me a good one for something like this. I propose to intercept Ernst Hein in an ultralight and shoot the motherfucker square between the eyes with my .22 Ruger."

Towson blinked. "A Ruger .22." He exhaled.

"A little beauty. An RSTF, the original standard semiautomatic model. Four-and-a-half-inch barrel. Cost $37.50 when it was first offered for sale in 1949."

"And if you fail?"

"I'll force him high enough for the shotguns to take over with safety. Twelve gauges with magnum-load double ought buck will do the trick. It will be good for people on television to watch someone take him on mano a mano and beat his ass. If not, they get to watch you shred him with shotguns."

Kissinger looked gravely about at his fellow defenders. "Major Khartoum correctly understands that ritual and symbol are a form of social glue. They hold us together. This man Hein is an abomination who would prevent us from having football tournaments on whim simply because he knows how to pull a trigger. Major Khartoum proposes to be our knight, facing the serpent with drawn sword."

Burlane said. "They say the Ruger semiautomatic .22 is the Mafia's weapon of choice for wasting people. When I found that out, I just had to have one."

Coelho, the former owner of the Brazilian side Palmeiras, said, "Let me make sure I understand this. What you propose in effect is a *catenaccio* of Rowayton with Major Khartoum as our goalkeeper and General Towson as our sweeper. The guardsmen on Wilson Avenue will be our fullbacks, and farther out, the state police on Witch Lane will be halfbacks dropped back on defense."

"Correct," Burlane said.

Coelho said, "While the fullbacks hold their places on Wilson and around the pitch, you propose to leave the goalmouth and challenge the center forward one-on-one. If you fail, Towson and his fullbacks will close fast."

Burlane grinned. "There you have it, Dr. Coelho. The defenders of Rowayton versus the devil's striker."

Kissinger, a goalkeeper himself as a schoolboy, said, "Of course, Dr. Coelho, we would ordinarily let our halfbacks handle Hein if they could, or failing that, our fullbacks."

Coelho smiled, "Mine would at Palmeiras, but I appreciate your argument."

Kissinger said, "In this case our keeper goes out to challenge him on behalf of our fans and because we have faith that our fullbacks can back him up."

Towson took a deep breath and exhaled through puffed cheeks. "Objections?" He waited. He considered his cigarette.

"Under the circumstances, it is a reasonable course of action," Kissinger said.

"Dr. Coelho?" Towson said. He took another hit on his Marlboro.

"We do it."

Towson said, "Okay then, Major Khartoum, we'll put you in goal, and I'll serve as your sweeper. We know Hein has access to nerve gas, and even though we have Mueller present, we have to assume he might use it again. We keep the townspeople well away from the field until we've taken care of him. They'll just have to stay inside and watch the action on television like everybody else. When it's safe we'll invite them over to watch the game. We'll have gas masks on hand for everybody on or close to the field, including the athletes. When we spot Hein, we all put 'em on.

"If he's coming from the east or south we'll have to have a perimeter of spotters to give us warning. That means spotters east of Wilson Point, here." He tapped the map with his forefinger. "Hoyt Island, here." He tapped it again. "And south of that, Cedar Hammocks, here." He tapped the map. "A spotter on Tree Hammock Island, here." Tap. "Someone on the northern tip of Shea Island, here; a spotter on the southwestern tip of Sheffield Island, about here; as well as the banks of the Five Mile River, here." Tap, tap, tap. The man who smoked Marlboros had been transformed into a man of action.

De Beauvoir, studying the map, said, "Mmmmmm. The same islands were used to warn the Rowayton patriots that Joe Hoyt was coming."

Kissinger bunched his face and ran his hand over his curly, short-cropped hair. "Almost all military defenses throughout history have depended on the idea of perimeters, Mr. de Beauvoir. The marines in Beirut lost their lives because they failed to establish effective perimeters. That should have been an elemental part of their training. The World Trade Center had no effective perimeters in place so lunatics were able to drive a van-load of explosives into the basement. The concept is as basic to warfare as it is in soccer: force your adversary to penetrate ever more formidable lines of defense. The tactics remain the same, only the scoundrels are different."

Burlane nodded in agreement. "I'll need help in finding a Kolb ultralight. The Kolb is one of the best American-made aerobatic ultralights, and because of its design, it has good visibility for the pilot. What self-respecting German wouldn't go for the Kolb? If I can't get a Kolb, I want a Rans Airaile. They're similar except the Rans has a tricycle landing gear."

5

3:15 P.M.
General Howard Towson scored—that is, his friend, Connecticut Governor Lowell Weicker, scored—a Rans Airaile for James Burlane, powered by a souped-up forty-horsepower Rotax. The Rans had a proper stick, just like a real airplane. Its colors, orange, orangish yellow, and black, made it look like a monarch butterfly.

Whether the engine was entirely legal was the adman's worry, not Burlane's. But for the moment, it was exactly what he wanted. He didn't want to be flying an old-fashioned Kasperwing, that's for sure. Heeding Muhammad Ali's advice, he wanted an ultralight that could float like a butterfly, so he could sting like a bee.

Using a hand mirror and a small pair of scissors, Burlane whacked off his shoulder-length mane of silver-gray hair and eliminated the handlebars from his mustache. He had once received a worse haircut from a Chinese barber who, confronted by a curly tangle of European hair, had no idea what to do with it.

When he was finished cutting his hair, Burlane unscrewed the cap from a plastic bottle of Lady Clairol chestnut-brown hair coloring that he had mixed in advance. He dipped his comb into the goo and, in a few minutes, was a brown head with a brown, ho-hum mustache. His hair was wet, but would dry. He grinned at the sight of the new Burlane.

Burlane proceeded with the business of putting a new nose in place. With a simple adhesive, it fit comfortably over his natural model. The artificial nose, which Burlane had used on several occasions, looked rather like the memorable beak that was the genetic inheritance of the character actor Karl Malden. He stuffed his Chicago White Sox baseball cap in his hip pocket; this was a size seven-and-a-half-inch baseball cap, not one with an adjustable plastic band in the back. He had his Bausch & Lomb sunglasses in his shirt pocket and his goggles for flying; he was ready.

Burlane positioned the Airaile just off the northeastern corner of the field by the tennis and paddle courts. He did this so he could swing onto the grass in front of the goalmouth, and take off toward the southern end of the field.

Burlane then used a felt-tipped marker pen to block out letters on the top of the wing of his plane. He paused momentarily to call Elizabeth Gunderson on his pocket transceiver to find out if the FBI had thought to check the FIFA limousine for tailing devices.

"Yes, I'm pleased to say they did, and we're told it was clean. Does Ladd McAllen get good marks for that one, Major Khartoum?"

"How about the heels of the shoes of Coelho and Torberg? Did he check those?"

Gunderson said nothing.

"Hein had to have some way of anticipating a move like this. He knew in advance Torberg would likely replace Dusenberry as chairman of the Emergency Committee. He also knows FIFA. The chairman of the Emergency Committee does not go with any fake. Humor me."

"I'll get back," she said.

Burlane, using a brush furnished by Jacques de Beauvoir's artist wife, began filling in the letters with black paint. If the adman bitched, he'd make FIFA take care of it. The lettering was sloppily done, but not bad considering how fast he had worked:

GBANKS.

Then, Gunderson was back on the radio. "Okay, all right, I have to hand it to you, Major Khartoum. There was indeed a tailing device in the heel of Sven Torberg's shoe. We're having the shoes driven north, but by now Ladd says Hein's probably got a fix on us. Ladd says good thinking."

"I guess we can expect the happy warrior any moment then, can't we?"

"That's what General Towson is telling his people. He says he's setting the defense. He's got guardsmen with shotguns on the roofs of the school and the library if you need help. He says they'll be tracking Hein every second; if you get in trouble just give the word, and he'll have them knock him down. There'll be more shotguns at the base of the foul ball screens."

"Solid, dependable fullbacks."

"That's what Señor Quelho says. We're all behind you, Major Khartoum."

"If I succeed, do I get a shot at the pretty girl?"

"If I were you, I'd just concentrate on the job at hand, Major Khartoum."

3:25 P.M.
As James Burlane waited for a call from one of General Towson's ultralight spotters, he watched the Dutch and the Americans take the field to loosen up with balls that had been thoroughly examined.

Burlane kept one ear on his transceiver as he listened to ESPN's first-team broadcasters describing the American and Dutch sides as the players warmed up on the field in Newport. The broadcasters said clever, security-conscious FIFA had decided to hold the game on an island.

Then, abruptly, the ESPN sportscaster fessed up: the viewers were really watching members of the soccer teams from Yale and Brown universities wearing American and Dutch national uniforms. The actual World Cup game was about to begin in Rowayton, Connecticut, more than 100 miles to the south. He apologized for the ruse, which, he said, had been necessary for security reasons.

Then, in a snap of the fingers, the world was watching and listening to ABC's World Cup announcers describing the action on a pitch fashioned out of adjoining softball fields in Rowayton.

Crews from the city of Norwalk, with Mayor Raymond watching anxiously over their shoulders, had sodded the six-foot-wide strip of the northwest infield that poked onto the corner of the soccer pitch. The workers, laboring feverishly throughout the morning, cut and lifted four-foot-wide strips of grass from near the library. They laid and packed the grass on the corner of the soccer field with virtually no visible seams; the ball bounced straight and true, and the footing was solid.

There would be no roaring of frenzied thousands, no whistling, jeering, or booing, no banners or human waves, no hot dog or beer concessions, but upon this rich and well-tended turf of Rowayton, American and Dutch athletes would see who was best at kicking a ball with their feet.

The Finnish referee set the game ball in the center of the field.

On the loudspeaker temporarily rigged for the occasion, a solemn and determined Henry Kissinger spoke in a deep, dignified, resonant voice that echoed across the grass and down the streets and sidewalks of the tranquil village:

"FIFA president, Dr. Antonio Coelho, has honored me with the privilege of thanking you residents of Rowayton for the use of your turf today. It is wrong to let uncivilized creeps squash such splendid international competition as the World Cup. We will not yield. We will have courage. Dr. Coelho?"

Coelho said, "When it's safe, and we give the word, you're all invited to come watch the match. Meanwhile, let's play football!"

Of course, Pat Duffy had wanted to play midfield for the national side. He had been an all-American halfback at the University of Santa Clara. But when he had tried out for the team, Coach Milutinovich had taken him aside and said that while he was good, it was no cigar as far as being a midfielder. But Coach M wanted the best athletes on the field. He wanted to try the ferociously competitive Duffy at fullback.

Now, with Luis Garcia and Denton Gjerde gone from the midfield, Duffy was moved forward. Duffy could defend, and he could attack if he had to.

Before the game, Coach Milutinovich had told his players they should defend, yes, but if they got a chance to move the ball up the field, they should do it. They had to shoot at the goal to score. He didn't want any part of organized thuggery masking as soccer. The Dutch didn't play that way. They were disciplined. They worked hard. They moved. They were skilled passers. They wanted to win, but they were honorable competitors. This was the kind of soccer that people liked to see. It was the kind of soccer Milutinovich wanted the American team to play, win or lose.

If the Americans didn't put their hearts into it, they were in for a long afternoon. The Dutch were rolling behind their superstar, Peter "the Painter" van Dyke, an artist in front of the goalmouth. Van Dyke, having fun with his name, wore a van Dyck beard.

Jerry Gotti watched him, kept an eye on the bearded one.

Van Dyke went about his duties in an almost leisurely manner. His face looked almost distracted, but Coach had said Gotti should not let that deceive him. Van Dyke was forever calculating angles and looking for weaknesses. He had an instinct for space. When an opening developed, he was there.

And when he shot, word was, van Dyke was quick as an adder's tongue.

Two minutes into the game, the Painter slid casually out to meet his mates as they brought the ball over the centerline.

Gotti watched him.

Van Dyke looped to Gotti's left, going half speed.

Then, a burst of speed to the inside . . .

Back to the middle . . .

Confusion in front of Gotti . . .

He couldn't see van Dyke.

Goal!

Jerry Gotti disconsolately retrieved the ball from the back of the net as the Dutch players celebrated the score.

Peter the Painter was so quick it was unreal. Gotti kicked the ball to the referee. A goal in two minutes. If this kept up, it was going to be a long afternoon.

They struggled. Oh, how they struggled. But the Dutch were very, very good, and on their game. It was tough for the Americans to get to the Dutch end of the field, much less remain there for any length of time.

Still without a shot on goal, they worked their way into Dutch territory, momentarily, in the twenty-second minute.

Pat Duffy, twenty-five yards out, was given space by the Dutch defender, who wanted to cut down on Duffy's opportunities for what the English called the "wall pass," in which a player taps a pass to a mate, races around the defender, and quickly gets the ball back. In the back alleys of Liverpool or London, the side of the buildings was used as an extra player. American basketball players called this a give-and-go.

Downfield, the Dutch goalkeeper, hustling for a better angle, shouting instructions to his fullbacks, was nearly knocked off his feet in a collision with one of his own fullbacks.

Duffy blasted one. A just-for-the-hell-of-it, nothing-to-lose blast. The spinning soccer ball, which had a wicked hook on it, sailed serenely past the outstretched hands of the horrified goalkeeper and into the far corner of the goal.

In the thirty-second minute, the Painter, demonstrating his extraordinary dribbling skills in front of the box, tapped a wall pass to a mate on the left wing, simultaneously juking his defender with his shoulders.

He stepped quickly into the space in front of the near post.

Where he got the ball back on a nifty backheel.

With Jerry Gotti right behind him.

Van Dyke, faking left with his head, coolly backheeled the ball into the net, where Gotti had been before he went with the fake.

The Netherlands 2, the United States 1.

In the thirty-second minute, a voice on Burlane's transceiver said, "This is Sergeant Donaldson on the tip of Sheffield Island. We've got a pale blue ultralight biplane approaching from due south about twenty feet off the water. It's headed straight for the bottom of Wilson Point."

Burlane said, "Anybody in the cockpit?"

"Sir?"

"Does it have a pilot?"

"One moment . . ."

"This is Sergeant Lemon on Tavern Island. It's empty, sir. It's a drone, now turning northwest toward the goalmouth."

Burlane said, "He's either using it for reconnaissance or it's a flying bomb. He'll have a videocamera in the nose so he can pick his targets."

Towson said, "Ms. Gunderson, Mr. McAllen, if you could have Mr. Linneman call an injury time-out, please, and get the players quickly off the field. I want them well out of harm's way until we're finished with this business. Get them under cover. Quickly please. Gas masks on everybody. Fullbacks stay alert."

"Sergeant Donaldson, is the drone low enough for shotguns?" Towson said.

"Yes, sir. Looks that way."

"I think the halfbacks on the bluff should bring him down, what do you say, Major Khartoum?"

"I say do it."

"Shotguns take it," Towson said.

As the pilotless aircraft appeared above the trees overlooking Wilson Cove, a volley of shotgun blasts sent it plummeting onto Bluff Avenue, where it hit with a jarring explosion."

"Good shooting," Burlane said.

"A flying bomb," Towson said.

"This is Sergeant Sanger on Hoyt Island. We have a bright red ultralight aloft somewhere around Norwalk Community College to the north of here. It's gaining altitude to the northwest. Can you see it?"

Towson said, "We certainly can. Thank you, Steve."

Burlane spotted the aircraft with his binoculars. It was impossible to tell if it had a pilot or was another drone.

Towson said, "Your opinion, Major Khartoum?"

"He knows we have shotguns. Now he's wondering if we have Stingers."

Towson said, "Stingers ready. You know your shooting order, fire only on command."

Burlane said, "I wouldn't use them all, if I were you. We don't yet know what he has up his sleeve."

Towson said, "Understood, major."

The ultralight was directly above Brien McMahon High School, north of Rowayton, gaining altitude, then above the Five Mile River as it circled west, then southwest, getting higher and higher, working its way above the soccer field.

Then, about 400 yards directly above the field, the ultralight suddenly plunged earthward in a near-vertical power dive.

"Fire Alpha," Towson said.

A streak of orange streaked upward.

A burst of silver deflected the Stinger.

"Chaff!" Burlane yelled.

"Fire Beta. Fire Charlie," Towson said quickly.

Two more streaks of orange shot skyward.

Chaff deflected the first.

Missile Charlie struck its target about 150 yards above the field, and the remote-piloted red ultralight, yet another flying bomb, burst into an incredible ball of orange.

"Sir, this is Sergeant Mills at Price's Point. While we were watching the Stingers, a yellow and black ultralight came out of nowhere and is flying up Five Mile River. Looks like a huge wasp. It's got a pilot in it, sir."

Towson said, "Be alert shotguns."

"Fucked up, sir. He had it timed perfectly. As the plane exploded above the field, he just whipped past us, hardly off the water."

"It's okay, Wes. He hasn't got us yet. Major Khartoum?"

"I heard, General." Burlane pulled his tinted goggles over his artificial nose. He revved the engine of the souped-up Rotax; it was like a lawn mower run amok. He released his brakes. "I'm on my way."

Towson said, "Good luck, Major Khartoum."

"Amen to that," said Gunderson.

Ernst Hein, with yachts on both sides and water zipping by 10 feet below him, licked his lips as he flew up the mouth of the Five Mile River just out of shotgun range.

Ja, ja, ja, Mueller, ja!

Hein could fire his Uzi pistol full automatic if he lucked onto a crowd of idiots or semiautomatic if he had to pick the *scheisses* off one at a time. If he could waste a jackrabbit on the dead run . . .

With the money he had made off Rodriguez and the stupid Englishmen, he would buy a retreat of dreams in Argentina. Nobody would ever find them. Nobody would ever know. He and Mueller would go fishing. They would hunt peccaries and jaguars. They would ride with the eagles in their ultralights.

Listen to me, Mueller. Hear me.

When they were in the mood, they would fly to Buenos Aires in Hein's Beechcraft. They would sip superb Argentine red wine on handsome boulevards, and afterwards, if they pleased, they would find pretty girls to fuck.

Do you hear me, Mueller?

Whatever Mueller had allegedly done, he had done on behalf of the people. He was a Vopo officer. He represented the people, something never acknowledged by the courts.

Duty.

It would be a proper, well-deserved retirement for Fredrich Mueller. To put Mueller in Stuttgart Stammhein was an abominable outrage. To allow him to rot there was unthinkable.

Honor.

The liars had said Mueller had turned on him. That was meant to provoke him, he knew. Well, all right, let them play their games!

I'm coming, Mueller.

They said they would have Mueller at the match to prevent random killing. That meant Mueller was there to see the action. Well, he wasn't going to let Mueller down. He'd give them a show they'd never forget. Mueller would love it.

For you, Mueller.

If they just let Mueller go, he would quit. Let them play football if they wanted.

Was that so impossible?

Either way he would not let the traitor Jens Steiner lead Germany in the championship match. *Nein, nein, nein.* If it came to that, there would be no championship match.

I ride the reckoning wind.

* * *

James Burlane's Rans Airaile bounded across the infield, gaining momentum. As he approached the box in front of the south goal, going full power, he pulled back the stick and was aloft. He headed skyward feeling loosey-goosey and good. The Airaile was quick to the touch and remarkably stable, but Burlane was grateful there was no wind.

Then, Lieutenant Gregg, stationed at the boat yards west of Rowayton and McKinley: "He just turned a hard right, sir, barely over the tops of the boat masts."

"This is Lieutenant Oliver at Rowayton Pizza. He's flying east down McKinley about six or eight feet off the ground. Low but slow."

"Shotguns hold your fire," Towson said.

Burlane, climbing, saw the unforgiving warrior in the cockpit of his Kolb Starfire, in dazzling yellow and black. The encounter was to begin above the southern end of the soccer field—just off the third-base foul line in the softball field closest to McKinley.

Towson said, "Shotguns up, fullbacks. All beads on the yellow and black. Above him, Major Khartoum. Get above him. Give it the juice. Give it the juice. Stingers at the ready if the wasp tries to escape high."

Gunderson said, "ABC has you on the tube, Major."

Kissinger said, "Let the people see, Major Khartoum. We can defend. We can."

Towson said, "Put it to him."

De Beauvoir said, "Do it, Major Khartoum."

Burlane tested his Ruger to make sure it didn't get hung up in the holster. The racket of the air-cooled, two-cycle Rotax pusher, above and back of his head, was horrific.

As he crossed over the south goal of the deserted pitch, Ernst Hein, aware of motion above him, glanced up and saw an orange and yellow and black Rans Airaile angling for attack from above, a butterfly turned hawk.

Hein was lucky to have seen him. He banked his plane tightly, climbing clockwise.

He saw GBANKS painted on the wing of the climbing monarch.

The pilot was the guy who had known the name of Roger Bannis-ter's rabbits.

He looked straight at Burlane through his goggles and nodded his head. He had beaten Banks in sports trivia, he'd beat him again.

James Burlane nodded back, then mouthed "mo-ther-fuck-er" as clearly as he could. He quickly slipped a Ruger butt-clip into his mouth.

Hein brandished his evil-looking Uzi assault pistol.

Burlane showed his Ruger.

In Burlane's ears, amid the screaming of the Rotax, Henry Kiss-inger: "Shoot, shoot, shoot!"

"Shoot, Sid!" Gunderson shouted.

Burlane shot and missed.

A shot from the Uzi slammed into the tail of Burlane's plane, slowing its ascent.

Hein was suddenly higher.

Shitaroonie! Burlane broke and headed for trees flanking McKinley.

Hein, above and behind Gordie Banks, had him. Had him dead to rights. Thinking one for you Mueller, and keeping his eye on the fleeing butterfly, he thumbed the Uzi onto full automatic and squeezed off a hail of 9 mm rounds

. . . into leaves and branches,

. . . as the fleeing Banks disappeared under the protective um-brella of a tree.

That Banks was able to do this without snagging a wing took remarkable piloting skill. *Scheisse!*

Ooof!

"Jesus, watch it, Sid!" Gunderson shouted in Burlane's ear-phones.

Burlane, on the far side of the tree, glanced back at Hein, who was replacing the clip of his Uzi.

Burlane put the Rotax full throttle and started climbing as steeply as he could manage.

Hein was right with him. Opposite him. Climbing.

In his ears, the steady, guttural voice of Henry M. Kissinger, "Get him, Major Khartoum. Get him."

Wasp and butterfly spiraled upward, wasp higher.

Gunderson said, "Watch above, Sid. He's coming back at you from above. Watch, watch, watch."

Hein had rolled back on Burlane in a loop.

Burlane banked sharply left to come back on him from the side . . .

. . . as Hein descended, on the backside of his loop, facing second base.

Burlane, passing him at a right angle, snapped a quick shot with his Ruger. *In your face, asshole.*

Hein twisted in the cockpit and nearly stalled the wasp. Then, he broke off and headed for the far side of the foul screen.

Butterfly followed.

In his earphones, General Towson said, "Nice work. I believe you scored a hit, Major Khartoum."

Mueller used to tell Ernst Hein to remain calm always. Emotion was lethal. Sentiment was death. To a real competitor, pain was nothing. A competitor played through pain. Concentration was the thing. At all times, follow the logic of victory. Hein had to concentrate.

Banks's slug had hit Hein in his left groin, about three inches up from his genitals. The slug throbbed and burned, but Hein didn't think it was a killing blow. Small caliber. A .22 maybe, same as Hein's Walther. Banks was a gutsy *scheisse* and a good shot. So was Ernst Hein.

For the moment, while Hein's body adjusted to the initial bolt of pain, he had to keep Banks's mind on his flying and off his peashooter.

Watch me, Mueller, just watch now. I am the best. I will not be defeated. I will concentrate. I will persevere. I will win.

There will be justice.

Watch me, Mueller.

*   *   *

Burlane, biting his lip, followed Hein around the foul ball screen.

Then, Hein banked right and led Burlane around the redbrick Rowayton library, turning in a ninety-degree snap roll to slip between the trees along Highland.

Towson said, "You hit him, Major. I'm sure of it."

"Lucked out, if I did."

"He nearly stalled," Towson said.

Gunderson said, "Watch the limbs, Sid."

Burlane too pulled a ninety-degree snap roll, as the branches passed over his head.

Ernst Hein was suddenly aware of the blood. His thigh and crotch were slimy with blood. He was sitting in a swamp of warm blood. His ass was soaked.

Banks had hit a pumper in his groin with a wild passing shot.

Hein pinched the artery with his left thumb, and headed back to the soccer pitch with his right hand. However much he tried not to let it bother him, the wound in his groin would inevitably affect his performance. He needed all the space he could get.

If Hein didn't do something about the artery, he'd bleed to death. How much blood had he lost? He could keep the artery pinched and retreat, or . . .

You always said to be decisive.

Banks was right behind him.

See this, Mueller. Watch this shot on goal.

Clenching his jaw, Ernst Hein pulled back the universal stick of his wasp.

"Watch it Sid!"

Burlane banked left, his wingtips barely missing Hein's. Burlane shouted, "Ooof!" into the microphone around his throat. The fucking psychopath had tried to ram him from above in a kamikazi run.

Was Hein badly hurt?

Burlane considered this turn of events as he circled clockwise for another run at the wasp.

Was Hein bleeding? Was that it?

They were now directly above the soccer field.

* * *

Ernst Hein peeled off on a counterclockwise circle exactly opposite of Banks. There would come a point, however briefly, when the arcs of wasp and butterfly would intersect.

He is a smart one, Mueller. He is good, and he suspects I am hurt.

Hein let go of the artery and the awful rush of blood resumed. He took the stick with his left hand.

I am bleeding, Mueller. I do what I have to do.

He felt weak. His strength was ebbing as his blood pressure fell.

Are you watching, Mueller?

With his right hand, Hein thumbed the Uzi onto full automatic.

Ride with me, Mueller, so that we may go fishing in the Andes.

Before him in a flash . . .

Banks.

He triggered a clip.

Yaaaaauuuughhhhhhh!

A blow to the left side of Burlane's head.

Burlane rolled the Airaile belly up, and headed for the turf. Like somebody had whacked him with a hammer.

"Major?" Towson yelled.

Pain stabbed at the side of his head. *Awwwwwww!*

"Sid!" Gunderson.

He pulled back on the stick and cut his power. He braced himself. Head pounding.

Grass in front of him . . .

Pain . . .

Airaile turning . . .

Bolts of pain . . .

He goosed the Rotax.

He bit his lower lip as the grass passed below him and the Airaile began to climb. He shook the cobwebs from his brain. Where was Hein? He shouted, "Where? Where?"

"Behind you." Gunderson.

He banked left.

He banked right.

* * *

Hein mimicked Gordie Banks's every move. A hit. He'd scored a hit in Banks's head or neck, he was sure of it. Banks had almost crashed into the pitch.

Ja, Mueller.

He popped a new clip into the Uzi.

Your head hurt, does it, Gordie?

He thumbed the pistol onto semiautomatic.

Shot on goal, Mueller.

Burlane banked left and simultaneously pulled a 90-degree snap roll . . .

. . . as a slug from the Uzi slammed into his ass. *Aaauuuggghhhh!*

His right cheek hammering with pain, he slipped through two trees along McKinley. Better his butt than the top of his head.

He poked at the bloody left side of his head. Half of his ear was missing.

He said, "Hits in the ear and ass. Cheek only so I'm okay."

Kissinger said, "Stay with him, Major."

"Do it, Sid," said Gunderson.

"Damned near buggered me," Burlane said. "Ear hurts like hell."

The inside of Hein's cockpit was slick with blood. The stick was covered with it. The Uzi was bloody. The clips were slippery, and it was hard to fly and reload at the same time. Hein's blood pressure was ebbing.

If Banks hadn't pulled a terrific snap roll at the last second, showing tails instead of heads, he'd be a dead man.

He's hurt too, Mueller.

He gave up on the Uzi and grabbed his Walther, which was loaded and ready.

Now, Mueller . . .

In the heartbeat before James Burlane pulled the trigger, he and Ernst Hein locked eyes over the barrels of their pistols.

Burlane fired first . . .

. . . and looped back on the wasp as it crashed onto the field.

Burlane yelled into the transceiver, "Fullbacks hold your places. He's dangerous, and he's still mine."

Towson said, "Fullbacks listen to your keeper."

Burlane said, "He's got a full-automatic assault pistol, fullbacks."

Towson said, "Ambulance be ready to roll."

Burlane landed quickly, not knowing if he had scored a hit with his last shot or not. He wondered if, in that final moment, Hein might not have been unconscious, or nearly so. His eyes had had a distracted, faraway look about them. Thinking of what, Burlane wondered?

Hein struggled to unsnap himself. He was still alive. He was not yet defeated. He could still score.

Was Mueller nearby?

Are you watching, Mueller?

The buckle came unsnapped.

I will yet score, Mueller.

He saw a man with blood on the side of his head and a pistol in his hand lurching toward him. This would be the gutsy *scheisse* Gordie Banks.

Watch this, Mueller.

It was a struggle trying to walk with a slug in your ass and pain shooting through your hip and down your leg, but James Burlane was several zones beyond giving a squat about pain.

In front of him, beside the wrecked Kolb, on his right knee, was Vopo captain Ernst Hein. He was crimson with blood. He rested his left forearm on top of his left knee. He held a bloody Uzi pistol by the barrel.

Hein backhanded the Uzi onto the grass in front of him. "Well done, Mr. Banks. The goal defended."

Burlane, pointing his Ruger at the middle of Hein's chest, kicked the Uzi to one side. "Let's see your other hand, asshole."

Loose ball . . .

Hein swung the Walther from behind his knee.

. . . in front of the goalmouth.

Burlane, firing wildly, dove on him.

With his left hand, Burlane grabbed Hein by the throat and

pinned him, squeezing for all he was worth; with his right, he grabbed the Walther and twisted it from Hein's weakened grip and pitched it aside.

Then, he sat on Hein's chest. He pinned Hein's arms with his knees.

Burlane's hurried final shot had entered Hein's left cheekbone and traveled down through his teeth and out of his neck just below his jawbone.

"Three shots on goal, and we blocked every fucking one."

Too weak to resist, his mouth filling with blood, Hein could barely talk. "I was unlucky. I hit Dusenberry's rib like Geoff Hurst's shot bounced off the bar in sixty-six." He spit a mouthful of blood. "Only no glory for me, eh, Gordie Banks?"

Burlane glared at him. "This isn't rugger. It's soccer. Association football. You're an expert on sports trivia, asshole, can you tell me Thring's third rule?"

Hein, eyes wide open, thought for a moment. He blinked.

"We're talking J. R. Thring of Cambridge University."

Hein shook his head. He didn't know. He spit more blood.

Burlane said, evenly, " 'Kicks must be aimed only at the ball.' *The Simplest Game*, 1862. No hacking. No shinning." With his right hand, Burlane whipped a red card from his shirt pocket, and waved it in front of Hein's face. "See this? This is for you, prick. We're doing our damnedest to play a civilized game. If scumbags like you won't follow the rules, somebody's gotta throw your ass off the field!" He threw the card down with disgust.

James Burlane, grateful that Ernst Hein hadn't knocked off his nose in their struggle, put on his White Sox cap, adjusted his sunglasses, and hobbled off the field.

Burlane ignored the ambulance that attended to Ernst Hein. He didn't give squat whether the Last Vopo bled to death or not. He had a World Cup soccer game to watch. This was the Round of 16, a knockout game, and the United States was in it, not solely because they were the host team, but goddamn it because they had tied two matches and beaten Brazil in their round-robin group. They'd earned the advancement fair and square.

The cheek of Burlane's ass and his ear throbbed with pain.

Burlane knew a medic could numb his butt with something that'd last the afternoon, and he'd pack some ice on what was left of his ear. He could still hear okay, and that's what counted. Of course, the eager reporters would triumphantly lift stills from the ABC game tape, but what would they get: a brown-haired White Sox fan in sunglasses with a Karl Malden nose and an accountant's mustache.

Gunderson, McAllen, Mayor Raymond, de Beauvoir, and Henry Kissinger came out to meet the gimpy Burlane so he could watch the game with the successful defenders of Rowayton.

They all looked amazed at Burlane's transformation into the new Sid Khartoum.

Burlane said, "If I wound up on the front of every newspaper and magazine in the country, it would put Mixed Enterprises out of business. Why should I do that? What counts is performance. We stopped Ernst Hein."

"Let them wonder," Gunderson said.

"You can tell the reporters you hired Major M. Sidarius Khartoum, if you like, but they don't need to know what Khartoum looks like, do they? Better that I watch the game somewhere on television."

De Beauvoir, grinning, said, "We can spirit you off to my house if you like. I've got a spare bedroom with its own bathroom. You can hole up there for a few days."

"Thank you, Mr. de Beauvoir, I accept," Burlane said.

As they left the field, the ambulance, which had been parked behind the library, rolled to a stop beside the stricken Hein.

They paused for a moment to watch an old man with bushy eyebrows run toward the ambulance with his wrists handcuffed in front of him. Burlane was surprised by his size; for some reason he had expected him to be larger. He was short and thick. He had bags under his blue eyes and a small nose that looked somehow patrician. He ran awkwardly, with an old man's stiff, unpracticed gait. His lips were pursed with determination. His face was grave. This was the murderous officer of the People's Police, minister of the People's Justice, and recipient of the People's Perks. Fredrich Mueller was surrounded by jogging guards.

Mueller called, "Ernst! Ernst!"

On the public-address system, the mellow, courtly voice of Dr. Antonio Coelho, sounding like a cultivated butler or the announcer at Yankee Stadium, said, "Ladies and gentlemen, if we might complete our chores with dispatch, please, so we can get on with the match. We have a football tournament to finish."

General Towson's guardsmen were already busy cleaning the debris from the turf, and the Dutch and American players were limbering up in front of their team benches.

The first of the Rowayton residents began arriving at the side of the field, still talking about the aerial duel between wasp and butterfly that some of them had watched from the windows of their houses.

When time had been called, the Dutch had the ball. Now, the Dutch would continue play from the same spot on the field.

The American and Dutch athletes took their places. Better footballs than bullets. After all was said and done, that was what the World Cup was all about.

The referee glanced at his wristwatch so the injury time-out could be added at the end of play. He placed the ball on the field and hopped quickly back. He blew his whistle with all the vigor he could muster.

Play on!

A doctor from the ambulance ran down Team Rowayton. She ordered Burlane to drop his blood-soaked pants and lean over a bat rack, while Mayor Raymond dispatched a cop to fetch him clean trousers and another shirt. She poked at the bullet hole with a needle-nosed surgical clamp. While it was no mortal wound, neither had the bullet exited; the 9 mm slug was lodged in butt muscle and would have to be removed when the game was over.

The doctor cleaned and dressed the wounds on Burlane's ear and rump, enjoying the speculative banter of the amused Kissinger, Gunderson, and de Beauvoir. Burlane, his bared buns the momentary center of attention, endured.

Then, as she stabbed him in the ass with the numbing needle, a cheer went up from around the pitch; Burlane turned to see a jubilant Pat Duffy being swarmed by his joyous teammates. Duffy had scored a second surprise goal!

The Netherlands and the United States were tied at two goals each! There was a long way to go, with Peter the Painter on the tear.

Was it possible?

Of course not.

Could such things be?

Dream on.

Pat Duffy, charged with energy and exuding confidence, now roamed the midfield with the authority of Franz Beckenbauer. Having scored two goals against the Dutch, Duffy was operating in the zone of the impossible, and he was determined to remain there for the rest of the game.

James Burlane, hating to have to watch the rest of the game on television, knew reporters and photographers would shortly be arriving en masse, eager to see the man who had taken on Ernst Hein mano a mano. It went without saying that with Sir Roger Dusenberry dead, Harry Beauchamp would step forward to claim that he personally was responsible for hiring the FIFA man who gave the terrorist the red card. He reluctantly hobbled to Jacques de Beauvoir's Saab and settled onto the front seat at an angle so his weight was on the good cheek.

Henry Kissinger was right, Burlane thought. It was a wonderful afternoon for soccer. Of course, the Dutch would likely win. He knew that. In the outskirts of Utrecht, he had once watched Dutch schoolboys play a soccer game, and they were amazing. But he was American born; as a point of honor, he wanted the luck-out Americans to show the world their best.

Besides, in beating Brazil 1–0, the Americans had repeated their World Cup upset of 1950. Joe Gaetjens had had his special moment against England in obscure Belo Horizonte; Luis Garcia's prize against Brazil had been televised round the world. Not a bad gift for the American fans—Burlane was sure that in East L.A. they'd be serving tacos Garcia.

Burlane, exhausted from the rush of adrenalin, felt suddenly hungry.

If the Germans won the championship, Burlane would buy his partner Ara Schott and Herr Jens Steiner all the bratwurst and

Beck's they could handle. He wasn't sure what the Belgians liked, but de Beauvoir would surely know. If the Norwegians won, he'd celebrate the occasion with boiled fish; Norwegians were big on boiled fish, he'd heard. If the Brazilians came through, he'd make a big, gesture-of-respect pot of *fijoada completa*. He was willing to consume chianti and pasta for the Italians, if necessary, and *tinto* and grilled beef for the Argies, although he was no admirer of their kicking and jersey pulling on defense. He would go with dry white wine and bouillabaisse for the French; mutton stew and Guinness stout for Ireland's best; gyros and retsina wine for the Greeks; tacos and Carta Blanca for the Mexicans. Whatever. If the Colombians won, he drew the line at cocaine, however; coke was out of the question.

For now, Burlane wanted pizza and cold beer. He was alive and living was good. His body was telling him: Enjoy! Smell a rose. Eat a pizza. One with all the crap on it. Perhaps de Beauvoir could have one sent from Rowayton Pizza to his house on Wilson Point. Later, perhaps, he could find out if there was, in fact, a repository of hormonal warmth under the efficient, ever logical, career-girl exterior of FBI agent Elizabeth Gunderson.

POSTSCRIPT

The World Cup is the most sought-after trophy in the world of sports, apparently by thieves as well as athletes.

The first trophy, designed by French sculptor Abel LaFleur, was a solid-gold goddess of victory, standing on a jeweled pedestal, arms upstretched. The trophy was officially the Jules Rimet Cup, named for the founder of the first tournament held in Uruguay in 1930, but it was popularly called the World Cup. The English, quite uppity in those days, declined to defend their reputation at this first World Cup even though the Uruguayans offered to pay for their transportation.

The 1930 tournament featured a dubious moment in which the referee blew the play to a halt—saying time had expired and the game was over—precisely when a French player was about to power the ball into an open goal. It turned out there was six minutes left. *Mon dieu!* After the enraged French protested vigorously, Argentina reluctantly agreed to return to the field for six more minutes, but the French had lost their opportunity.

The 1934 championship game in Rome, played before Benito Mussolini, was opened with Fascist salutes by the two finalists, Italy and Czechoslovakia. Italy pleased Il Duce with a win and the World Cup moved to Rome.

The successful Italian defense in the 1938 tournament held in France began with a shocking draw by little Switzerland of the heavily favored German side, which was loaded with players from powerful Austria (whose territory had been consumed by the German army). To make matters worse, Switzerland won the replay 4–2 and sent the Germans packing.

Jules Rimet personally hid the trophy under his bed during World War II, as the next World Cup tournament was not held until 1950 in Brazil, when awesome England—the Italians called them *i maestri*, "the Masters"—entered the fray for the first time. After beating Chile 2–0, they were upset by the Americans, and sent home by Spain. In the final match, Brazil needed only a tie with Uruguay to win the 1950 championship, but 200,000 wildly cheering Brazilians, then the largest home-stadium advantage ever assembled for any sport, were rudely silenced by the Uruguayans, who came from behind in the second half to win 2–1.

Just before the 1966 tournament in England, the trophy was stolen from a public exhibit in London. A dog named Pickles upstaged Scotland Yard by finding the golden goddess under a bush in a park.

The much-traveled Rimet trophy was retired in 1970, given to triumphant Brazil, the first country to win the championship three times.

In 1983, the statue was stolen again, this time in Brazil, where it was allegedly melted down for the gold; the Brazilian football association replaced it with a duplicate.

An Italian sculptor, Silvio Gazzaniga, designed the trophy that has been the World Cup since 1974. Gazzaniga's cup, made of eighteen-karat gold, is fourteen inches tall and weighs eleven pounds. The cup clearly does contain a globe, but it is otherwise difficult to describe. What appear to be two human or anthropomorphic figures under the globe, said the artist Gazzaniga, are "athletes at the stirring moment of victory."

So does the winning side get this Cup?

No.

FIFA keeps this trophy in Zurich.

The champions get a gold-plated replica.

World Cup Atlas '94

THERE ARE 6 GROUPS, 24 TEAMS, AND 9 SITES

SAN FRANCISCO	CHICAGO	DETROIT	BOSTON
Groups A&B	Groups C&D	Groups A&B	Groups C&D

LOS ANGELES	DALLAS	ORLANDO	WASHINGTON
Groups A&B	Groups C&D	Groups A&B	Groups A&B

NEW YORK/NEW JERSEY
Groups A&B

GROUP A

A1 United States
A2 Switzerland
A3 Columbia
A4 Romania

GROUP B

B1 Brazil
B2 Russia
B3 Cameroon
B4 Sweeden

GROUP C

C1 Germany
C2 Bolivia
C3 Spain
C4 South Korea

GROUP D

D1 Argentina
D2 Greece
D3 Nigeria
D4 Bulgaria

GROUP E

E1 Italy
E2 Ireland
E3 Norway
E4 Mexico

GROUP F

F1 Belgium
F2 Morocco
F3 Netherlands
F4 Saudi Arabia